KALPA IMPERIAL
THE GREATEST EMPIRE THAT NEVER WAS

KALPA IMPERIAL
THE GREATEST EMPIRE THAT NEVER WAS

Angélica Gorodischer

Translated by Ursula K. Le Guin

Small Beer Press
Easthampton, MA

Kalpa Imperial by Angélica Gorodischer was published by Ediciones Minotauro, calle Humberto 1 545, Buenos Aires, Argentina, in 1983, in two volumes: I, *La Casa del poder;* II, *El Imperio mas vasto.* It was reprinted in one volume by Ediciones Gigamesh, Rda. San Pedro, 53·08010 Barcelona, Spain, in 2000.

A portion of this novel, "The End of a Dynasty, or The Natural History of Ferrets," was published in *Starlight 2*, edited by Patrick Nielsen Hayden.

Small Beer Press
150 Pleasant St., #306
Easthampton, MA 01027
smallbeerpress.com
weightlessbooks.com
info@smallbeerpress.com

Distributed to the trade by Consortium.

PCIP

Gorodischer, Angelica, 1929-
        [original title in Spanish. English]
        Kalpa Imperial / Angelica Gorodischer,
        Translated by Ursula Le Guin.
        p. cm.
        LCCN 2003105105
        ISBN 1-931520-05-4
        Translation of: original in Spanish.
        1. Latin America -- fiction   I. Title
        2. Fantastic fiction
        PQ 7798.15 .O76 2003   869.3

First edition   2 3 4 5 6 7 8 9 0

Printed with soy inks on 50# Dexter Offset Natural recycled paper by Maple Press of York, PA.
Text set in Centaur. Titles set in Trajan.
Cover painting by Rafal Olbinski.

BOOK ONE:
THE HOUSE OF POWER

BOOK TWO:
THE GREATEST EMPIRE

BOOK ONE

THE HOUSE OF POWER

PORTRAIT
OF
THE
EMPEROR

The storyteller said: Now that the good winds are blowing, now that we're done with days of anxiety and nights of terror, now that there are no more denunciations, persecutions, secret executions, and whim and madness have departed from the heart of the Empire, and we and our children aren't playthings of blind power; now that a just man sits on the Golden Throne and people look peacefully out of their doors to see if the weather's fine and plan their vacations and kids go to school and actors put their hearts into their lines and girls fall in love and old men die in their beds and poets sing and jewelers weigh gold behind their little windows and gardeners rake the parks and young people argue and innkeepers water the wine and teachers teach what they know and we storytellers tell old stories and archivists archive and fishermen fish and all of us can decide according to our talents and lack of talents what to do with our lives—now anybody can enter the emperor's palace, out of need or curiosity; anybody can visit that great house which was for so many years forbidden, prohibited, defended by armed guards, locked, and as dark as the souls of the Warrior Emperors of the Dynasty of the Ellydróvides. Now any of us can walk those wide, tapestried corridors, sit down in the courtyards to listen to the fountains run, go into the kitchens and cadge a doughnut from a fat, grinning cook's helper, pick a flower in the gardens, admire ourself in the mirror galleries, watch maids go by with baskets full of clean laundry, tickle the foot of a marble statue with an irreverent finger, say good-morning to the crown prince's tutors, smile at the princesses playing ball on the lawn; and then go on to the door of the throne room and simply wait our turn to come right up to the emperor and say to him, for instance, "Sir, I love plays, but my town doesn't have a theater. Do you think you might tell them to build one?"

Ekkemantes I will probably smile, since he too loves plays, and fall to talking enthusiastically about the poetic tragedy by Orab'Maagg recently presented in the capital, until one of his counselors reminds him with a discreet cough that he can't spend an hour chattering with every one of his subjects because it would leave him no time to rule the Empire. And probably the good emperor, who seems born to smiles and good nature, though he wielded weapons like the black-winged angel of war when it was a matter of eradicating from the Empire the greed and cruelty of a damnable race, will reply to the counselor that chattering for an hour with each of his subjects is one way of ruling the Empire, and not the worst way, but that the lord counselor is right, and in order not to lose any more valuable time, he'll dictate a decree to the lord counselor and sign it himself, ordering that a theater be constructed in the town of Sariaband. And very likely the counselor will stare and say: "My lord! Building a theater, even a theater for a very small town, is an expensive business!"

"Oh, that's all right," the emperor may say, "let's not obsess about money. A theater's never expensive, because what goes on inside it teaches people to think and understand themselves. There's some jewel in the palace, some fortune down in the basement, to cover the cost.

And if nothing turns up, we'll ask all the actors in the Empire to send the profits from one day, one evening, one show, to help build a theater in Sariaband, where some of them will act some day or where some day they'll see their son act, or their daughter, or a student who they've been trying to teach the hundred and eleven methods of expressing sorrow on the stage. And when the actors agree, we'll build a theater of the pink marble from the quarries of the province of Sariabb, and we'll ask the sculptors of the Imperial Academy to carve statues of Comedy and Tragedy to flank the doorways."

And the play-lover will go off happy, whistling, his hands in his pockets, his heart light, and maybe before he reaches the doors of the great throne room he'll hear the emperor shouting after him, promising to come in person to the opening of the theater, and the lord counselor clicking his tongue in disapproval of such a transgression of protocol.

Well, well, I've let words run away with me, something a storyteller should take care to avoid; but I've known fear, and sometimes I need to reassure myself that there's nothing to fear any more, and the only way I have to do that is by the sound of my own words. Now, back to what I was getting at when I began, we all now have the right to use as if it were our own house, which it is—in that palace, in the south wing, in a salon that looks out on a very pretty hexagonal garden, there's a shapeless heap of dusty, dirty old stones. Everywhere else in the building you'll see carpets, furniture, mirrors, paintings, musical instruments, cushions and porcelains, flowers, books, plants in vases and in pots. There, nothing of the kind. The room's empty, bare, and the marble flags don't even cover the whole floor, but leave an area of beaten earth in the middle, where the stones are piled up. There's nothing secret or forbidden about it, but many of you, looking for the way out, or a quiet place to sit down and rest and eat the sandwich you brought in your backpack, will have opened the door of that room and asked yourself what on earth that heap of grey rocks was doing in such a well-kept, clean, cheerful palace. Well, well, my friends, I'm going to tell you why there are storytellers in the world: not for frivolities, though we may sometimes seem frivolous, but to answer those questions we all ask, and not as the teller, but as the hearer.

Long is the history of the Empire, very long, so long that a whole life dedicated to study and research isn't enough to know it wholly. There are names, events, years, centuries that remain dark, that are recorded in some folio of some archive waiting for some memory to rescue them or some storyteller bring them back to life, in a tent like this, for people like you, who'll go back home thinking about what you heard and look at your children with pride and a little sadness. As well as being long, the history of the Empire is complex: it's not a simple tale in which one thing happens after another and the causes explain the effects and the effects are in proportion to the causes. Nothing of the kind. The history of the Empire is strewn with surprises, contradictions, abysses, deaths, resurrections. And I tell you now that those stones lying in an unused room of the emperor's palace are, precisely, death. And resurrection.

For the Empire has died many times, many deaths, slow or sudden, painful or easy, silly or tragic—died and re-arisen from its death. One of those deaths, thousands of years ago, was deeper and darker than the others. It wasn't silly, nor tragic, but mindless, senseless, heartbreaking: men killing one another for the most futile and dangerous of the passions, power, so they could attain the Golden Throne, sit on it, and stay sitting on it as long as possible. An ambitious general killed an inept emperor. The emperor's widow, who had always lived in his shadow and whose name is forgotten, avenged her husband and at the same time cleared her own way to the throne by killing the general with his regicidal sword before he could take over the palace. Then she cultivated the resentment of the leaderless soldiers, something she was good at since she was quite familiar with resentment herself; she incited them against the officials and had every general of the Imperial Army killed so that none of them might conceive the same idea as her husband's assassin. The dead emperor's brothers armed themselves and ran to the palace to defend the helpless widow, so they said—in fact, to try to seize the throne from her. There was an uprising in the eastern provinces, where a bankrupt nobleman who claimed descent from an ancient dynasty asserted his right to rule the Empire. Somebody strangled the empress in her bed and stabbed her children to death, though it was said that one girl escaped the slaughter. From the bogs and forests of the south came hordes of the dispossessed, sacking the cities, improving on the confusion left in the wake of the armies. In the north a charlatan said heavenly voices had ordered him to proclaim himself emperor and kill all who opposed him, and unfortunately many believed him. Within months war was everywhere, a war in which men ended up not knowing and not wanting to know who they were fighting against, in which it wasn't a matter of kill or die but kill and die. Plague made its appearance. Within a year the population of the Empire was reduced to less than half. The rest of them went on fighting, killing, burning, and destroying. In the capital, some officers of what had been the proudest army of all time found a girl they said was the emperor's daughter, sole survivor of the night of the assassins. Perhaps she was, perhaps she wasn't. The girl took the throne, not among parades and fanfares but among flames and screams; once there she tried to impose order, first in the palace, then in the streets and houses of the city, and looked as if she might succeed. But the men in uniform got worried. If instead of being their puppet, this supposed daughter of the dead emperor strengthened her rule, none of them would get to be emperor. They did all they could to make sure her plans failed and her orders were disobeyed. And when they saw that the girl was cleverer and stronger than they'd expected, they met in secret and talked all one night. And she died. Don't ask me how, I don't know, nobody knows. She was very young and she may have been beautiful even though she'd lived so long in hiding, half starved. Her reign lasted fifty-four days.

Well, well, each of you has an imagination; not a very big one, or you wouldn't need me; but you have one. So think about the death of the Empire. Look at the gutted cities, the burnt fields, the deserted streets; listen to the silence, the howl of the wind knocking loose stones from ruined buildings. There's no food, there's no drinkable water, no vehicles, no medicine or merriment or textbooks or music or communications or factories or banks or elegant shops or poets or storytellers. There's nothing, not even a symbol of power to fight over: the Golden Throne is lost, it doesn't exist, or if it does it's buried under a mountain of broken bodies and rubbish. Even war is dead, and nothing's left but oblivion. The population of the Empire is sparse, reduced to brutalized bands of nomads who wear rags torn from corpses and shelter under tottering walls that support only the remains of a roof; they eat what they can find, any animal they can catch, or, if winter deprives them even of that, they eat the weakest or unwariest of the band.

And so they lived for generation after generation. Until, from being naked wandering animals, these sick, wrecked creatures slowly began to become people once again and learned to make fire, cook meat, sow grain, shape clay, and bury their dead. They also, unfortunately, learned to fight again. The tribes increased. There were sorcerers, warriors, chiefs, hunters, strange men who hollowed out canes and blew in them to make sounds, and women and girls who danced languidly to the rhythm of those sounds.

Well, well, my dear friends gathered round me listening, let's consider now, let's think that it all might have gone in a different direction, that people might have organized themselves in a different way from the old Empire. Perhaps in little kingdoms, perhaps in independent, sovereign cities, perhaps in societies of herders and farmers living close to the earth, perhaps in theocracies, perhaps in hordes of raiders, who knows? Death is rebirth, but we don't know what kind of rebirth until it's happened and it's already too late to meditate on past events and wonder if it's not possible to learn something more about ourselves. So then, now we'll see why the Empire was reborn as if from a dream and why it began again to be what it had been. I'm going to tell you about a boy who was born into one of these tribes hesitating between the plow and the sword, an inquisitive boy called Bib, who was particularly good at getting sounds out of hollowed reeds. If anybody had been sensitive and keen enough, if they'd had time for anything beyond food, fire, and safety, they'd have seen that Bib had other gifts, some of them quite notable: disobedience, for one. He was rash and, as I said, inquisitive. Insatiably inquisitive. When the other children were sleeping in the sun in hammocks woven of withies, Bib's little round head was raised to watch the leaves on the trees moving in the wind. When the other children were climbing around on their mothers, Bib slipped off to the door of the hut and watched what was going on outside. When the other children were playing in the mud or with the animals, Bib went off to the ruins and dug in search of strange objects, which he cleaned and hid in a secret place where he could study them and arrange them without being bothered.

He was forbidden to go to the ruins. They were off limits to everybody, especially the kids. All the same, people went there, sometimes, when a cauldron or a lance or an axe got broken, something irreplaceable. At such times the men and women would ask permission of the Chief or the Eldest to go look for what they needed. No, no, I don't know why the ruins were off limits, but I can imagine. It was because those high walls, those labyrinthine rooms, those huge grilles of ironwork, standing or fallen in the undergrowth, those great wide openings like mouths of wild beasts, were so different from the fragile one-roomed huts of clay, windowless, roofed with straw—so different that the people of the tribe knew them as the houses of Fear.

Bib was small and weak, he'd been sick a good deal, he'd been near death several times, he wasn't built for lance-throwing, but he knew already that fear dwells in men and not in things, not even ruined palaces. He didn't know, of course, that those buildings, which even fire, madness, and time had left imposing, were palaces. Nor had reasoning brought him to think that fear belongs to men not to things, nor had he ever said it clearly to anyone, not even himself. Yet he knew it. If his people hadn't believed those who killed the most animals and enemies and had the most sons and the biggest store-house were strong, wise, and clever, they might have seen that Bib was the strongest, wisest, and cleverest person of the tribe.

When the other boys went on their first hunt with their father, grandfather, uncle, or big brother, Bib went hunting too. And then for the first time the men and women of the village looked at him and thought maybe Voro's boy was something more than an idler who spent all day and half the night wandering who knows where and blowing in a hollow reed that had five holes bored in it instead of two like the ones played for the dances when the long days of sunlight began. For Bib, small and weak as he was, brought back more game than any of his companions, even Itur who was almost a warrior already, with a scarred face and shoulders as wide as a ram's back.

It was the only time in his life that Bib went hunting. Well, he'd proved he was a man and from now on nobody should try to give him orders. He left the dead animals for others to skin and roast or salt for him, and refused to show the weapon with which he'd killed them. That wasn't important, though the people, particularly the men, would have liked to know what made those peculiar wounds. It was unusual, but not important: every boy on his first hunt was expected to make his own weapons, which gave him a certain right to do whatever he pleased with them afterwards, including hiding them from the others.

But the next day, my friends, to the amazement and maybe the scandal and certainly the dread of all the villagers, Bib left his hut and walked to the ruins and without asking anybody's leave entered the great doorways and was lost in the shadows, as if swallowed up by Fear. He came back in the evening, carrying a load so heavy that he staggered at every step, went into his fragile, windowless hut, gave his mother a lot of queer, shining things, and told her to use them. She had no idea what they were for.

"This one's for putting food in, and it won't ever break," Bib told her. "See? I hit it and it doesn't break into bits like earthenware. The best bowls, even the ones Lloba makes, get broken, or they crack and let the soup run out. Not this one. Don't be scared, nothing will happen if we use these things. This one's for stirring with; don't use a hollowed-out stick any more, this is better, and it won't break or rot, either. . . . You could put this one on the fire for cooking soup or meat, but you'd better keep water in it, because it gets too hot and it might burn you. . . . This one's for cutting leather: you put a finger here, and one here, and spread out the leather with the other hand, and do it like this. . . . This one's to reflect the sun—no, not there, you have to hold it here, and that side faces up. Don't drop it. It does break. Magic? Why? Those are just our faces, yours and mine. All right, we can put it down like this and it won't reflect anything. . . . This one's for keeping things in, but it's better than a bag because you can keep things separate, arrowheads here, fishhooks here, knives here, feathers here, and this big part down below for winter clothes. . . . This is to sit on, or you can stand on it and reach the lower branches of trees. . . . This is for holding meat when you want to cut it, see? And this is for you to put around your neck instead of that string of yellow bones Voro gave you."

"But they're from animals he killed hunting, before you were born," said his mother.

"That doesn't matter," Bib said. "They're ugly, they're just old dry bones. This is harder, and prettier, and it shines in the light—see?"

And Bib went on explaining to her what each thing he'd brought back was for. Meanwhile, outside, the oldest and bravest and smartest men of the tribe were talking about what the boy had done. Around nightfall, one of them left the group, came to Bib's hut, and called to him.

"I'm here," Bib said, appearing in the doorway.

"Bib son of Voro," said the man, "what you have done is evil."

"Why don't you go to bed, old man?" said Bib.

The man was outraged: "You're going to die, Bib!" he shouted. "We're going to burn your house and roast you inside it with your mother and all those accursed things!"

"Don't be stupid," the boy said, smiling.

The man went on shouting, he opened his arms and hurled himself at Bib, but he never reached him. Bib raised his right hand and in that hand was a little, shiny weapon. Bib fired and the man fell dead.

Nobody else said anything about killing the son of Voro or burning his house full of things taken from the ruins. The villagers went right on believing that Fear dwelt there, but they'd rather face it than Bib's weapon. That was why they agreed to let him divide them into groups and take them off to excavate the ruins every day, after they'd tended to the animals and the little children and the sick. Gone were the days when they had to get permission to enter the ruined palaces seeking the point of an iron grille to replace a lance-head. Gone too were the times of fear, though they didn't know it and would have denied it. Though it's true that they refused to rebuild the apartments and move into them, and that Bib couldn't convince them that they'd live better and more safely there, it's also true that under the boy's direction they hauled loose stones, fallen beams, and rusted grillwork, and used them to build themselves new houses with solid walls and roofs, proper doors and windows and interior partitions.

But Bib didn't let them touch the biggest of the ruined buildings: "That's my house," he said. "Some day I'm going to live there."

The men and women of his tribe told him not to, the demons of darkness would appear in the night and carry him off. Bib laughed because he knew there were no demons of darkness. They no longer threatened him.

Well, well, where's all this leading us? You'll soon see, my good friends, you'll soon see: it leads to something farther along in time, when all the villagers lived in stone houses and ate off gold plates and served water in crystal jugs, some of them blackened, others cracked or with a broken lip, and in silver vases or cups, on carved tables which had been carefully cleaned and sanded. And they slept in beds which were missing the headboard or a post or a leg, with old cloaks laid over the straps, but real beds, wide and long, that filled the back rooms of the stone houses. The old people never got used to such things and just as they sometimes asked for their old clay bowls to eat from, so they sometimes secretly slept on the floor beside the big beds. But Bib said that powerful, valiant people slept in beds, not on the ground like the animals that serve only to provide work and food for their masters; and the young people and children liked feeling powerful and valiant.

And so when winter came the men had finished building a wall that surrounded the new houses, the animal pens, the granaries and the ruins of Fear. The wall was gated and locked, with a great iron door that had taken them a month to carry and set in place. So when snow and hunger drove other tribes to seek food, attacking, killing,

Angélica Gorodischer

stealing, Bib's people resisted them. They chased down the surviving assailants and brought some of them into the stone city. Nobody knew it, not even the son of Voro knew it, but the Empire was being reborn.

Winter passed, spring came and passed, summer came; the stone city was changing fast, growing. They had to knock down part of the wall and rebuild it much farther out. Among the ruins were flat stones they used to pave the walkways between houses, and when they ran out of stones from the ruins they went looking for more in other ruins or natural quarries. It became necessary to construct landings on the river, and to cut wood into boards and fit them together into big boats instead of hollowing out logs to make canoes. It became necessary to bring more stones to erect more houses, and to clear the central place so that people could meet there to exchange what they made or harvested. Somebody made a circular platter turned by the pressure of a foot on a lever, put clay on it, and in a few moments shaped a vessel to contain liquids. A woman who had a sick child who couldn't walk took two of the rollers they used to drag the flat stones over the ground and put a platform on them so the child could be moved. A man with a big family built up the walls of his house and added an upper floor and an inside staircase. The young people sat under the trees with the old people and asked what were the delicate, rare tools they kept finding in the ruins, what were they used for. Sometimes the old folks knew, sometimes they didn't, and then the young ones found out for themselves by trying, hurting themselves, getting it wrong, and starting over. Protected and sheltered, well fed, safe from enemies and wild animals, the population of the city grew in number and in strength. What's more, by the rainy season the people who came to them weren't attacking, but came looking for refuge or for work or to offer what they made and what they knew. And when the rains ended and the fields turned deep green and men and women were harvesting grain and fruit, something very important happened.

The young man they still called Bib really did want to go live in the big stone house in the ruins, because the dreams he'd dreamed as a child and the thoughts he'd thought as he grew to manhood were all still there, still alive within those walls, which in his eyes loomed ever grander. Not much was left of the other ruins of Fear, since everything that had been there, buried or not, was being used for living or for building in the city. Only the great central edifice stood as before; and there Bib worked, paving the ground with flagstones or uncovering the old faded tiling, setting beams in place to support upper floors, repairing, reinforcing walls and lintels, studying and trying to guess the purpose of the pipes of soft metal that stuck out between the joints of the stones.

In that big house, in a room shut off by its fallen ceiling, one day toward the end of summer Bib came upon a gigantic chair, heavy as a mountain. It shone like the dishes he'd brought to his mother on his first day of manhood, and was covered with hard beads like those on the necklace that she'd worn since then instead of the string of teeth from animals Voro had killed in a long-ago winter before he was born. The chair was so high, so imposing, so solid, so tremendous, that it scarcely seemed made for a man. Bib thought it might be for a giant. He also thought he was a giant. Certainly not in body: Bib was still a weak little man, not very tall. Yet he thought himself a giant, and the chair was made for him. He climbed the three steps of its base and seated himself on it. Alone, in the ruined place, in almost total darkness since light entered only through the hole the son of Voro had made in the ceiling that had fallen across the old doorway, there he sat, a bold, inquisitive, disobedient barbarian, on the Golden Throne of the Lords of the Empire.

Well, you'll have to believe me when I tell you that once he'd sat in the seat of power, Bib became a giant. No, my friends, I don't mean that he grew taller or fatter. He was just as he had been, smaller and shorter than most men of his age, but he thought intensely of himself not as an isolated person but as part of something that no longer existed and that needed him in order to exist. And that, my friends, that's the kind of thinking that turns us into giants.

Why go on about this old story? There's plenty to do in the streets and houses of the city; there's plenty to do in the cities and fields of the Empire, and some of you may be thinking that this storyteller's too caught up in the tale he's telling. Well, well, there's some truth in that, but be patient; there's not much more. It remains to be told that autumn came to the city of stone, and gave place to winter. And when the snow fell, the city was named Bibarandaraina, and received tribute from many new cities, weaker, poorer, smaller, more hastily constructed, which it in return defended and protected. In the center of this capital stood the ancient palace, now occupied by Emperor Bibaraïn I, called The Flute-Player, initiator of the Voronnsid dynasty, one of the founders of the Empire. None of you will ever find a portrait of The Flute-Player in the history books or the interminable galleries of images of the many men and women who sat on the Golden Throne, for no painting or sculpture of him remains, if there ever was one. We storytellers who sit in the town squares or in tents to tell old tales, only we can picture what he was like. And if you want something to remember him by, all you have to do is go into the palace of the good Emperor Ekkemantes I, find the room that gives on the hexagonal garden, and gaze at the last vestige of another palace, one that was destroyed, like the Empire, by war, and that, like the Empire, was brought back to life, thousands of years ago, by that man who was too weak, too inquisitive, too disobedient.

He was a good emperor. I won't say he was perfect, because he wasn't; no, my friends, no man is perfect and an emperor less than anybody, because he holds power in his hands, and power is as dangerous as an animal not fully tamed, dangerous as acid, sweet and fatal as poisoned honey. But I do say he was a good emperor. He knew, for example, the right side of the coin from the wrong side, and that's already a great deal to know. Of course he sometimes chose the wrong, for the birth of an Empire is something too big for the thoughts, the feelings, and the acts of a single man. And so it was that the first thing he did was organize an army—wrong—in order to keep down disorder in the semibarbarous cities and towns and to protect those that were already his subjects—right. After that he had the ruins and remains of the old Empire brought to light wherever there was a trace of them, which was all across the whole territory, and returned them to their place and splendor, and thanks to them he could trace out the borders of the provinces. And then he selected the cleverest men and set them to deciphering the sound and meaning of whatever they found written on paper, on cloth, on marble or on metal. Soon after, schools were founded, and as people had relearned to make fire and bury their dead, so they relearned to read, to write, to make laws, to compose music, to design gears, to polish glass, to solder metal, to measure fields, to cure sicknesses, to observe the sky, to lay roads, to count time, and even to live in peace.

All this happened in one lifetime, yes, my dear friends, it really did. A long life, very long, but one life. Emperor Bibaraïn I married twice and had fourteen children, six boys and eight girls. He never learned to read and write: he said he didn't need to, and maybe he was right. But he didn't remain ignorant of anything about him. His second wife, the Empress Dalayya, learned reading and writing at fifteen, and at thirty had written four volumes of chronicles in which was recorded all that the excavations revealed about the old Empire, with precise details, and interpretations which were mostly mistaken but full of beauty and imagination. One of his sons was a mathematician and another a poet who sang of his father's incredible life and the death of the old Empire, as he, who had seen it reborn, felt it might have been. All the children were intelligent, enlightened, and competent. And one daughter was as inquisitive and disobedient as a boy called Bib, in a tribe of semi-nomadic barbarians, had once been.

They say, I can't verify it, my good friends, but they say that when death came the old Emperor Bibaraïn saw it coming and smiled and asked it to wait a bit for him, and death waited. Not long, but it waited. The old Lord of the new Empire seated himself on the Golden Throne, called his wife, his children, his grandchildren, his ministers, and his servants, and told them he was dying. Nobody wanted to believe him; his eyes were so bright, his head so erect, his voice so clear, that nobody could believe him. Nobody except a girl who'd been ordered to wash her hands and comb her hair and put on some clean clothes before she came to see her august father. Having done none of these things, she tried to hide behind her older brothers. But she believed him. Old Bibaraïn I, The Flute-Player, smiled and said that he declared the inheritor of his throne to be his daughter Mainaleaä. He named her mother the Empress Dalayya as regent until the tangle-haired girl reached her majority. And while a scribe labored with quill and paper so that the emperor could sign the decree of succession and the order to maintain the ancient palace as long as possible, the old lord took his flute and began to play. When the scribe brought him the decree, the emperor signed it and then went on playing the flute until he remembered that death was waiting for him. He raised his eyes in the midst of a very high note, looked at death, and winked. Death came to him, and the old lord died, playing his flute, seated on the Golden Throne that had belonged to the lords of the greatest and most ancient empire ever known.

THE
TWO
HANDS

What Blaise Pascal said: *Car il est malheureux, tout roi qu'il est, s'il y pense.*

The storyteller said: Between the dynasty of the Oróbeles, called the Dark Princes, and that of the Three Hundred Kings, of whom there were in fact only twelve if you count the child who reigned for a single day, the imperial throne was held by a nameless usurper. He came from the south, was drawn into the palace by the tides of war, and never came out again. Some people say he's still there, which is not impossible, as you'll see. The tale of his life and works is banal, sorry, and inconclusive. Have any of you ever gone near the imperial palace? Have you seen the towers, the immeasurable terraces, the black walls, the fountains? No, nor have I, and even now it's very hard to do so. That's why this story belongs to other people. I'm the one they give presents to and butter up to get me to tell about old, forgotten things. But this time, though it probably won't work, I'm going to try—why not?—to say nothing.

What the Archivist said: I live my life, gentlemen, in folio. I have seen nothing and read everything. Your life, too, is written down, it's catalogued, classified, and archived, and if your wife wants to know about your childhood she need only come to me: I can take it down from the proper shelf and spread it out before her. Now, as for the Dark Princes, gentlemen, there were seven of them. They were aristocrats, not strong enough to be good rulers. They married within the family, uncle with niece, cousin with cousin, brother with sister. The last of the Dark Princes was a babbling, snivelling idiot, uselessly married to one of the most beautiful women that ever walked the earth. He was blind to that. He took little interest in the history of his race and less in that of his people. He ate little, slept less, and welcomed every fortune-teller, augur, priest, mage, alchemist, inventor, and charlatan who asked to see him. He was called Orbad and appeared in imperial decrees as the Great, the Powerful, and above all, the Mysterious. But he had very little resemblance to Or, or it may have been Oróbel, the first of the Dark Princes, a black-skinned, filthy, frightful giant of a man, who fouled the marbles of the palace when he came back from hunting or fighting or chasing after women. One day somebody came to the palace who did look like Or, and I wonder if it wasn't actually Or himself, and the next day Orbad the Great, the Mysterious, the Idiot, was dead.

What the chambermaid said: The empress was so beautiful! I can't remember what her name was any more, but she was so beautiful, and a virgin all her life. Such a pity! I can say that, I've buried three husbands and never bothered to be faithful to any of them. Well, so, she came, the empress came to the imperial palace, two days after the coronation of Orbad the Mysterious. They say she came from that fortress where they raised beautiful women the way they raised cattle, where they never let any stranger enter except a certain Smith. But that seems unlikely, because Smith himself explained afterwards why no woman ever left there. But maybe it was true, maybe she escaped from the Alendar, or they let her escape. She arrived in a carriage and with a retinue. She was veiled and dressed in purple. That very day they got her married to the emperor. They got her married, I say, because when she saw him, white as a worm, feeble, with red eyes and trembling hands, she found him disgusting. But she was well brought up, she'd been educated for the throne. She spent her wedding night sitting on a footstool, in a white tunic bordered with gold, a wreath of flowers on her head, waiting, by the light of a single lamp. The next night she waited again; I brought her fresh flowers for the wreath. And after that she didn't wait any more. She always locked her door from inside, though there wasn't any need. When the warrior came, two years after that, she was just as beautiful as ever, and she saw him from the balcony. She still locked her door, but the warrior was very strong. I never saw her again.

What the officer of the guard said: If you've been in the service awhile you get a kind of nose for it, like a dog; you learn to know who to let pass and who gets stopped. You know who's dangerous, who's harmless. You just know it, it's not something you figure out. He was one of the ones you let pass, and yet he was dangerous. It never happened like that before. Either they were wandering fortune-tellers, and they were allowed into the palace, we had to let them in, or they were adventurers hoping for a gain, and those we stopped at the gates, or sometimes we killed them out in the thickets because we were bored or it was hot and we were in a bad mood. We saw a cloud of dust and the watch said it was a big force. But they camped on the other side of the river. The dust was settling. He came alone, on foot. My height, younger than me. He was armed, but dressed like a priest, not like a soldier. He walked slowly up to us and said he wanted to see the emperor. My men looked at me. I knew that he could go in and that he shouldn't go in. To gain time I told him that he couldn't go in carrying weapons. He clapped his sword down on the ground and took two daggers out from under his robes. I asked him what he wanted and he told me that he held the emperor's future in his hands. I'd heard that story often enough, but this time I believed it. I let him go in. I put a subaltern in charge of the guards and followed the warrior. A porter showed him the way. The soldiers in the passage led him into the great room, and there he saw the emperor. Orbad the Mysterious was a weakling who cried at everything. He cried this time, too, when the warrior showed him his life. I mean, he went up the steps to the throne without bowing or saluting and asked for a bowl of clear water. The emperor, quaking in his boots, made a gesture and they brought the man a bowl of clear water. He took it in the hollow of his hand and put it under the emperor's eyes and the emperor started crying. I left. They say he saw the future, but somebody lied. Because they say he saw himself, the emperor, ruler of the whole world, covered with glory and honor, and the next day he was dead; or he didn't see any of that, or he saw it but it was false. Anyhow, the next day he was dead. Then the warrior climbed up on the wall and made his rings shine in the sun and his troops across the river saw him and came and surrounded the palace. And the warrior went back to the throne room and took hold of the scepter and the crown and said that now he was the emperor.

What the fisherman said: I never saw any emperor. We live down the river, in houses on the mud. We fish at night. We salt the fish and sell it. We marry women from other houses on the mud. We have kids and they grow up and help us fish. When our kids are grown up we die.

The storyteller said: At first he was just one of the usurpers in the long, long history of the Empire. He seemed no different from his predecessors: he had Orbad the Idiot buried with pomp, his troops took over the fort, and life went on as before. The man who was now emperor stopped often before the door of the woman who had been empress, but he never spoke. He worked day and night, and under his rule good turned to evil with amazing speed. He did a lot for the Empire and everything he did led to ruin, which didn't seem to bother him. He had a dam built, for instance, and thousands of families had to escape the flooding and wandered about with nowhere to settle and died of hunger in the wilderness. He enlarged the frontiers, and the conquered territories rebelled and the killing went for years. He was so busy that he ate and slept in the throne room, where officials brought the problems of the Empire to him and came away with ruinous solutions. And then the woman who had been empress died and was buried in the Garden of the Dead, and the emperor shut himself up in her apartments, where he was more comfortable, having at least a decent bed to sleep in, and where he was alone. Fewer and fewer functionaries came to see him. They were afraid of him. It got so they sent one man with messages from all the others, and finally not even that; they left notices about this and that in front of the door. A few hours later, they'd find the emperor's decrees and orders in the same place. Fear is contagious. Soon the whole Empire trembled just at the the title, not even the name, of the man locked in the innermost room of the palace, at whose feet blood flowed as easily as water in a river. I can imagine him sitting there in the half-darkness seeing nothing but the destiny of the Empire. They might have forgotten him, but he didn't let them forget. Locked away in that room, he went to war at the head of the armies, he executed the condemned, he raped women, he built advance posts, he burned harvests, he sowed fields with salt, he changed the course of rivers, he declared wars, he dried up marshes, he invaded nations. Never were there so many ministers with such short terms of office, so many deaths, so many women made pregnant. Never had the streets been so empty or the labor camps so full. Never had there been so many denunciations, so much torture, so much grief. And it went on for twenty years. A long,

long time, surely, for the man locked in the room, and a long time for those outside it. Yet it's a fact that nobody got in to see him. Plenty of people had seen him earlier, of course, and in twenty years there were plenty of bold or audacious or simply well-meaning people who tried to see him. And so there arose a legend, a multiple legend: everybody in the palace, in the city, in the Empire, knew somebody who knew somebody who had seen the emperor. In the marketplace, the gambling hall, at a table in the coffee shop, there was always some blowhard who could describe him in great detail. If you listened to them you'd end up knowing that the emperor was fair, dark, tall, short, fat, thin, bald, hairy, feeble, muscular, old, and young. Oddly enough, every one of them said that he had empty eyes, veiled eyes, eyes that seemed to gaze through an opaque liquid. Twenty years, maybe a little more, maybe a little less, twenty years he reigned from inside that room and never let himself be seen and never let anybody in.

What the Archivist said: All that's as true and as false as any tale. In the first place, a great many people had known him before he shut himself up in the inner room of the palace, and they weren't all dead, like the woman who had been empress. In the second place, it's possible that some people who claimed to have seen him during those twenty years were telling the truth. If we can imagine him locked up in the half-darkness, his empty eyes fixed on something unseen, it's just as easy to imagine him wandering about the palace, through the city streets, in the small hours when everybody's asleep or trying to sleep. And in the third place, he received one visitor. Of this there is no possible doubt. I know that it would be pleasing and suitable to say that his visitor was a mighty warrior or a great sorcerer, so that history could repeat itself and philosophers could draw conclusions from it. But what would become of the Annals of the Empire if we archivists started spinning fantasies like the storytellers? No. It was a beggar, lean, lousy, filthy, leprous. He arrived at the palace along with the crowds of curious yokels that came from every corner of the Empire to see the house of power. He told a porter that he wanted to see the emperor, and the porter laughed, holding his big paunch and showing the cavities in his back teeth. But the beggar stayed, and nobody drove him away. He stayed day after day, night after night, sitting in the anteroom, waiting. The women gave him something to eat now and then. He slept in his rags on the marble pavement. Everybody got used to seeing him there, and his presence was suitably recorded in the proper folio, until the emperor took notice of his presence. Nothing strange about that; the emperor knew everything. He knew much more, now that he'd gone into the bedchamber to die, however long and slow his death agony, than when he galloped over the plains of the South, or paced the palace corridors pausing a moment before the locked door of the woman who had been empress, or when he called the ministers together in the throne room. And one morning the door was opened, and the beggar went into the bedchamber. A maidservant bringing breakfast saw, and showed the others, the tracks of the leper's dirty feet crossing the threshold of the emperor's room. They stood about in the anteroom, silent, and I tell you it wasn't long before the door was opened again. The beggar came out, passed through the anteroom, the courtyard, the gates, and was lost to sight forever. Next day the notices and dispatches disappeared as usual, but there was only one decree, an insignificant one concerning the cleanliness of public wells. And the next day, nobody picked up the notices, and the day after that, and the day after that. On the fourth day the stench was intolerable, but none of them dared go into the room. They simply left off hanging around that door, first the ministers, then the secretaries, the officials, the priests, the scholars, finally the cleaning staff. Grass grew in the dirt that gathered on the marble, until at last, when the stench was fading, the first of the Three Hundred Kings seated himself on the throne of the Empire.

The storyteller said: No, I don't know who the visitor was, nor do I know what the two of them said in that room. Since I'm not an archivist I could make up a thousand identities, a thousand conversations, but what's the good? I'm an old man and every day it gets harder for me to talk for long. Anyhow, people make up things for themselves, they don't need me as much as they think they do. I've heard many versions, and I'll tell the two that I've dreamed most about. In the first version, the visitor was the emperor himself, the man he would have been if he hadn't been a soldier, a captain, a general, a usurper. In that case, they wouldn't have needed to talk at all. In the second version the visitor was death. In that case, it's useless to try and imagine what they said. I think both versions are true, just as true as all the other versions running around the Empire. Because who's the only one who can see the hidden emperor even without seeing him? Who's the only one who can take on the vilest appearance without losing his power and glory? Who's the only one totally indifferent to the destiny of a man and an Empire simply through being who he is? I ask you that, and then I fall silent and go away, leaving you to ponder the arrogance of an old storyteller: who is it that talks with blind poets, with fishermen who die every day in their huts on the mud, with unhappy women, with tellers of tales?

THE END OF A DYNASTY, OR THE NATURAL HISTORY OF FERRETS

The storyteller said: He was a sorrowful prince, young Livna'lams, seven years old and full of sorrow. It wasn't just that he had sad moments, the way any kid does, prince or commoner, or that in the middle of a phrase or something going on his mind would wander, or that he'd wake up with a heaviness in his chest or burst into tears for no apparent reason. All that happens to everybody, whatever their age or condition of life. No, now listen to what I'm telling you, and don't get distracted and then say I didn't explain it well enough. If anybody here isn't interested in what I'm saying, they can leave. Go. Just try not to bother the others. This tent's open to the south and north, and the roads are broad and lead to green lands and black lands and there's plenty to do in the world—sift flour, hammer iron, beat rugs, plow furrows, gossip about the neighbors, cast fishing nets—but what there is to do here is listen. You can shut your eyes and cross your hands on your belly if you like, but shut your mouth and open your ears to what I'm telling you: This young prince was sad all the time, sad the way people are when they're old and alone and death won't come to them. His days were all dreary, grey, and empty, however full they were.

And they were full, for these were the years of the Hehvrontes dynasty, those proud, rigid rulers, tall and handsome, with white skin and very black eyes and hair, who walked without swinging their shoulders or hips, head high, gaze fixed somewhere beyond the horizon, not looking aside even to see their own mother in her death-agony, not looking down even if the path was rough and rocky, falling into a well if it was in the way and standing erect down inside the well, maintaining the dignity of the lords of the world. That's what they were like, I'm telling you, I who've read the old histories till my poor eyes are nearly blind. That's what they were like.

Livna'lams's grandfather was the eighth emperor of the Hehvrontes dynasty; and his father—well, we'll be talking about his father presently. That is, *I'll* be talking, because you ignorant boors know nothing of the secret history of the Empire, occupied as you are in the despicable business of accumulating money, decorating your houses out of vanity, not love of beauty, eating and drinking and wallowing your way to apoplexy and death. I'll talk about him when the time comes. For now, suffice it to say that the pride of the Hehvrontes had elaborated a stupid, showy, formal protocol unequalled at any other period of the Empire except that of the Noörams, who were equally stupid but less showy and more sinister. Luckily for people like you, the Noörams killed each other off, and nobody believes the story that a servant saved from the bloodbath a newborn son of the Empress Tennitraä, called The She-Snake and The Unjust, though nobody can disprove the story either. . . .

The Protocol of the Hehvrontes involved everything. It filled the court and the palace and filtered down into public charities, the army, schools, hospitals, whore-houses—high class whore-houses, you understand, since anything that fell short of a considerable fortune or a sonorous title lacked importance and so escaped the protocol. But in the palace, oh, in the palace! There the black-eyed, black-bearded lords had woven a real nightmare in which a sneeze was a crime and the tilt of a hatbrim a disgrace and the thoughtless twitch of a finger a tragedy.

Livna'lams escaped none of it. How could he, the crown prince, the tenth and, I'll tell you now, the last of the Hehvrontes, only son of the widowed empress, on whom were fixed the eyes of the court, the palace, the capital, the Empire, the world! That's why he was sorrowful, you say? Come, come, my good people, ignorance has one chance at good sense: keeping its mouth shut. Or so say the wise. But I say that if you're utterly, hopelessly ignorant, there isn't room in your skull for even that much sense. Come on, now, why would the Protocol make him sad? Why, when nine Hehvrontes before him had been perfectly happy, well maybe not nine but definitely eight—had been so happy that, attributing their beatific state to that very protocol, they devoted themselves to augmenting and enriching the hundred thousand minute formalities that distinguished them from everybody else? No, he too might well have been happy and satisfied, being a prince, made like any other prince for the frivolous and terrible uses of power. But he wasn't. Maybe because the men in his family line had changed, since his grandfather took as his empress a Southern woman reputed to be not entirely human. Or maybe because of the ceremony which his mother, the Empress Hallovâh, had added to the Protocol of the Palace. Or because of both those things.

So, now, let me tell you that the Empress Hallovâh was very beautiful, but I mean *very* beautiful, and still young. The young heart is wide open to life and love, say the wise, and then they smile and look into the eyes of the child eager to learn, and add: and also open to sickness and hatred. The empress always dressed in white, long white tunics of silk or gauze with no ornament, nothing but a fine, heavy chain of unpolished iron links round her neck, from which a plain locket hung on her breast. She was always barefoot, her hair loose. In expiation, she said. Her hair was the color of ripe wheat. Remember that she was a Hehvrontes by marriage only. By birth she was from the Ja'lahdahlva family, who had been moving upward rapidly for the last three generations. She had grey eyes, a fine mouth, a slim waist. She never smiled.

Precisely one hour after sunrise, seven servants, each dressed in one of the colors of the rainbow, entered Prince Livna'lams's room and woke him by repeating meaningless words about fortune, happiness, obligation, benevolence, in fixed phrases hundreds of years old. If I were to try to explain these words to you and tell how each man dressed in a different color each day so that the one who came in wearing blue today tomorrow would wear purple and yesterday wore red, if I tried to describe their gestures, the other words they said and the clothing they dressed the boy in and the tub they bathed him in and the perfumes assigned to each day, we'd have to stay here till the Short Harvest Feast, spending what's left of summer and the whole autumn and sitting through snow and frost to see false spring and then the ground white again and the sky all thick with clouds until the day when the shoots must be gathered before the sun burns them or the hail destroys them, and even then we'd have trouble getting through the ceremony of the Bath and the Combing of the Hair, and not just because of the torpid sluggishness of the tiny intellects inside your skulls.

The prince opened his eyes, black Hehvronte eyes, and knew he had twenty seconds to sit up in bed and another twenty to get out of bed. The servants bowed, asserted their fidelity and respect in the formula proper for that day of the year, undressed him, and surrounding him closely escorted him to the bath, where other servants of inferior rank had prepared the tub full of scented water and the towels and sandals and oils and perfumes. After the bath they dressed him, never in clothes that he had worn before, and again surrounding him in a certain order, they escorted him to the door of the apartment, where another servant unlocked the lock and another opened both leaves of the door so that the boy might cross the threshold into the anteroom. There the lords of the nobility, clothed in the colors of the imperial house, received him with more bows and more formulas of adulation, and informed him of the state of the weather and the health of the Empress Hallovâh, which was always splendid, and recited to him the list of activities he was to perform today in the palace, and asked him what he wished to have for breakfast. The prince always gave the same answer:

"Nothing."

This, too, was by way of expiation, said the empress, except that it was a farce like all the rest, since nobody expected the child to die of hunger. Yet it wasn't a farce, because Livna'lams was never hungry. The nobles pleaded with him to eat so that he'd grow strong, brave, just, handsome, and good, as an emperor should be. The little boy assented, and they all went on to a dining room where a table was spread and eleven servants looked after the plates, the silver, the goblets, the platters, the napkins, the decorations, the water the crown prince drank and what little food he ate, while the noblemen looked on and approved, standing behind the chair of ancient, fragrant wood covered with cushions and tapestries. Every dish, every mouthful, every sip, every movement was meticulously planned and controlled by the Protocol of the Palace. And when all that was done, another servant opened the door of the room, and other noblemen escorted the emperor-to-be, and now came the moment, the only moment in the day, when the son and the mother met.

Even misfortune has its advantages, say the wise. Of course the wise say stupid things, because even wisdom has its foolishness, say I. But there's no question but that being down has its up side. If Livna'lams hadn't been such a sorrowful prince, in that moment he might have been frightened, or angry, or in despair. But sorrow filled him till he couldn't feel anything. Nothing mattered to him, not even the Empress Hallovâh, his mother.

She would be sitting dressed in white on a great chair upholstered in white velvet, surrounded by her seventy-seven maids of honor, who wore bright colors and were loaded with gold and jewels, crowned with diadems, shod with embroidered satin slippers, their hands and wrists beringed and braceleted. As the prince came, in all the ladies bowed deeply and the empress stood up, for though she was his mother, he was going to be the emperor. She greeted him: "May the day be propitious for you, Prince."

He replied, "May the day be propitious for you, Mother."

Even you ignorant louts who don't know beans about anything let alone palaces and courts can see how differently they behaved towards each other. But then, while all the ladies in waiting stayed bowed down to the ground in submission, the Empress Hallovâh acted as if she felt tenderness towards the child: kissed him, stroked his face, asked him how he'd slept, if he'd had good dreams, if he loved her, if he'd like to go walking in the gardens with her. The prince would take one of the woman's hands in his and reply: "I slept very well and my dreams were happy and serene, Mother. I love you very much, Mother. Nothing would please me more than to walk in the gardens, Mother."

When this section of the Protocol was complete, the prince and the empress walked side by side holding hands to the great glass doors that opened on the gardens. As they reached them, the woman would stop and look at her son: "Though we are happy," she would say, "we cannot enjoy our good fortune until we have completed our duties, painful as they may be."

"I was about to suggest to you, Mother," the prince would reply, "that as leaders and protectors of our beloved people, we owe our happiness to them, and our principal task is to see that justice is done to the living and the dead."

"The dead can wait, Prince."

At this point in the dialogue the ladies, still all doubled over curtsying, felt some relief at the thought that soon they'd be able to straighten up their backs and necks.

"That is so, Mother; but not the people, who await our judgment on which of the dead were great men and which were traitors."

The ladies straightened up. The prince and the empress were already in the gardens. Sun or snow or rain or wind or hail, lightning, thunder, whatever the weather, the two of them, the little boy and the woman in white, walked every morning to the central fountain, where eight marble swans opened their wings to the water falling from a basin of alabaster. South of the fountain, paths ran through a grove, and following one of them deep into the shadows—green in the sunlight, dark in storm—they came to what once had been a statue. Had been, I say. There wasn't much of it left. The pedestal was intact, but the pink-grained marble had been scratched all over with a chisel to erase the inscription, the names and dates. Above that nothing remained but a shapeless lump of white marble, whether pink-grained or not you couldn't tell, it was so battered and filthy. It might have been the figure of a man; looking carefully you could make out the stump of an arm, a ruined leg, a truncated, headless neck, something like a torso. In front of it the prince and the empress stood and waited. The noblemen arrived, then the ladies, then the officers of the palace guard and the soldiers, magistrates, lawyers, and functionaries. And behind them came the servants, trying to peer over the heads of the gentry to see what happened.

What happened was, day after day, the same, always exactly the same. Some moments of silence, till everything within the palace walls seemed to have fallen still. And then suddenly, at the same instant, the joined voices of the mother and son: "We curse you!" they said. "May you be cursed, may you be damned, hated, loathed, despised forever!

May your memory waken only rancor towards you, your face, your deeds. We curse you!"

Another silence, and the empress spoke: "Treason degrades and corrupts all that it touches," she said. "I vow to heaven and earth and all the peoples therein to expiate for the rest of my life the guilt of having been your wife, of having shared your throne, your table, and your bed."

Again everyone was silent. The boy prince took a whip which one of the noblemen offered him, a pearl-handled whip, seventeen strands, tipped with steel hooks. With it he struck at the statue, what was left of it: twenty blows that echoed through the grove. Sometimes a bird got the notion to start singing just at that moment, and this was considered a lamentable occurrence to be discussed in low voices during all the rest of the day throughout the palace, from the throne room to the kitchens. But we know that the birds and beasts, the plants, the waters all have their own protocol, and evidently have no intention of changing it for a human one.

And what happened next, you ask? Oh, good people, everything had been arranged, as you can imagine. Or can't imagine, since if you could imagine anything you wouldn't have come here to listen to stories and whine like silly old women if the storyteller leaves out one single detail. So, next, another nobleman received the whip from the hands of the prince, who then approached his mother. The empress stooped, because her son was still a little boy, and held out the polished locket that hung from her neck on the chain of black iron links. She opened it. The boy spat into it, onto a face and name cut in the white stone and half scratched out with a sharp tool, the face and name of the dead man, the emperor, his father.

No, I'm sorry, but I can't tell you the name of the ninth emperor of the Hehvrontes dynasty, because I don't know it. Nobody does. It's a name that is not remembered. His guilt and treason, so they said, had been so horrible that his name was never to be pronounced again.

Moreover, that name was erased from the annals, the laws, the decrees, from history books, official registries, monuments, coins, escutcheons, maps, poems. Poems, because the emperor had written songs and poems ever since he was a boy. Unfortunately he'd been a good poet, good enough that the people got hold of his verses and sang them, back in those happy days when he reigned in peace. And to tell you the truth, many of his poems survived despite everything, and it's said that Livna'lams heard them sung in distant provinces when he himself was emperor. But memory is weak, and that's a blessing, so say the wise. And I know, because I know a lot of things, that it was a wise man who said or wrote that time's mirror loses all it reflects. Memory is weak, and people had forgotten where those songs came from. What mattered was that the name be forgotten. And it was.

So the empress left the despicable locket open on her breast, turned her back on the broken statue, and started back to the palace with her son. Then came the procession. Everybody, the most important persons first, the others following, finally the servants, passed the statue, and all did their utmost to express hatred and contempt. Some spat on it, some kicked it, some struck it with sticks or chains or their belts, some smeared it with mud or muck, and some, hoping that their exploit would reach the ears of the empress, went so far as to bring a little bag full of yesterday's turds and empty them out on the marble.

On their return to the galleries of the palace, the prince and the empress saluted each other and parted. She would spend the rest of the morning in meetings with her ministers; in the afternoon she was occupied with affairs of justice and official proceedings. The little boy met with his teachers and studied history, geography, mathematics, music, strategy, politics, dance, falconry, and all the things an emperor has to know so that later on he can do everything that makes him feel that doing it makes him the emperor.

I said he was a sorrowful prince, young Livna'lams; he was a bright one too, alert, intelligent. There's another of the advantages of sorrow: it doesn't dull the intellect as depression and rancor do. His teachers had soon discovered that the boy learned in ten minutes what might take most boys an hour, not to mention totally moronic princes incapable of learning anything. And as he was seven, an important age, and as the noblemen were always present during his studies to supervise the process, they had arrived at a tacit agreement to depart, secretly, from the Protocol: the teachers taught what they had to teach, Livna'lams learned what he had to learn, and then everybody could go do what they pleased—the schoolmasters could burrow into their books, or write boring treatises on themes they believed to be original and important, or get drunk, or play dice, or plot crimes against their colleagues, and the prince could seek a little solitude.

Sometimes he found it in the music rooms, sometimes in the stables or the libraries. But he always found it in the far corners of the palace gardens. Only if he was extremely lucky could he touch an instrument, talk to the horses and the mares with young foals, or read a book, without a music teacher appearing, or a riding master, or a librarian, bowing and scraping and asking to be of service or just standing around waiting for orders. But almost never, or in truth never, was there anyone under the garden walls, among the dense thickets, the hidden benches, the bricked-up doors, the dry fountains, the pergolas. I don't know what the prince did there. I think he just let time pass. I think he saw and heard things that had not been included in the Protocol. I think that, sorrowfully as ever, he tried to love something—beetles with hard, iridescent wingcases, sprouting weeds, the dirt, stones fallen from the walls.

Now listen carefully, because one day something happened. The day was grey and muggy, and what happened was this: the prince heard voices. I don't mean he went mad or was divinely inspired. He heard somebody talking, and it alarmed him.

Weren't the librarians and the riding masters enough? Was he going to have to start hiding even from the gardeners? He looked around, thinking that was it: some idiot had discovered these forgotten corners of the garden and decided to acquire merit by getting the paths sanded, the trees pruned, the benches restored, and worst of all, the thickets cut down.

"I think you're as crazy as I am," said a mild, slow voice.

A burst of laughter, and a second voice said, "Friend, I can't say you're wrong." This voice was deeper, richer, stronger.

Those aren't gardeners, Livna'lams said to himself. Gardeners don't talk like that, or laugh like that. And he was right. Do any of you have the honor of being acquainted with a gardener? They are admirable people, believe me, but they don't go around making comments on their own or other people's mental condition. They stay close to the ground, and know many names in different languages, and nothing in this world impresses them much, since they see life in the right way, as it should be seen, from below looking up, and in concentric circles. But what do you know about all that and how could it interest you? All you want to know is what happened in the palace garden that day when the prince heard voices.

All right, all right, I'll tell you what happened, just as truly as if I'd been there myself. Those aren't gardeners, the little boy said to himself, and so nobody's going to come and clear out the thickets; and that pleased him. And since he was pleased, he got up from the steps he'd been sitting on and walked, trying not to make noise, towards the place where the men were talking. Now, he wasn't used to walking silently in an overgrown garden; he might manage to be noiseless in the palace corridors, but not here. He trod on a dry stick, a pebble rolled under his foot, he brushed up against a bush, and then, there in front of him, was a huge man, the tallest, broadest man he'd ever seen, very dark, with coal-black beard and hair and eyes. The man took hold of the prince's arm with a gigantic, powerful hand. The prince squeaked out, "How dare you, you insolent fellow!"

The giant laughed. It was the deep, tremendous laugh Livna'lams had heard a minute earlier. But he didn't let go. "Ah ha ha ha!" he went, and then, "Come see what we've got here!"

He wasn't talking to the prince but to the owner of the other voice, who was standing behind the big man. This one was shorter and slighter, lanky, also very tanned, cleanshaven, with tangled black hair, bright black eyes that looked amused, a wide mouth and a long, delicate neck.

"I think it might be best to let him go," he said in a lazy, quiet voice.

"Why?" said the giant. "Why should I? No telling how long he's been listening. Better not let him go. Better give him a good beating to teach him not to spy, so he forgets that he even came around here this morning."

"No beatings," said the other man. "Unless you want us shorter by a head."

The big fellow considered this possibility, and you can bet your puny little life savings that he didn't like it; he opened his fist and let the boy go. The prince brushed off his silken sleeve and looked at the two men. He wasn't afraid. They say princes are never afraid but don't believe it, it's a lie. They're afraid not only when they ought to be but sometimes when there's nothing to fear, and there have even been some who have lived in fear and died of fear. But Livna'lams wasn't afraid. He looked at them and saw they wore coarse clothing like fieldworkers or bricklayers, ordinary sandals, a worn pouch hanging from the belt. He also saw that they weren't afraid of him, which didn't surprise him—what was there to fear?—and that they didn't seem disposed to bow or do homage or await his orders in silence. That did surprise him.

"Who are you?" he asked them.

"Oh, you'd like to know that, wouldn't you now!" said the great big fellow.

This totally non-Protocolish reply, this rude and blustering reply, didn't offend the prince at all. He liked it.

"Yes, I'd like to know," he said, crossing his arms.

"But I'm not going to tell you, snotnose."

"Hey, hey, Renka," said the other man.

"And I'd like to know what you're doing here, too," said the young prince.

"We'd just finished our work, Prince," said the shorter man, "and we were taking a break."

"How did you know who I am?" said the prince, at the same time as the big fellow said, "This tadpole is a prince?"

The man answered Renka first: "Yes, which is why I told you that if you gave him a lick they'd have our heads," and then, to Livna'lams: "By your clothes."

"What does a bricklayer know about what a prince wears?" the boy asked.

"Listen, tadpole," said Renka. "Listen up, because I don't care if you're a prince. We aren't bricklayers. We're adventurers, and therefore philosophers, and therefore although we aren't going to beat you up, being fond of having our heads attached at the neck, neither are we going to play monkey tricks and bob up and down in reverence to Your Majesty."

At this the boy did something really wonderful, really magnificent. He uncrossed his arms, threw his head back, and laughed with all his heart.

"We aren't clowns, either," said Renka, deeply insulted.

But the other man, who was called Loo'Loö, which isn't a name or if it's a name it's a very unusual one, threw his head back too, and holding his sides he laughed right along with the prince. Big Renka looked at them, very serious, and scratched his head, and when Livna'lams and Loo'Loö quit laughing and wiped their eyes, he said, "If you want my opinion, you're both crazy. I'm not surprised. Philosophers and princes have a definite tendency to go crazy. Though I never heard of a tadpole with sense enough to go crazy."

The boy laughed again and then all three sat down on the ground and talked.

They talked about a lot of things that day, but when the sun was high in the sky the prince stood up and said he had to go, they'd be expecting him in the palace for lunch.

"Too bad," said Renka. "We've got cheese," and he gave a loving pat to the pouch that hung from his wide belt, "and we're going to buy wine and fruit."

The prince took this as an invitation. "But I can't," he said.

"How come?" said Renka.

Young Livna'lams turned away and set off. After a couple of steps, he stopped and looked back at the two men. Loo'Loö was still sitting on the ground, chewing a grass-blade. "I don't know," he said. "Tomorrow, when your work's done, will you come here again?"

"I say no," said Renka. "I say we've sweated enough in this damned part of this hellish city, but he insists on staying, and since I'm kind and generous and have a heart as tender as a dove in love and can't watch a friend suffer, I let him have his way." He sighed.

"Until tomorrow, then," said the prince.

The two waved goodbye.

"What'll you get to eat, tadpole?" Renka shouted after him.

"Fish!" the prince called back, running towards the palace.

He had never run before. You realize that he was seven years old and this was the first time he'd ever run? But within sight of the palace he slowed down, and walking as the princes of the Hehvrontes walked, he entered the dining room where the nobles, the knights, the servants were waiting for him, the whole jigsaw puzzle all ready to be put together. The prince sat down, looked at his empty plate, and said, "I want fish."

It was like an earthquake. The Protocol in no way prevented an hereditary prince from ordering whatever he wanted for lunch, but nobody had ever heard this hereditary prince open his mouth to express any wish, and certainly not a wish for some particular food, since he'd never had any appetite. It cannot be determined whether a cook actually had a nervous breakdown and two footmen fainted, but the story is, and it seems to be true, that when informed, the empress raised an eyebrow—some say it was the left eyebrow, others say the right—and lost the thread of what she'd been saying to one of her ladies of honor. The young prince ate two servings of fish.

Next day—no. I'm not going to tell you everything that happened next day, since it was just the same as the day before. Except for one of those things the Hehvrontes couldn't prescribe in the Imperial Protocol: it was sunny. How do I know that? Ah, my little man, that's my privilege, you know. And I have a further privilege, which is that you don't know what I know nor how I know it. So it was sunny, and the lanky fellow was lying in the grass, half hidden by some shrubbery, and big Renka was standing watching the overgrown path that led from the palace. It led to the palace, too, but Renka was watching for somebody coming.

"Think he'll come?" he asked.

Loo'Loö was watching a lazy lizard, maybe, or the weeds over his head. "I'd like to say he will," he said.

Now even you people, with all the sensitivity of paving-stones, have figured out that the two adventurers, we'll call them that for now although only one of them really was one, had been drawn toward the young prince by more than mere chance. We may ask ourselves—ask yourselves, because I've done it already and come up with the answer—whether chance rules humankind or if all our acts are fore-seen, as if by the demented Protocol of the Hehvrontes. And it's no use asking this curious question of the wise, because some will insist that everything is chance, others will say it plays no part, and maybe all of them are right, since they all suspect, behind chance or non-chance, the workings of a secret order. The lizard scarcely moved, enjoying the sunlight, elegant and silvery as a new coin.

"He'll come," said the lanky man. I don't know—this I don't know—whether he believed in chance.

"He'll come," he said again, and put his hand on the old leather bag that hung from his belt.

And he came. He said, "Hello!" and stood there.

He just stood there because he didn't know what else to say to them. To escape from the Protocol was thrilling, and he'd had a wonderful time the day before, but today our young prince realized that it might be dangerous, too. Yes, dangerous: think a little, if you're capable of thought, and you'll see that it's safer to obey a law however stupid it may be than to act freely; because to act freely, unless you're as wicked as certain emperors, is to seek a just law; and if you make a mistake, you've taken the first step towards power, which is what destroys men.

And so that you can understand me once for all, I'll tell you that the little boy said nothing but hello because the Protocol didn't tell him how to behave towards these two men who were humble laborers, and adventurers and philosophers, according to Renka, but who were also something else, something indefinable, mysterious, great, attractive, and frightening.

"Hello, kid," said Renka.

The other man said nothing.

"I'll tell you something," said the big man. "I didn't call you tadpole because I've decided that maybe you aren't a tadpole." He smiled. "Maybe you're a ferret. Do you like ferrets?"

"I don't know," the prince said. "I've never seen a ferret."

He sat down near Loo'Loö, and Renka sat down too.

"I've got a present for you, Prince," said the lanky man.

"Silence!" Renka thundered. "I'm about to give a lecture on ferrets!"

In that moment, Livna'lams thought that he didn't like being a prince, and that instead of commanding and deciding and giving orders he'd rather obey Renka, even if that meant he had to wait for his present.

"Ferrets," said the black-eyed giant, "are small, tawny animals with four paws and a snout. They use their front paws to dig their underground cities, to hunt rats, and to hold food and baby ferrets. They use their hind paws to stand up, to mount females, and to jump. They use all four paws to run, walk, and dance. They use their snout for sniffing and to grow whiskers on, for eating, and to show their kind and benevolent feelings. They also have a furry tail, which is a source of pride to them. Justified pride, moreover, for what would become of a ferret who wasn't proud of being a ferret? Their congenital trait is prudence, but with time they acquire wisdom as well. For them, everything in the world is red, because their eyes are red, that being the appropriate eye-color for ferrets. They are deeply interested in engineering and music. They have certain gifts of prescience, and would like to be able to fly, but so far have not done so, prevented by their prudence. They are loyal and brave. And they generally carry out their intentions."

Renka looked at his companion and the little boy, smoothed his beard and mustache, and said: "I have done. We may apply ourselves to other tasks."

Livna'lams clapped his hands. "Good, Renka, very good! I like ferrets! I agree to being a ferret! And now, can I see the present Loo brought me?"

"Why not?" said Renka.

The lanky man opened his pouch and took out a folded, yellowish piece of paper. The prince put out his hand for it.

"Not yet," said Loo'Loö.

"You're a very young ferret," Renka said, "proud, prudent, but not yet wise enough."

The prince was taken aback, perhaps embarrassed, certainly confused. But you know what? He wasn't sorrowful. Of course since Renka was right and he was a very young ferret, he didn't know he wasn't sad any more, just as he hadn't known that the deep-hidden core of his imperial body had been a core of sorrow. Loo'Loö unfolded the yellow paper once, twice, three times, seven times, and when it was entirely unfolded it was circular. From the center dangled a long, fine, strong thread. Loo'Loö unwound it. Then he pulled on it, and the circle became a sphere of yellow paper, delicate, translucent, captive. Livna'lams held his breath. "Now what?"

"Now you blow into it," said Loo'Loö.

"Where?"

"Here, where the string goes in."

The prince blew. The yellow sphere bounced up. Loo'Loö put the end of the string into the little ferret's paw, and the balloon rose up into the air.

You have memories, you people listening to me—try to remember and spare me the labor of describing what the prince felt when he saw the yellow sphere rise up so high, and ferret-pride filled his heart. Do you feel anything, can you recapture some faint memory of those days? The prince returned to the palace with a stiff neck, and with a little folded yellow paper hidden in his fist. And with an appetite.

No, nobody knew anything, not yet. The days went by all alike, all settled beforehand, perfect, dry, and hard, as they had been since the first of the Hehvrontes. The ceremony of contempt took place every day at the ruined statue in the wood among the trees in which sometimes a bird sang; but it didn't matter to the prince. He no longer hated his nameless father, if ever he had hated him as they had told him he should do, because he loved Renka and Loo. Every misfortune has its lucky side, say the wise. And I'd add that every good thing has its disadvantages, and the disadvantage of love is precisely that it leaves room for nothing else, not even the prudence of ferrets.

On the day after the day of the yellow balloon, Renka taught the ferret-prince a poem which told about the night wind, forgetfulness, and a man who was sitting at the door of his house, waiting. Next day they told fortunes. Next day they got down on all fours on the dirt and crawled around looking for ferrets, but couldn't find any.

"Too bad," said Renka. "I've wanted for a long time to go down into their subterranean cities."

Another day Renka and Loo'Loö taught Livna'lams how to braid leather thongs, and he wanted to teach them how to play the rebec, but they laughed at him and told him they already knew how. Then he told them how he passed his days in the palace and they listened gravely. Another day it started raining while the three of them were discussing the several ways of rowing upstream in rough water, and the two men built a shelter with branches and covered the ferret-prince with their heavy smocks and the three of them sang at the top of their voices and completely out of tune with the ceaseless song of the rain. Another day the adventurers described the hunting and trapping of tigers, and Renka displayed a scar on his shoulder which he declared was from the claws of a tiger which he had strangled with his bare hands, and Loo'Loö laughed a lot but told Livna'lams that it was true: "Whereas I, Prince, have never hunted tigers. What for?" said he.

That night before he went to sleep the little boy thought about hunting tigers. He thought that some day he'd challenge tigers, all the tigers in the world, and Renka and Loo would be there, backing him up.

Another day they played sintu and Loo'Loö won every round.

These days the prince got through the tasks his teachers set him so quickly that he often had to wait a long time for the two men in the deserted corner of the gardens, and when they came he'd say, "Why did you take so long?" or, "I thought you weren't going to come," or "How come I can always get here before you do?"

Renka and Loo'Loö explained that they had to finish their work and it took a long time because there were a lot of latrines to clean in the servants' quarters of the palace. It occurred to the ferret prince, of course, that two men as unusual as Renka and Loo shouldn't be cleaning latrines, but should be doing important things while wearing clothes of silk and velvet. But they told him he was mistaken; because, in the first place, jobs considered despicable by the powerful are those which favor philosophical discussion; in the second place, keeping servants' latrines clean is more important than it seems, since servants notice that some-body's paying attention to them and their well-being, which puts them in a good humor, and so they wait diligently on their masters, who in turn are satisfied and so incline towards benevolence and justice; and finally, because coarse linen is much more comfortable than embroidered velvet, being warm in winter and cool in summer, while rich fabrics are chilly in winter and suffocating in summer. The ferret prince said that was true. And it is. It is, of course it is, and it's why the wise say that gold is sweet in the purse but bitter in the blood. But who takes any notice of the wise, these days, except storytellers or poets?

Renka and Loo'Loö agreed with what the wise say, being wise themselves, even if they didn't know it. What happened in those days proves it. In those days that were all alike, yet different from the earlier days that had been all alike, there occurred two notable events. Notable is scarcely the right word, but I use it because I can't find a word to signify total change in all respects, external, internal, political, cosmic. The first notable event was provided for in the Protocol and occurred annually; the second was not, and occurred once only. Now listen to me while I tell you the first event.

One morning the ferret prince arrived later than usual at the abandoned corner of the garden, and this time it was the brown men in linen and leather who asked him why he'd taken so long. The little boy told them that he hadn't had lessons that day because it was the anniversary of the death of his uncle, the younger brother of his mother the Empress Hallovâh, the Lord of the Shining Glance—for such was the name he had merited in death for what he had been in life, scion of the now very powerful Ja'lahdahlva family—the sixth anniversary: and so the prince had had to attend the ceremony of remembrance and homage.

Renka spat on the dirt. "Bah," he said. "All that wasted on unscrupulous scum."

"Don't talk that way, Renka," said Livna'lams.

"Why shouldn't I, little ferret?"

"My uncle was a great man."

Renka spat again. "You're sure about that?"

The ferret prince thought hard about this uncle whom he hadn't known, and about the memorial observance. He thought about the noblemen and lords and magistrates all dressed in black, the veiled ladies, his mother in white. He remembered that his mother the empress wept only this one time in the year, and remembered the words of the elegy which it was his duty to speak. He remembered the gold urn that held his uncle's ashes, and the portraits of a fair man with eyes so clear they were almost transparent, wearing not linen, but brocade. He said, "No."

"Ha!" said Renka.

"What was the ceremony like, Prince?" asked Loo'Loö.

The prince told him, but don't expect me to describe it all to you, because it isn't worth it: it was nothing but the reverse of the ceremony of contempt for the nameless emperor, and it was a farce. As was the other one, as you'll soon see by what I have to tell you.

The second notable event of those days that were all alike happened to the two adventurers and the ferret prince one morning when a storm made its presence felt by thundering on the other side of the river, though it didn't break till the afternoon, which got dark all at once, as if the world were a kettle and somebody had decided to beat on it after throwing cold water onto hot grease. But all morning the storm just crouched, waiting, and the three of them were crouching too, silently watching a busy scarab beetle rolling tiny balls of mud.

"Why's it doing that?" asked Livna'lams.

"Making a nest," said Loo'Loö.

"What's happening," said Renka, "is that the Lord of the Scarabs is provident, and when he knows that the moment has come, when his hard wings tremble and his jaws clack, he hurries to gather little balls of mud."

"But what for?"

"Don't rush it, because he doesn't rush it. He's ready, but he doesn't let himself be rushed," Renka went on. "When he's got a lot of little balls of mud, I don't know exactly how many because I've never been a scarab, but enough, he goes scuttling off to where a Scarab Lady is, and he finds her, infallibly. If there's another male beetle around, he opens his jaws wide and bites off its head. Then he brings the Lady of the Scarabs to where the little mudballs are, and they do together what they have to do, and she lays eggs and he covers them with the mudballs and hatches them, and she goes off, airhead that she is, hoping to meet another Scarab Lord. It's even possible she may say nasty things to him about the first one."

The ferret prince put out a finger towards the beetle.

"Don't bother him," said Loo'Loö. "He'll feel very bad if you interrupt him."

"Great Ladies do things like that," Renka said, "and I don't like Great Ladies, not that I've known many."

"Come on, Renka," said Loo'Loö, "let's not start that again."

"I'm going to tell you a secret, little ferret," Renka went on as if nobody had said anything, or as if somebody might have said something but he hadn't heard it—"Your mother, the Lady Hallovâh, is a Great Lady, and your uncle Lord Hohviolol, scion of the ambitious Ja'lahdahvas, was a shameless, feeble, greedy, vicious turkeycock who, instead of dying in a soft bed of a fever like an honest man, should have been stoned to death in the public square. And your father was not a traitor."

Now, you good people listening to me, know this: the ferret prince was not surprised. Know it as surely as I do, as if he himself had come from death across the years to tell us. Know that, instead of surprise, he felt the core of sorrow in him was gone, and in its place was a core of anger. And he was aware that it wasn't Renka who had made that change just now, but that he'd been making it himself, slowly, for a long time, with infinite patience and secrecy, but not alone. No, not alone. Strange as it seems, his mother the Empress Hallovâh had helped him in his great task, and so had the Protocol of the Hehvrontes.

"That's enough, Renka," said Loo'Loö.

And now the ferret prince *was* surprised. What surprised him was hearing the familiar voice speak in an unfamiliar tone, as if the strings of a lady's lute were to play a march to battle. And what surprised him was the look on the face of the lanky, gentle man who was or wasn't named Loo'Loö as he looked at him, at the prince, while he spoke to Renka. He heard and saw a tone and an expression that seemed familiar, though he didn't know why.

"Renka, will you tell me everything?" said Livna'lams the Ferret.

"Sure I will, little ferret," said big Renka.

"You will not," said Loo'Loö.

The two men faced each other, and the ferret prince remembered the tigers. Not that Renka was a tiger—he was a mad elephant about to charge. The prince had seen an elephant gone wild, seen it sweep men and arms and wagons aside, trampling on whatever got in its way, heard its furious trumpeting while it killed and while it died, defeated at last. The other man, Loo'Loö, was the tiger, a splendid, supple tiger, serene and dangerous, defending his territory against everyone and everything. The ferret prince thought for a moment that the tiger was going to spring and sink his claws in some vulnerable part of the elephant's hide. But they both held still, watching each other.

"I don't want that," said Loo'Loö.

"You don't, eh? Why did we come, then? Why are we here?"

"For other reasons."

"Ha!" Renka said again. "They're terrific, your reasons, it's a real treat the way you can string reasons together, pal."

"There are some things it's better not to meddle with," Loo'Loö said quietly. "I thought we agreed about that."

"We did," said Renka. "A long time ago. So long ago I don't remember. But now we know him, and we've raised him to the rank of Ferret, right? He'll be emperor some day, right?"

"Yes," said Loo'Loö, smiling, and his smile filled the world of the ferret prince the way Renka's laughs and bellows filled it, but with light, not thunder.

"So," the big man said, "he needs information, he needs to know something more than music and politics and which foot to put first when he enters the council hall and which color of pen to write with on the third day of the week. I'm going to tell you something, pal: he needs to know everything, he needs to hear and see and touch and smell and taste and suffer everything so he can find out some day what kind of emperor he's going to be—right? At whatever cost."

"I agree," said Loo'Loö. "But I don't want that."

"You're lying!" Renka roared. "You're lying, there's nothing you want more!"

Again the ferret prince thought the tiger and the elephant were on the point of destroying each other. But again Loo'Loö smiled.

"I don't want it," he said. "He's very young and shouldn't be troubled. He should be let alone, like the beetles. And the ferrets."

"He's no beetle, he's only a boy. But a prince, worse luck for him," said Renka. "Beetles know a lot more than he does. Not to mention ferrets."

And that, strangely enough, seemed to settle the question. Loo'Loö turned the fierce, steady stare of his dark eyes away from Renka and sat down on the ground and listened. And Renka told all, as he had said he would. And now I'll tell it to you people, who will never be emperors. I'm not telling it in the hope that you'll understand me, or understand the ferret prince, but only because the wise say that words, being daughters of the flesh, spoil if they're kept locked up.

"Your father was a good man, little ferret," Renka began, "I can tell you that, since I was his friend for many years, and his only friend for many more years."

Yes, Livna'lams said to himself, yes, that's how it must have been, that's how it was. And he listened. Renka told him about a handsome man, black-eyed, black-haired, a tranquil, moderate, just man, an emperor who protected his people and composed songs and built cities and enriched farmlands. A man who won the love of everyone who knew him, except his wife, who loved another man.

"An idiot," said Renka. "Which doesn't reflect much credit on your mother. An idiot, shameless, vicious, boastful, cowardly, greedy, and ambitious, which reflects even less credit on her. I'm sorry, but it's better that I tell you, so you don't find it out little by little, and keep telling yourself no, no, no, and filling yourself up with so much pain that finally the only way out is to say yes, yes, yes."

"Let's stop there," said Loo'Loö. "You can go on about his father, since the only way to stop you would be to cut out your tongue, and I don't know that I want to. I don't think I do. But don't talk about his mother."

Renka laughed his usual laugh, just as when he told about his adventures or made fun of himself because he'd lost at sintu. "I always said you were crazy, partner," he said.

But believe me, the conversation didn't end there. Renka said nothing more about the Empress Hallovâh, but he told the ferret prince how, when war came, when the enemy approached the borders of the Empire, his father the emperor called the generals together and the army marched away. Flowers rained down, said Renka, armfuls of flowers, on the soldiers, and the emperor, who wasn't an ambitious coward like the other man, who was hiding in the palace pretending to be sick, and was sick, with fear—the emperor marched at the head of his troops. They fought on the border, Renka said, and they were all brave, but the bravest was the Ninth Emperor of the House of the Hehvrontes. But the other man had stayed behind in the palace, very pale, very blond, very scared, being looked after by his sister the Empress Hallovâh. And both of them expected and hoped that the emperor would die in battle.

"Not that it would have done them any good," said Renka, "since although she didn't know it, she already had you in her belly, little ferret."

And he went on with the story: Not only did the emperor stay alive, he defeated the enemy. Then, when news came that the invaders were retreating, when victory was certain, the two in the palace had to find another way: treason, since death had failed them.

"But the traitor wasn't your father," Renka said. "It wasn't him!"

And he told how somebody had made sure that the ministers found supposed proof of the emperor's treason.

"I said it was somebody," he insisted. "I didn't say it was her."

"It doesn't matter," said Loo'Loö. And, to the prince, "It really doesn't matter who it was, prince. What matters, since Renka wants it so, and maybe I do too, is that you know that *he* didn't betray you. Even though he didn't know either that you were going to be born."

"The proof," said Renka without looking at either of them, "was a letter, a secret copy of the secret letters kept in a very well-hidden drawer which now, inexplicably, wasn't well hidden. In this letter the emperor offered unconditional surrender and permanent submission to the enemy in exchange for gold, enough gold to fill his chests, enough to buy luxury, folly, vice."

The ferret prince sat up and looked, not at Renka, but at Loo'Loö. "Didn't he come back to say it wasn't true?"

It was Renka who answered: "A good question. Yes, little ferret, sure, he came back. But he came back in hiding, as if he really had been a traitor, because it's a very short step from the ministers to the generals, from the generals to the troops, and from the troops to the people. Good sense is inversely proportional to the number of brains, so say the wise. If you don't understand that, it means that the more people there are to think a thought, the uglier and more crippled and deformed the poor thought gets. So, if the ministers believed it, why not the generals and the troops and the people, eh? And why not, if the emperor's personal seal was on the letter, eh? Of course somebody had access to his seal, who knows who, pal. Who knows . . ."

The three were silent for a long time, listening to the rumbling of the black, indecisive storm on the other side of the river.

"And then?" Livna'lams whispered.

"I don't know anything more," said the giant.

"It's true," said Loo'Loö. "It's true, we don't know anything more. Nobody does."

"He died?" asked the little ferret.

"Maybe so, maybe not," said Renka. "Nobody knows. People say different things."

"What things?"

"They say somebody surprised him trying to enter the palace and killed him, nobody knows who, just somebody. They say nobody killed him. They say somebody else, I don't say who, some friend of his, warned him in time and so he got away. They say he killed himself. They say he didn't kill himself and went wandering over the fields, into the mountains. A lot of people say they've seen him disguised as a shepherd or a beggar or a monk, and in more than one city they've stoned and killed some poor fool who never dreamed of being emperor and had nothing to do with the Hehvrontes. They say that when your mother learned she was pregnant with you she wept and screamed and beat her belly to try to force you out. But you were very small and very well protected and all she could do was put on white clothes and go barefoot with her hair down and no jewelry. They say that the other man beat her when he found out, because she'd promised him to have nothing to do with her husband and to keep herself for him, and because your birth meant that it wouldn't be their blood, pure Ja'lahdahlva blood, but your father's Hehvrontes blood that would rule the Empire. There was, evidently, one solution."

"You're just guessing," Loo'Loö said.

Renka burst with a "Ha!" and the storm echoed him. "The solution was to wait it out, then say you'd been born dead and show your poor little corpse around for public mourning. What saved you, Prince Ferret, was a prostitute. The other man caught a deadly fever from her. For over two years he lay in bed, really sick this time, burning up. And in that condition no man could engender sons, as everybody knows. Doctors and treatments and drugs that made him howl and writhe did no good. He died."

The storm shouted something very loudly in the distance but the ferret prince didn't know the language of storms the way gardeners do, and didn't understand it. Maybe he didn't hear it. Imagine, if you can: his world had changed utterly.

The wise say everything has its season, and each stage in a man's life has its sign, and it must be so, since the wise know what they're talking about and if sometimes we don't understand them it's not their fault but ours. What I say, and this is something I thought myself and never read or heard, is that in the ferret prince's life the years of sorrow had ended and the years of anger had begun. The worst thing about sorrow is that it's blind, and the worst thing about anger is that it sees too much. But the prince's anger wasn't the kind that flares up and dies down in a few minutes, not like the stupid raging of a drunk or the fury of a jealous husband. It was growing unseen, unknown, hidden, in him, as he had grown in the Empress Hallovâh's womb. Now and then it made a little movement that showed it was there, as when Renka spoke for the first time of the nameless emperor. But then it would quiet down till it seemed not to exist. And since the anger wasn't fully formed yet and the sorrow was gone, all that was left was indifference, which is a heavy burden for a child of seven.

So it was that the little ferret went back to the palace that morning and performed all the acts expected of him and said everything that he was supposed to say and knew he was going to say. So it was that he went on playing his role in the life of the palace and in the ceremony of contempt, too, day after day, beside his mother in her white dress. So it was that he went on studying and taking part in official duties, escaping late in the morning to meet Renka and Loo'Loö and play and laugh and explore the ruined garden with them and sometimes ask them about his father. They always answered his questions, especially big Renka.

And all this time the anger never ceased; he felt it burning inside him, and his mother guessed it. The empress didn't know exactly what was going on, but every day she felt more uncomfortable with her son, and when she didn't see him, when he wasn't there, still she seemed to hear and see him through the walls and rooms of the palace. Occasionally he looked directly into her eyes, and that was the worst of all. Or he turned his head away so as not to look at her, and that was worse than the worst of all. She increased what she called her expiation, spending the nights on the bare marble floor of her rooms instead of in bed. When that did no good, she ordered the richest food for her table, but lived on bread and water for forty days. That did no good either. She kept on coughing and shaking with fever, shivering in her white clothes. The forty days of fasting and penitence were just ending when one morning in the ceremony of contempt the ferret prince looked up at his mother and, instead of spitting on her medallion, spat in her face.

Perhaps the lords and ladies and magistrates didn't notice, perhaps they did. Nobody said anything, nobody looked surprised, nobody moved, including the Empress Hallovâh. She decided, however, to kill her son. And so, on the pretext of her illness, she had a doctor come to her room, and asked him for a drug that would cure insomnia and help her sleep soundly at night, and the silly fool gave it to her with a lot of advice about the dosage. The empress kept the drug in a sealed glass flask and waited for the moment to use it.

She didn't use it, obviously, since you've all heard of Emperor Ferret, his life, his works, his madness, and his magnificent death. Fooling herself, telling herself she had to know when it would be safe to give Livna'lams the poison, she had him watched by one of her servants. And so she was informed of the existence of Renka and Loo'Loö.

If you've ever lived with somebody in trouble, or if you've ever been in bad trouble for a long time, you know the relief unhappy people feel when they find something or somebody to blame their trouble on. That's exactly what the empress felt. They say she even smiled. I'm not certain I believe it, but I know they say she smiled. And I know she sent for the captain of her bodyguards and ordered him to wait for her in her chambers with ten armed men and the executioner. Then she went barefoot, dressed in white, splendid, her eyes bright and her hair loose and her cheeks burning red, to perform the ritual farce at the broken statue among the trees.

Late that morning, the ferret prince and the two adventurers were playing a game of skill in which the one who was quickest and most skillful at making a fifteen-foot rope ladder would win the right to make three wishes, which the other two had to grant. Renka and Loo'Loö had brought the ropes all carefully measured and cut, and the big man handed them round, making sure that all three had the same number of pieces in the same condition. And it looked as if Loo'Loö was going to win.

"Captain, these two trespassers are to be taken and executed at once," said the empress appearing between the leafless bushes, her feet bruised by loose stones, her face very white, her hands very shaky, her cheeks very red.

Renka looked up and smiled. Loo'Loö stood up. Anger filled the young prince, forever.

The captain took a step forward. The weapons were raised and aimed. The empress cried out aloud.

It was a desolate, furious cry that had struggled to get loose for years, a cry far deeper and stronger than she was, a noise too big to come from that weak throat, those lips cracked with fever.

"Wait!" she said, defeated, when she could speak.

Nobody moved, nobody spoke, and a long while, a very long while passed in that unmoving silence.

"Who are you?" said the pale empress.

"Two humble workmen in the service of Your Majesty's palace," said the enormous brown man. "I'm called Renka and my pal's called Loo'Loö, a very unusual name. So unusual that I've often thought it isn't really his name. But I've never been able to find out, because he knows how to keep a secret."

And then Renka smiled still more broadly, pleased with his speech, perfectly happy and cheerful, as if he weren't in danger, as if there weren't ten men pointing their weapons at him and Loo.

The captain of the guard, on the other hand, was disconcerted; he didn't yet know why he was there and whether he ought to kill these two fellows, or go silently away, or await further orders from his lady. A captain of the guard is invariably a brainless brute, but some, not always the least brutish, acquire a certain training, which in the best cases may lead to subtlety, making them act as appropriately as if they were capable of thought or reason. This captain knew, knew in his guts, that he was out of place in whatever was going on here. And so he signaled his men to lower their arms and step back, and he himself stepped back a few paces, and they waited behind the empress in case she needed them.

"You must die," she said, but she didn't sound as if she believed it.

"We all have to die, my lady," Renka said, still smiling. "In our case it's a pity, because there's a lot of foreign countries we haven't seen yet, a lot of rivers to cross, a lot of wine we haven't tasted, a lot of sweet women to cheer us up and for us to cheer up, nights. In your case, who knows?"

That was an insult, in case you didn't notice, and yet the captain didn't stir from where he stood. It was the ferret prince who spoke: "I pray you, Mother, take care," he said. "It is not my wish that these men die."

That wasn't an insult, it was an order. Remember what I told you at the start, remember that Livna'lams was heir to the throne, and when he was a little older or when his mother died, he'd be emperor. The empress kept her gaze fixed on one of the two men; she didn't look at her son, and paid no heed to the captain and his men or the executioner.

"But, thanks to the generosity of the prince," she went on as if nothing had been said, "your lives will be spared, on the condition that you leave the palace and the capital at once and never set foot again in the eastern provinces."

Renka got up; he made a heap of the unfinished rope ladder and shook the bits of hemp off his hands. "What do you think of the deal?" he asked.

"The lady is generous," said Loo'Loö.

"Oh really?" the big man sneered. "She's so generous, maybe you should ask her for another favor."

"It's all right, Renka. Let's go," said Loo'Loö, still looking at the empress.

"No," said Prince Ferret. "I don't want you to go. Renka, Loo, stay here."

"I hate to let a ferret down, but this time there's no help for it. We're going, young 'un."

"It is an order," said Livna'lams.

"Aha, ha, ahaha!" Renka boomed. "I don't like saying this any better, but there it is: Nobody gives us orders."

Loo'Loö turned to Prince Ferret. "Renka's always joking, Prince," he said. "But we can't stay here. Not now. It wouldn't be a good thing."

The future Tenth Emperor of the Hehvrontes dynasty understood. "Where will you go?" he asked.

"Oh, my little ferret," said Renka, "who knows, since we don't know? All the provinces aren't in the east, you'll find that out when you're emperor. In the western provinces there are mountains, in the north there's snow, in the south are marshes where barbarians live who'll kill you at a word and give their life for a friend. So long, prince, be a good emperor, and don't ever forget the things you've seen and heard."

Renka put his immense, dark hands on the prince's shoulders and looked down at him smiling, and then drew away from him and turned to go without a glance, even of mockery, at the empress. Loo'Loö, instead, bent down and hugged the little boy, and Livna'lams rested his head for a moment against the man's chest.

"Good-bye," Loo'Loö said, and looked at the pale woman, and went.

The two men disappeared among the branches. When the sound of their steps could no longer be heard, Prince Ferret called to the captain of the guard.

"Highness!" said the brute, squaring his shoulders and clicking his boot-heels.

"You will answer to me with your life for the lives of those two men," said Livna'lams in his high little boyish voice, in which you could already hear the tone of an emperor giving orders. "You will follow them without their seeing you. Others will be following you without your seeing them. You'll look out for them without their knowing it, and you'll be watched without your knowing it. And you will not come back to the palace till they're safely across the border of the eastern provinces."

The captain saluted again and marched off with his soldiers and his executioner. Prince Ferret looked at his mother with a certain icy curiosity, and she endured his gaze until she was doubled over by a spasm of coughing. Then they walked back to the palace, he leading, she following with bruised, bare feet.

You've all read something somewhere or heard something about Emperor Ferret's reign. Whatever you've read or heard, I tell you that he was a just man. He was mad, but he ruled well. Maybe you have to be a bit touched to be a ruler, good or bad. For, as the wise say, a sensible man looks after his garden, and a coward looks after his money; a just man cares about his city and a crazy man cares about the government; and a wise man studies the thickness of fern-fronds.

He was the last emperor of the Hehvrontes dynasty. During his reign, the Protocol so laboriously constructed by his ancestors began to deteriorate, and unforeseen phrases and unrehearsed gestures entered palace life. Very soon after the two adventurers left, while he was still a child, he stopped attending the ceremony of contempt for the nameless emperor, his father. Some say that the day before he stopped going, he had a long conversation with his mother, or rather that he talked for a long time and she listened, but this isn't written down anywhere and frankly I don't believe it. What is recorded in the history books is that the Empress Hallovâh never went back to the wood either, and so the ritual ceased. She locked herself up in her rooms, where she slowly withered away, seen by no one but her maids, giving her orders through an opaque screen. Young Livna'lams succeeded to the throne when he was ten, upon the death of his mother, whom he did not go to see when she was dying. He had her buried with all due honor, but he did not attend the funeral.

He married when he reached marrying age. He had a principal wife who was crowned empress, and six secondary wives. But he never slept with any of them, or as far as I know with any woman, or man, or animal—nobody, nothing. He ordered all the noble families with children to leave the court and the palace; they could keep their goods and privileges, on condition that they never return as long as he lived. And more: any servant, soldier, magistrate, official, who had children or whose wife got pregnant, had to leave the court. And at the same time as he gave such orders, he was dealing out justice wisely, distributing land, founding schools and hospitals, beautifying the capital, the cities, and the towns, making food and water and medical help available to everybody, peacefully consolidating the borders, protecting the arts, and helping anybody who needed help.

Unfortunately, one of his untouched secondary wives got pregnant. She was very beautiful, stupid, and soft-hearted, and had a lovely voice.

He didn't punish her, as everybody thought he would. He let her go, free, rich, and healthy, with her lover, an assistant fencing-master in the officer training program, who was also beautiful, stupid, and probably soft-hearted, though quite unable to sing. Three days after that, Emperor Ferret signed an insane decree: every man who wished to stay at court must be castrated. He was mad, no doubt of it; but the men who preferred mutilation to leaving the court were madder. And there were plenty of them, since it was from among them that Obonendas I, the Eunuch, arose. He wasn't a bad emperor, though many would disagree.

Emperor Ferret never lost his anger, though in fact it didn't keep him from being sensible, just, mad, and possibly wise. And he was never a coward, for our songs still tell the glory of his death, even after so many years, lifting their triumphant rhythms in taverns and town squares, quarries and sawmills and battlefields. But that—as they say another storyteller used to say—is another story.

THE
SIEGE,
BATTLE,
AND VICTORY
OF SELIMMAGUD

The storyteller said: He was called Rabavt-tuar and was engrossed in the praiseworthy task of stealing absinthe when the imperial soldiers caught him. They said he was a deserter and carried him off. He tried to explain to them that he wasn't a deserter because he'd never been a soldier. He'd been born in the back room of the Thousand Delights Inn, the son of a Southern prostitute and, presumably, somebody else, though nobody ever knew who. What happened between then and his seventeenth year, when the soldiers found him robbing the experimental farm and hastily declared him a deserter, is a sordid history that has nothing to do with Selimmagud. As a child he lived with a snake charmer—"snake" being a euphemism for certain creatures that hide under rocks along riverbanks. The snake charmer, who may have been his father, though many tellers of tales insist it's unlikely, wasn't a bad fellow, and provided food and a bed whenever such luxuries were at his disposal. In return the boy assisted him in his act in circuses and small-town theaters and looked after his beloved little slimy pets. The snake charmer was called, or called himself, Bollopoppoll; he never washed, insisting that bathing destroys the natural protective agents of the skin; he got drunk frequently; he loved dark women and rings with colored stones; he died in a ditch with his heart split open by a knife wielded by somebody who mistook him for somebody else. But while he was still alive with nothing to eat and nowhere to sleep, which happened increasingly often, he sent Rabavt-tuar out to steal.

The soldiers who took him prisoner had been no luckier in life than he had. There were five of them, under the command of a sergeant whose consuming interest as a military man consisted in flaying and burning prisoners as slowly as possible. He did this without the general's knowledge, so he had to make do with the few prisoners he could smuggle into camp without being seen by the guards. But none of them lasted as long as he would have liked, and this, plus the wound in his left thigh, which wouldn't heal and kept oozing a stinking yellowish fluid, convinced him that the world owed him something and that it was his duty to take it by force. It was this sergeant who ordered that the prisoner's hands be tied behind his back. The soldiers were on horseback. The rope was long. A soldier on each side of him held each end of the rope, while he walked between the horses. The sergeant led the troop, keeping his hand on the damp, sticky left leg of his trousers. There were no other prisoners in camp.

Rabavt-tuar wore blue pants and nothing else. He was barefoot, so by the time they got to the camp his feet were cut and bleeding. The heavy darkness in the sergeant's heart lifted a little, just a tiny bit, when he saw that.

They put the boy in a tent and left him there, tied up. He lay on the hard ground to sleep. Wanting to go to sleep, he thought about Sonora's daughter so he could dream about her, but it wasn't till dawn that he dreamed, and then it was a dream about those damned snakes. He was putting them into a sack he'd taken from the experimental farm, and one of them was always escaping and the others were howling and tearing up the sack with the horns on their little wedge-shaped heads.

Then the trumpets sounded. The sun had not yet risen. He sat up laboriously; his wrists, his feet, his eyes, his stomach hurt. A veteran of the Jerimadian Wars said that no symphony can compare with the sounds of an encampment waking up. He didn't say it in those words, to be sure, and he had to be blind drunk to contemplate his past with the slightest benevolence, and yet he loved army life, and sometimes could express that love to other people.

As for the little thief, hero, traitor, prince consort, whatever you want to call him, he thought he'd been forgotten. But no, they hadn't forgotten him. The sergeant with the sore in his left thigh remembered him; he sent a surgeon to look after him. Since the general was a soft-hearted man, and the sergeant had his own plans, not yet very clear, but exciting plans, he wanted the general to know that everything possible had been done for the prisoner. The surgeon attended to the boy's lacerated feet, untied his hands, and gave orders that he be given something to eat.

The day went by. There was a lot of noise in camp, but no fighting. Rabavt-tuar was scared of getting mixed up in a battle. There had been no battles for months and months. The besieged city remained silent.

Along in the afternoon the prisoner heard the general's voice. He knew it was the general because nobody else was talking and only that one voice could be heard amidst the tramp of feet, the crunch of boots on sandstone. Though he couldn't make out what it was saying it was a deep voice, not loud. It talked on and on and then was lost in the distance along with the tramping feet. He started worrying again that they'd forgotten him. Then he thought about the sack he'd left at the farm, a good cloth sack, machine-woven at Threeworlds, stolen from a bakery; he thought about Sonora's daughter, and about escaping. But when he went to look he found an armed guard at the tent door. He sat down on the ground and waited, that being all he could do. Food was brought to him. And at nightfall the sergeant came in, wearing clean trousers he had just put on. He looked at the boy and said, "The general wants to see you."

He spoke between clenched teeth, so that the thief felt he was being spat on.

Behind the sergeant came a soldier who he thought was not one of the ones who had arrested him, carrying some clothes: sandals, white pants, a white shirt, a green sash. And they brought him a wash-basin with water, soap, sponge, towel, and razor. The sergeant stood there watching him the whole time. Then the sergeant called, and two soldiers came to take him to the general's tent. His feet hurt when he walked, even in the soft leather sandals. He was clean, combed, shaved, and uncomfortable.

The general's white tent was right in the center of the encampment. Banners fluttered on high poles on either side of the entrance: the imperial flag and the flag of the Seventh Imperial Army of Assault.

"In," they said, and pushed him in.

There was nobody but the general in the tent.

The general was the doomed son of the Duchess of Coldwinter and Marshal Koopt, a miserable marriage if ever there was one. The duchess preferred women, the marshal preferred men. They had fourteen children, eight boys and six girls. The general, their fifth son, had joined the army at fifteen; he was thirty now, the bravest man in the whole world.

Inside the tent the ground was covered by a crimson carpet with gold arabesques. There were seven standing lamps, all alight. There was a marble fountain with a golden flower from which the water sprang. There was a hearth where logs were burning, platters of fruit, cushions, a couch.

The general was lying on the couch wearing a tunic of pink gauze, a crown of wildflowers on his head. A short sword hung from his belt of gilt links. His fair, sleek hair drooped down to his waist. He had gold rings on his fingers, gold bracelets on his wrists. His feet were bare.

"Come in," he said, and stood up.

He was no taller than the thief, and as thin as the thief, but he was a General of the Empire and had won two hundred battles. He walked around Rabavt-tuar and settled back onto the couch.

"What were you doing in the experimental farm?" he asked.

"Stealing."

"Stealing what?"

"Eggs."

"What for?"

"To sell."

"Would you like to have a lot of money?"

"Yes," said the thief.

"A lot—really a lot?"

The thief didn't answer.

"It's easy enough," said the general, stretching out on the couch. "I expect you know who I am?"

"The general."

The general laughed. "Of course, dear boy. There are lots of generals in the Empire, but only one General Sabirtowol, Duke of Frilusa, Viscount Albantares, Baron Rocaparida, Lord of Previostoros, of Uzimal'ou, of Valabá, and another hundred and seventy-two titles which I can't remember. Those are the battles I won."

The thief knew who the general was, obviously. It's possible that in the whole Empire, so vast that the emperor himself wasn't sure of its boundaries, there was nobody who didn't know who the general was.

"I'm going to give you a chest full of gold," the general said, yawning. "It's a long time since I met a suitable man. We don't take many prisoners, and so many of them get themselves killed trying to escape. And you can understand that it's unwise for a general to sleep with his officers, still less with his soldiers."

He got up again and came close to the thief, unbuttoned his shirt and untied his sash. "Come on," he said. "We'll use the pillows, the couch is too narrow."

He ordered the thief to strip, come on, hurry up, while he stretched himself out on the cushions. He lifted his tunic to his waist, his gold bracelets clashing.

The thief approached. He thought as hard as he could about Sonora's daughter, without looking at the general. He knelt down between the general's legs. As the general was a hermaphrodite, to the extent that it's said that at twenty he impregnated himself and bore a child as androgynous as himself, the thief's task presented considerable difficulties. He had to arouse the general's masculine organ in order to get at the general's feminine organ. Little by little he stopped thinking about Sonora's daughter and remembered his dream about the snakes tearing up the cloth sack from Threeworlds. By now he was convinced that slimy little creatures with wedge-shaped heads were hiding between the general's legs. He collapsed onto the pillows, sobbing.

"Imbecile," said the general. "Useless fool."

He pulled the tunic down to his ankles and sat up, leaning on one elbow. "No gold for you," he said. "None. I'll have you hung by your thumbs a foot above the ground. With a sign on your chest saying 'Thief—Impotent—Coward.' And I'll order my soldiers to spit at you."

Stark naked, the thief reached out to the general's side, snatched the sword from his belt, and, still sobbing, cut his throat. The blood of the bravest, handsomest general of the Empire soaked the cushions and the carpet. The thief dragged the cushions over the body and lay down on them. No question of sleeping: the lamplight burned in his eyes, and he couldn't let go his grip on the sword. He stood up and put out the lamps. He wiped the sword on the carpet and waited in the reddish darkness.

When the trumpets sounded, the blood had long since stopped flowing and the tent was dark. A soldier parted the curtain at the entrance and announced that the general's clothes were being brought.

"No," the thief said, low-voiced. "Armor. Weapons. Helmet."

The soldier went off. The naked thief sat astride the cushions that hid the body of General Sabirtowold, Duke of Frilusa, Viscount Albantares, Baron Rocaparida, Lord of Previostoros, of Uzimal'ou, of Valabá, and a hundred and seventy-two more titles.

The soldier returned carrying the general's armor, shield, helmet, and weapons. The thief got dressed. He hid his dark hair under the plumed helmet and wrapped himself in the cape, concealing his face in the folds. He came out of the tent and ordered that his horse be brought. They led up the finest charger in the camp. He mounted and gave the order: "Make ready for battle!" The trumpets sounded.

The thief made a speech to the troops. It wasn't hard for him. In ten different provinces he'd almost always convinced the police of his innocence, so why shouldn't he convince several thousand soldiers who'd been doing nothing at all for months that it was time to launch an attack? The soldiers of the Imperial Seventh Regiment liked fighting. Each of them was certain he'd survive and if anybody had to die it would be the next fellow. They didn't know who Abraham de Moivre had been, or Augustus Morgan, or Stanislas Noisescu. And it had been too long since they'd done any looting and burning and getting drunk among the ruins. They formed into three divisions and marched out onto the plain.

"First the battering rams," the thief said to the general's staff officers riding at his side.

He was right. The walls of the city had resisted every weapon the Empire had invented. They must attack the gates. But the officers hesitated.

"We'll lose a lot of men," one said.

The thief laughed, behind the folds of the cape. He raised his clean and shining sword and galloped towards the city. The soldiers followed, shouting the general's name.

They never got to use the battering rams. The enemy opened fire from the walls. The plain was strewn with mutilated bodies. The sergeant who had taken prisoner a certain Rabavt-tuar in the depths of an experimental farm, and who had hoped that being young and strong he might last longer than the others, was one of the last to fall. He was galloping—so he thought—behind his general, when at the top of the talus a hail of projectiles mowed him down; he survived for a few minutes, long enough to realize that he had no legs and blood was bubbling out of his gaping belly and to curse the man who led him to his death.

If the thief had stayed to look around, he would have seen trickles of blood running from mouths and wounded chests and broken heads and he would have seen how these trickles ran together and formed streams, rivers, waterfalls among the stones.

Not a man remained alive beneath the walls. Not one, except the thief. He threw off the cape, tied it to the clean and shining sword, and waved it before the gates. The gates opened. The thief entered the city of Selimmagud.

CONCERNING
THE
UNCHECKED
GROWTH OF CITIES

The storyteller said: They gave all kinds of names to it, they made up all kinds of origins for it, and all of them were false. The names were mere inventions of obscure, scheming little men whose sole ambition was to get one step higher on a miserable official ladder or obtain a place among the palace lickspittles or a little extra money to satisfy some petty vanity. And the origins were laborious artifacts constructed to display some influential personage as a descendant of the hero who was supposed to have founded it in a fit of divine madness. Lighthouse of the Desert, it was called, and Jewel of the North; Star, Mother, Guide, Cradle. All those words, which you will have noticed are closely related, were worked up into pompous, hollow descriptions. Thus, the younger brother of Ylleädil the Great, starving and half frozen, pursued by the men who had dethroned the Warrior Emperor, coming to the foot of the mountains unsheathed the imperial sword in order to take his own life, but instead of plunging the blade into his heart he thrust it into the ground and cried, "Here shall arise the new capital of the new Empire!"—That's one of the stories. Or it's a helpless maiden who came to that same place, where the Spring of the Five Rivers still rises, and dug with her hands in the rain-wet dirt and made a well and buried herself alive in the mud mixed with her own blood, rather than allow a lascivious emperor to dishonor her. Usually the emperor is not named, though sometimes a name is daringly mentioned, all perfectly plausible, since there was no lack, indeed a steady supply, of lascivious gentlemen on the imperial throne. But this particular emperor, they insist, repented—already we're losing credibility—and raised a monument to the girl who had slipped through his fat fingers, moreover he provided housing for the people who looked after the monument. Others frown, cough, raise their eyes to Heaven and explain how Ylleranves the Philosopher, also called the Nose, not for the organ that grows in the middle of the faces of commoners and emperors alike but for sticking his in where it didn't belong—how Ylleranves recognized the place as the location of the Garden of Perfect Beauty told of in mystical books, and sought to build there a perfect city inhabited by a new and perfect generation who would regain the Golden Age of mankind. Of course the Nose didn't have time to achieve all this since he was still young when his bodyguards cut him into ribbons and gave the imperial throne to Legyi the Short, who was no worse than Ylleranves because it would have been hard to be a worse emperor than the Nose, but who was just about as bad, although he and the Empire both had a bit of good luck when he married an energetic, intelligent, fair-minded woman. Yes, gentlemen, yes: the Empress Ahia Della, who left the Empire sons, grandsons, great-grandsons as just and sensible as herself, to everybody's great relief.

All these works of the imaginative inventions unfortunately got into chronicles, which were made into books which everybody respected and believed, principally because they were thick, hard to hold, tedious, and old. And they got into legends, those tales that everybody says they don't believe in because they can't take them seriously, and that everybody believes in precisely because they can't take them seriously. And they were sung in ballads, which are insidious because they pass so easily about town squares and the ports and the dance halls. And none of it was true, none of it, none of the romantic origins, none of the melodious and fantastical names.

I'm the one who can tell you what really happened, because it's the storyteller's job to speak the truth even when the truth lacks the brilliance of invention and has only that other beauty which stupid people call mean and base.

You see the city? You see it now, as it stands? It starts up from the plain, all of a piece, the backs of the houses turned to what was a desert. It has no great gates, no battlements or towers or encircling walls. Enter one of the holes in it—a street—and climb. Seen from above, the city's an irregular many-colored square peppered with dark points, bright points at night. The streets and buildings and balconies and facades are all mixed up together, factories stand next to mansions, shops next to embassies. Very few of its inhabitants know all its streets and ways. I won't go so far as to say it's a labyrinth. If I had to describe it in a few words, I'd say: A colony of fear-crazed ants, escaping from a ferocious spider, build a hiding place. They climb straight up the mountain, with a desperate rashness not lacking in vainglory. They lay their foundations on stone or sand, it doesn't matter: the point is to go up, up as far as possible. They succeed, as you might expect. The mountains are buried under walls, balconies, terraces, parks; a square slants down, separated from a steep drop by stone arcades; the third floor of a house is the basement of another that fronts on the street above; the west wall of a government building adjoins the ironwork around the courtyard of a school for deaf girls; the cellars of a functionary's grand mansion become the attics of a deserted building, while a cat-flap, crowned with an architrave added two hundred years later, serves as a tunnel into a coalhole, and a shelf has become the transept for a window with golden shields in the panes, and the sky-light doesn't open on the sky but on a gallery of waterwheels made of earthenware. A street that winds now up, now down, ends abruptly in a widow's garden; a marketplace opens into a temple, and the cry of the seller of copper pots blends with the chants of the priest; the windows of a hospital ward for the dying open onto an ex-convict's grog shop; the druggist has to cross the library of the Association of Master Stevedores in order to take a bath; a curly palm growing in the office of a justice of the peace reaches outside the building through a gap in the stonework. There are no vehicles because nothing wider than a man's shoulders can get through the streets, which means that fat people and people carrying big loads have a terrible time even getting to the butcher's to buy some nice tender lamb for next day's dinner.

And it wasn't founded by the sword of a hero nor the sacrifice of a virgin, and it never was called Queen of the Dawn. Down there in the catacombs, currently painted with glow-in-the-dark colors, where dissolute teenagers dance and people who're going to die get drunk—down there, when the Empire was young and struggling to unite, lived outlaws, smugglers, and assassins; and from there a mule-path led over the mountains and across the marshes to cities and towns where these gentlemen practiced their noble professions. Alas for the wretched beauty of the truth!

A bit up the hill from the mouth of the catacombs stood a palace belonging to a person you've all heard of though you don't know anything about him: Drauwdo the Brawny. It wasn't really a palace but a big, ill-shaped, lopsided shed, wide and low-roofed, windowless, with an opening on the south side that you had to crawl into on all fours, a huge fireplace inside, and all round it a ditch filled with sharpened stakes pointing upward.

Drauwdo was stupid, cruel, ignorant, and vain, and these qualities caused his downfall. Yet in his own way he was strong, valiant, and these qualities brought him briefly and violently to the top. He captained the outlaws and assassins; and around him, though not thanks to him, a ragged band took shape, that used assault and murder to get what they wanted—clothes, food, furniture, gold—above all, gold. The chief handed out rewards, a woman, an extra handful of jewels, a piece of land. And his followers imitated the chief and built stone houses, if you can call them houses, though most of the bunch went on huddling in the caves and tunnels.

One of the not uncommon learnéd and progressive emperors one day leaned over a map of the Empire and by one banal gesture ended the ascendancy of Drauwdo the Brawny, the stupid, the vain, the cruel, the in-his-own-way valiant.

"Here," the emperor said, and put his manicured, bejeweled finger on a spot on the coastline of a cold and foggy sea far to the north. He looked at his engineers and geologists and the captains of his merchant marine and went on, "If we build a port here, transporting merchandise to the east will be much quicker and cheaper."

So the engineers and geologists set to work, the ship-captains waited, and Drauwdo, though he didn't know it, was doomed.

They laid out a road from the far-off capital to the mountains, and Brawny's bandits rushed happily forth from their stone houses and catacombs and killed the foremen and the workmen and robbed them of the little they had. Drauwdo congratulated his men and divided the loot equally among them. You see now why I called him stupid.

The emperor said, "Bandits?"

And a little captain, not particularly brave but not at all stupid, having received orders from a colonel who had received them from a general who had received them from a minister who had them from the emperor's own lips, readied an ambush and, in three hours, without wrinkling his uniform or losing a man, disposed of Drauwdo and his assassins, his followers, his cavemen, and his smugglers—every last one of them, as he believed, and as he informed his superior officers; which accelerated his rise in the shock troops and also considerably hastened the hour of his death.

But in fact one of Drauwdo's men had escaped, fleeing in time to hide himself in the deepest caves. Oh, well, he wasn't even a man, he was a kid they called Foxy, a prentice bandit, an insignificant leech, born and raised in the sewers of some city. Under Drauwdo he'd had nothing but dirty jobs to do and got slapped around and laughed at. But when the heads of Drauwdo and the other outlaws appeared along the road under construction, stuck on pikes, rotting in the sun, crawling with green-gold flies, there was Foxy's head still stuck on his own neck, thinking the kind of thoughts such a head has learned to think.

The road went round the mountains, crossed the plain, and cut across the marshes, which were drained and made fertile. The port was built, ships arrived, loaded wagons rolled along the way, and Foxy sat in the mouth of a cave and waited.

By the time the illustrious emperor died and was succeeded by his even more illustrious son, the cave was empty and nobody sat waiting in its dark mouth. But just below, on the roadside, were inns, eating-houses, hostelries, and shops that sold axles, wheels, reins, fodder, cloaks, everything a wagon-driver might need. The owner of all this was a thin, dark, close-mouthed man with a foxy face, who had begun by selling wild fruit to the road-workers and had quickly made a fortune. He was called Nilkamm, a Southern name, but a name all the same, and he sat behind the desk of the principal inn watching his guests come and go, keeping an eye on his employees, calculating whether it would pay to build another hotel a bit farther on, maybe on the hillside, one with a lot of rooms and a terrace on the flat, and bring in some women from the capital.

And when the young empress bore her second child, a daughter, Princess Hilfa of the unlucky name and unlucky life, Mr. Nilkamm'Dau was president of the Chamber of Commerce of his city, married to the widow of a magistrate from the capital, living in a big house built on foundations of stones from the misshapen houses of Drauwdo the Brawny's followers; and the bawdy houses, the gambling houses, and the dubious hostelries had, nominally, another owner.

It was now, by the way, a city: a city with wide but crooked streets that led to no port, no beach, no viewpoint, only to other crooked streets that ended in a dilapidated wall or an empty lot strewn with rubbish. There were more starving cats than there were glossy ponies with silver-mounted harness; there were more suicides than schoolmasters, more drunks than mathematicians, more cardsharps than musicians, more travelling salesmen than storytellers, more snake-charmers than architects, more quacks than poets. And yet, ah yet! it was a restless city, a city that was looking for something and didn't know quite what, like all adolescents.

It found what it was looking for, of course, found it with interest, as it got it all and lost it all and got it back and was the Jewel of the North and the Mother of the Arts and the Travellers' Lighthouse and the Cradle of Fortune; as the legends grew of the unlucky heroes and persecuted virgins and wise visionaries and all that stuff, sublime, incredible, ridiculous, fake.

The man was called Ferager-Manad. He was a sculptor and arrived richly dressed in a coach pulled by the first glossy ponies with silver-mounted harness the city had ever seen, attended by three servants. No doubt he'd spent his last penny on the coach and the ponies and the servants, since he wasn't a very good sculptor and it was a long time since anybody had ordered an allegorical group or a monument or even a little bas-relief for a modest tombstone. All the same he certainly hoped to meet with good fortune in the city, because it was only twenty days since the death of Mr. Nilkamm'Dau, first mayor of the city, president of the Chamber of Commerce and of the Resident

Founders Club, creator of the first Municipal Census, the first school, the first hospital, the first library, the first asylum, and the Department of Storage and Distribution of Meat, Leather, and Grain. Mr. Nilkamm'Dau's widow, now twice widowed but no longer young, needed to provide further motives of admiration and respect as soon as possible, since, having secretly despised him for his lowly origin and because he was from the South, she now found herself with a fortune larger than she had ever calculated on even during nights of insomnia, and had resolved not only to show off a little of the money but also to excuse her scorn by thanking her silent husband for being rich and dying. A mausoleum, she thought, what a good idea. A mausoleum was what they needed, she, her dead second husband, and the humble cemetery in the suburbs. Let's see, she said, a sculptor, a sculptor from the capital, an artist trained at the Imperial Academy, who'll make a monument of pink and black marble crowned with mourning figures and covered with garlands and vases and surrounded by bronze palings with little pots where aromatic herbs are burning. And she chose a name at random, because she thought she'd seen it before and because it was on the list of graduates of the Academy.

You've all seen the result: the beautiful marble ladies with marble tunics and floating marble hair gathered weeping about a prone figure, one of them lifting her hands to heaven, calling upon him who has left us. But the cemetery's gone, taken over by the city that obliterated and forgot it. The crypt is a candy warehouse, and the mourning figures lean over the watertank that supplies the Registry of Real Estate. Yet this isn't what matters in the order of events. The stone is worked, modeled, polished, the empty eyes of the statues gaze unseeing at people. What matters are the people, who have eyes that sometimes see. What matters is that the sculptor was a widower and poor and the woman who commissioned him was a widow and rich. They got married, not before the funeral monument was finished, as that would have been unseemly, but they got married the instant the aromatic herbs were set alight, and the sculptor paid his debts and acquired more servants and more carriages and more horses, and no longer worked in marble or bronze but became a patron of the arts, which is far less tiring, less risky, and more respectable.

So the artists arrived. The first were mere rowdies and idlers who'd heard that there was a rich patron of the arts in that city who might provide them food and lodging while they sat around in cafés till dawn talking about the poems they were going to write, the pictures they were going to paint, the symphonies they were going to compose, sneering at the world which had so far failed to understand them and despising the rich man who insisted that he did understand them and who, before paying for their bed and wine and soup, made them listen to him describing his own works of art and, even worse, giving them advice. But later on came another sort, who only sat around in cafés occasionally and spent most of their time shut away in silence weaving words or mixing sounds or colors. Among these artists who came to the city, early or late, some lacked talent, some lacked discipline, some lacked dedication, but all had a good deal of imagination. The city ascended and twisted yet again: it gained not elegance but a certain eccentric, unexpected beauty. Windowed galleries were built, which you reached by stairways that took off from anywhere, from the middle of a street, from the second-floor balcony of a house, even from other stairways; circular houses were built, labyrinthine houses, underground houses, tiny studios, huge music halls, chamber theaters, concert stadiums. The fashion changed, and the austere suits of businessmen and the gloomy high-necked gowns of their wives gave place to purple and green blouses, paint-splashed smocks, capes, tunics, stoles, naked torsos, sandals, boots, embroidered slippers, bare feet, flowered kerchiefs, cothurns, gold chains, rings worn in one ear, necklaces, bracelets, headbands, tattoos, bodices, colored beads glued on the forehead, anklets, cameos. Schedules changed too: the city that used to get up early, hurry through breakfast, work, eat lunch quietly at home, go back to work, eat dinner with the family and go to bed as the stars came out, little by little disappeared. Offices and institutions opened now about noon, afternoon was the busy time, cafés and restaurants were always crowded, and at night the city glittered. From the distant port far to the north they saw above the mountains a halo of light that never went out but only paled with the rising of the sun.

But let's not forget Ferager-Manad and his wife. She got no chance at a third husband, a pity, if you think of what a stunning funeral monument she could have raised to this one now that she had so many sculptors at hand to choose from. She died of a stroke one summer evening and I'm sorry to say that her widower didn't give a thought to mausoleums but only to going out every night with his protégés to try new drinks and new girls while they discussed pure form or the transcendent contents of line. Having filled several years with productive discussions and investigations, he died of pneumonia and was buried, unceremoniously because little remained of the immense fortune his wife had left him, and not where he belonged, because the door of the mausoleum surmounted by mourning figures had stuck shut and couldn't be opened.

Now we mustn't forget the capital. The imperial throne was occupied by Mezsiadar III the Ascetic, a well-meaning man, who spent so much time and so much energy in doing good that he succeeded in doing as much harm as twenty emperors of egregious iniquity. Mezsiadar wished all his subjects to be good, a dangerous wish. Gone were the peaceful days of the dynasty of the Danoubbes, founded centuries ago by Callasdanm the Fat, an emperor neither good nor bad, who understood, perhaps through laziness, that men and women are neither good nor bad and that it's best to let them go on being that way. The current rulers were the Embaroddar, of whom it was said,

"Black great-grandfather, white grandfather, black father, white son, black grandson, white great-grandson," because if one of them reigned well the next was certain to be a disaster, and if one reigned badly people took comfort in the knowledge that the next would bring blessings to his people. The Embaroddars knew the saying too, and as Mezsiadar II had been a good emperor, Mezsiadar III was certain to bring misfortune to all; except that he had decided otherwise; which was precisely why he did exactly what was expected of the members of that long dynasty, which happened to be on the point of ending, though nobody at the moment knew it.

Mother of the Arts is what they were calling the city then, and its inhabitants (poor twits) took great pride in such a fine name. Mezsiadar the Ascetic heard about this "Mother of the Arts" business and was suspicious, not because he distrusted the arts but because by inclination and conviction he was suspicious of everything. He asked for information, and the city officials (poor twits) wrote an enthusiastic and detailed memorandum. So as a precautionary measure Mezsiadar the Ascetic had them beheaded.

"What?" cried the emperor, reaching page 174 of the 215-page memorandum. "Where is piety? Where is decency? Where is prudence, modesty, frugality, selflessness? Where?"

Mezsiadar III the Ascetic was afraid of himself and his nights were sleepless. This, I think, explains it all. After ordering that the city functionaries have their heads removed, he sat alone in the shadows, in a bare, cold room, and thought intensely about the many-colored city that came alive at night, about the barefoot dreamers and the naked models, about promiscuity, absinthe, idleness; he thought about what goes on in darkness, he thought about caresses and murmurs, he thought about carpeted rooms, hoarse voices, stringed instruments lazily twanging, about narrow staircases leading up to stifling rooms where the shapes of bodies can be only guessed and an exotic odor tickles the nostrils, he thought about tongues, breasts, thighs, genitals and buttocks, in paintings and songs, fleshy, swaying, bulging, teasing, heavy, foully desirable. That night he sent dinner away untasted, lay down on his comfortless bed, and fell into a fever. Next day two army battalions left for the city.

When the last of the artists, actors, poets, musicians, what have you, had been killed or had escaped, the soldiers painted all the facades of buildings greenish grey, cut back the vines, and sprayed disinfectant on the garrets, the glass-roofed studios, and the music rooms. Paintings and lutes and books were all dumped into a great bonfire, which for the last time brightened the night sky over the mountains. The city remained a barracks as long as Mesziadar the Ascetic lived, though that didn't help give him peaceful nights or fewer headaches and belly cramps. On the contrary. His arms, shoulders, and head broke out in a pustulent eczema, which he considered to be a punishment for his failure to discover at once what was going on in the mountain city. So he sought information on all the other cities in the Empire, now very numerous; but what was going on in the other cities of the Empire doesn't enter into my story. A nobleman of his entourage turned the pages of the innumerable reports for the emperor, since his hands were tied to the arms of his chair to prevent him from scratching. He didn't die of the itch, nor did he die while reading reports; he died a few years later, when nothing was left of the eczema but scars, and the palace doctors said his liver had burst, who knows why.

He was succeeded by Riggameth II, a "white" Emperor, who had hated his father deeply since boyhood and went on hating him even after his death. Thus he tried to undo everything the Ascetic had done. Though Riggameth lived into old age he didn't have time to undo absolutely everything, but he managed a good deal. For one thing, he kicked the army out of the grey city.

The soldiers and captains and lieutenants departed. Some people painted their houses white or pink or green. A boy composed a song, a woman sketched a landscape, and neither got hanged for it. A theater opened, one or two vines put out buds. And though never again was it the Mother of the Arts, the city acquired a reasonable quota of musicians, actors, and poets.

And then in the arcane order of events, two women appeared. One of them would have gained the Ascetic's entire approval since she was a widow, pure, and stupid; she had known only one man in her life, and had considered the experience a prolonged torture. The other woman he would have had burned in the public square as indecent, which she was, as immodest, which she was, and as promiscuous, which she also was.

Neither woman was young, and both remembered the city as it had been before the pious intervention of the late emperor. The widow enjoyed gardening and embroidery, the other one enjoyed men. The widow venerated the memory of Mezsiadar, the other one spat when she heard his name. The widow was digging in her garden to plant a shoot of *trissingalia adurata* when she found her hands wet with hot water that seemed to be rising up from deep in the earth. The other had been a model and lover of painters and sculptors, and then had opened an inn for officers; the money from artists and from army men had run out and she was wondering what kind of business to start up, something entertaining, a place where lots of people would come, where she could talk with lots of clients and maybe, too, why not, maybe, even though she wasn't the girl she used to be, maybe . . .

It was thus that the springs of the thermal baths were discovered. One woman found her garden full of salty water which killed off her plants, and in disappointment put her house up for sale. Another woman bought it, thinking that the big front room could be used as a tea-room; but since the water kept welling up, she called the neighborhood schoolmaster and asked him what it was.

The first hot bath of the city was established in the garden court of a recently purchased house which hadn't yet become a tea-room. The widow who liked gardening brought suit, charging that the other woman knew what was rising from under the ground and had fraudulently paid much less than the property was worth. But the other one laughed, and even offered money in compensation, and when the widow wouldn't take it left the affair to her attorneys and turned her attention to her business, so that she didn't notice, or if she noticed didn't think it very important, that the widow lost her suit. She got rich, in any case, very rich—I don't mean the widow but the other one, of course—and ended up running more than a dozen thermal establishments, until she married, sold some of them, hired managers for the rest, and went travelling. Her husband was a penniless nobleman, a very handsome man, very quiet, very elegant, who was even rather fond of her. And it was she who built the Fountain of the Five Rivers.

A spa city can't be grey. It became white. Hotels sprang up, consulting rooms, rest homes; there was soft music playing to relax patients resting in their rooms or getting massages or working out in gyms or lying in mudbaths; crystal tinkled in lampshades, vases, glasses; and nobody from the emperor on down found anything to complain about, nobody except the invalids, who whined because they were invalids, because the massage was too rough or too mild, because the water was too cold or too hot, too deep or not deep enough, because they didn't have enough blankets or too many blankets. But the invalids kept coming, often from a great distance, to spend their money in the city, so everybody listened to them smiling and tried, if there was time enough, to satisfy them.

Now I'm going to tell you about Blaggarde II, the Listener, an emperor who had dreams and visions and heard voices speaking from stones, but wasn't a bad ruler, all the same. Or could it have been because he saw visions and heard voices that he wasn't a bad ruler? A small problem, which a teller of tales doesn't have to pretend to solve; so let's go on. For at least three hundred years the warm mineral waters had sprung up from the earth, and people had built ingenious and beautiful devices for the liquid that had enriched them and brought them peace. The Fountain of the Five Rivers never ceased to run; statues of dancing women spouted transparent jets from their mouths; stone figures of chubby children cupped their hands under bronze spouts; great alabaster cups, winged monsters with open beaks, improbable bouquets of marble sent streams of water falling into tanks and thence into bathing ponds and swimming pools and artificial lakes, when Blaggarde II marched south to put down the rebellion. We know now how that expedition ended and what effect it had on Blaggarde the Listener, his dynasty, and the history of the Empire. But what the chronicles don't always say is that the wound that finally brought the emperor to his death remained unhealed ever after the day of the last battle. No surgeon succeeded in closing it even temporarily. A year after the expedition to the south, somebody told the emperor about the waters which cured all ills, in the mountain city called, at that time, Star of Hope; and the Listener took to the road once again, not south this time but north, not on horseback in full dress uniform but lying in a litter and covered with woolen cloaks and blankets, not with songs but with lamentations, not surrounded by soldiers but by doctors and nurses. And he found a charming white city, sprawling but solid, where voices and music never got too loud, where nothing was done in a hurry, and where almost everybody who walked the streets or leaned on the windowsills had eyes as dull as those of the Lord of the Empire.

He built himself a palace. A real one this time, not a shapeless stone den but a palace bristling with towers, flanked by terraces and gardens looked out upon by the tall blue-paned windows of the dining rooms and retiring rooms and the tall red or yellow-paned windows of the gaming rooms and party rooms: a palace of limitless apartments and interminable corridors, with its own water-fountains for the sick emperor.

Blaggarde the Listener did not lay aside his duties. He no longer wore a coat of mail nor went to war, and day and night his life drained from the oozing wound, but he never ceased to busy himself with the tasks of empire. He saw his ministers first, then his secretaries. He had to keep in touch with the administrators and people in contact with the distant capital. Then noblemen appeared with their relatives and servants. And when the emperor brought the empress and his children to live with him, noblewomen came too, and teachers, palace provisioners, more noble families, and bodyguards and lickspittles and all the rabble that surrounds the powerful.

Once again the city changed. Many buildings came down to make room for the great houses of lordly folk; whole blocks were cleared for parks and gardens; the streets were widened so coaches could pass; the desert was watered to grow fruits and greens and flowers for a population now covering the mountains and overflowing onto the plain. Not everything was destroyed, though. Some things remained: the waters that cured all ills, or almost all, the Fountain of the Five Rivers, the underground tunnels of Drauwdo the Brawny, a few inexplicable foundations of rough stone, the mausoleum built by the city's first mayor, and here and there an eccentric staircase in the middle of a street.

The emperor's wound stopped oozing, but its inflamed lips would not join, even when painfully sutured or even more painfully cauterized. The emperor realized, or maybe the stones spoke and told him, that his life would end here. So he signed a decree making the mountain city the capital of the Empire. The whole Empire looked towards the new capital. All roads led to the mountains, across what had been the desert; all ambitious men dreamed of living there and some managed to do it, and for many centuries after that time there was no capital so splendid, so rich, so active, so beautiful, so prosperous. The dynasties of the Selbiddoës, of the Avvoggardios, and of the Rubbaerderum governed the vast Empire from that city, sometimes well, sometimes pretty well, sometimes badly, as usual; and the water went on welling up, and some palaces fell down and others were built, and some streets were closed off and others were opened up between the houses and the parks, and women bore children, poets sang, thieves stole, tellers of tales sat in tents and talked to people, archivists went on classifying ancient writings, judges sat in judgment, couples loved and wept, men fought for stupid things that in any case weren't going to last long, gardeners produced new varieties of eggplant, assassins lurked in shadows, kids invented games, blacksmiths hammered, madmen howled, girls fell in love, unhappy men hanged themselves, and one day a girl was born with her eyes open.

It's not so rare as most people think. Kids do get born open-eyed, though it's true that they generally arrive with their eyes sensibly closed. But everybody believes that the open eyes of a newborn baby signify great events, fortunate or unfortunate, in the life of that child. And her parents committed the blunder of repeating that belief out of vainglory, and of repeating it to her, in order to prepare her for her destiny; and the girl believed them. If it had been anything else she probably would have smiled, as girls smile at the stupidities of their parents, and forgotten all about it; but if you're told your life is going to be full of tremendous events you're likely to believe it. When Sesdimillia was ten, she looked around and wondered where the great events were going to come from, the fame, the tragedy, the martyrdom, the bliss, the glory. The city worked and played and lived and died, and up there stood the shining imperial palace.

"I'm going to be empress," she said to herself.

Her chance of coming to the throne was slight, as her ancestors weren't royalty or aristocrats, only moderately prosperous merchants. But she got there.

When she was twenty the old Emperor Llandoïvar died at the age of a hundred and one and was succeeded by his great-grandson Ledonoïnor, all his children and grandchildren having already died. The new emperor came very near to marrying the daughter of a duke with whom he used to play in the palace gardens when they were little children. But Ledonoïnor the Vacant wasn't called that for nothing. He didn't love the duke's daughter because, it seemed, he loved nobody and nothing and had no interest in anybody or anything. Nor did he love the dark-haired, active, efficient, handsome, hard girl who oddly enough held the post of Chief of the Internal Vigilance Forces in the palace, which she had won two years ago, disguised as a man, demonstrating greater skill and strength in armed and unarmed combat than her many male opponents. But two months before the emperor's wedding with the duke's daughter, an assassin somehow made his way into the palace and raised his sword against Ledonoïnor I, and the girl shortened him by a head with his own weapon, and the emperor married her, because when he promised her whatever reward she wanted for saving his life she said to him, "Marry me, sir." Though there was no proof and no witnesses it was said that she had provoked the assault, had paid the would-be regicide, and had promised him he'd go free. It's quite possible; what then? Greater infamies than that take place in the palaces of emperors, from which everybody suffers, nobles and commoners, rich and poor. In this case nobody suffered, not even the duke's daughter, who took it hard at first, but who married a man she could love and hate and who could love and hate her. The emperor didn't suffer because he didn't know how to suffer. The empress got what she wanted. And the people were all right because she governed well, really well.

Fortunately Ledonoïnor the Vacant spent his time walking through the gardens and galleries with his empty eyes fixed on emptiness and his soul empty and inert in his empty body and left her to rule, efficiently, harshly sometimes, but always with style. Every now and then she called him to her apartments, and nine months later the Empire had a new prince, and so it went for five years, until the emperor died of a tumor in his belly, probably because there was so much emptiness in there that it could grow as it liked till it suffocated him.

And a short while after, another rebellion arose in the south. The widowed empress put on the men's clothes she used to wear and her armor, and marched like so many other rulers to defend the unity of the Empire. She defended and won it in a single engagement, the Battle of the Field of Nnarient, on which the South bowed its fierce, rebellious head. She won the victory because she was brave, because she believed in what she was doing, because she knew to control armies, and because the leader of the rebellion was a fool. Handsome, ardent, but a fool.

The Treaty of Nnarient-Issinn was signed, unique in the history of the Empire: the South submitted unconditionally and swore fealty to the empress. She moved the capital to the border between the rebel territories and the states of the North, and married the ardent fool. Putting the capital on the border was a bold strategic move which assured peace for many years more than could have been expected when dealing with the South. Such was not the case with the empress's marriage to the rebel chief. She married him because it was her destiny, or so say those who believe in the destiny of those born with their eyes open. I say she married him because she was one of those empresses who had enough power to do whatever she liked. And they were happy, and provided the Empire with more princes and a fresh royal lineage, but you can read all that in any historical treatise or booklet of love poems, and in any case it doesn't matter to us.

What matters to us is what happened in the city in the mountains. People drifted away from the palaces, the great houses, the elegant shops, the parks and gardens and avenues. The nobles left, the gentle-folk, the rich folk, the field marshals, the ladies, the antiquaries, the jewelers, the cabinetmakers, they all left. People of no importance stayed on, some sentimentalists, owners of small businesses, owners of spas, people who had been there, like their parents and grandparents, for a long, long time. The mansions were divided and subdivided again and again, doors were cut in unexpected places, and ramps and stair-cases led up to higher floors that were no longer part of a house but a whole house, or several houses. Every bedroom, every spacious draw-ing room was made into two or even three apartments for humble families by putting up partitions and screens and enclosing balconies as kitchens. Corridors cut through rooms and, after various contortions, opened onto the street. The facades deteriorated, losing their paint and carvings. Some windows were sealed, others cut open; the street doors were no longer used, and their hinges and knockers didn't work. As this went on the streets grew narrower because so many lean-tos and sheds and enclosures were built up against outside walls, and the city acquired a silence, a mystery, it had never had before. Yet it wasn't a silence of menace, but of resignation. It went on so for years and years, growing ever more jumbled, more intricate, more improbable. Whole neighborhoods stood silent and abandoned. A street of elegant, unchanged houses, or of mansions bulging with labyrinthine apartments, behind which were precarious structures in what had been a park, led suddenly to a string of low, gloomy shop-buildings. And then came semi-detached palaces, and lonesome avenues where the grass grew and where many-colored awnings, now stiff with dirt, that had once sheltered the nobility at their games, now protected opticians, fortune tellers, dentists, masseuses, academies of physical fitness, dyers, and seamstresses.

For a time the palace of the Empress Sesdimillia stood closed but well maintained by servants who had remained behind for that purpose; but though the children the empress had with Ledonoïnor the Vacant and those she had with the Southerner respected her wishes, her grandchildren didn't care much about a palace they'd never seen, and failed to replace the caretakers when they got old and died. One night somebody stole the great bronze and golden bell from the main door, and that was the signal for general looting. Not violent, brutal looting as in war, but a mild, intermittent, natural, easygoing depredation, not totally secret but not overt, that went on till nothing was left of the palace but the walls, the roofs, a few doors, and the stone and marble pavements.

The mysterious, peaceful, labyrinthine city continued to offer its waters to those who came seeking a cure for something, though they were far fewer than in the times of the Listener. The skeleton of the deserted palace was about to be knocked down when a mayor asked permission of the capital to take over what was left of it and turn it into a cultural center. They sent word that he could do as he pleased, which is exactly what this mayor, who had written poetry and plays as a young man, did. He repaired the ruinous building at a low cost, remodeling the rooms for readings, concerts, lectures, plays, dance, and exhibitions of art. There was a natural history museum, two libraries, and an historical archive. The people of the city never took a great deal of interest in so much art and culture, but the invalids and the convalescents paid money to go in and see plays or hear music, or merely out of curiosity, and so for many long years the great doors were never locked.

The Empire didn't entirely forget the mountain city during this period, because its curative waters kept it in mind, and because vehicles carrying freight went on using the north road to and from the port, but indubitably its fame, importance, and attractiveness had declined.

It was just another city: people knew somebody who lived there or had lived there, people had a relative who went to take the waters there, people consulted the annals in the archives seeking information on the various imperial capitals, people remembered a trip, a conversation, a name. And that was all. The city didn't die, but it rested, it dozed. I'd say it was making ready for something.

Have you heard tell of Heldinav'Var? Of course you have, of course you have. I'll bet my boots and buttons you've forgotten all the virtuous emperors, but who is there, eh? that doesn't wink and grin as soon as they hear that name, Heldinav'Var? Well, I'm about to disillusion you, because I'm not going to talk about that lecherous and vicious emperor. Who did have some good qualities, though most people don't believe it, or don't want to. No, I'm not going to talk about him but about one of his relations, Meabramiddir'Ven, Baron of the Towers, Seneschal of the Walls, and a lot of other equally meaningless titles—and the emperor's first cousin. That, now, is meaningful. It means, for instance, that he nursed certain pretensions about sitting on the imperial throne some day, despite the fact that he was ninth in succession. Heldinav'Var was a swine, but he wasn't stupid, which was one of his good qualities. It's always good not to be stupid, and when it's the emperor who isn't stupid, people can have hope; not security, of course, but still, hope helps. Heldinav'Var was Crown Prince and his father the Emperor Embemdarv'Var was dying. The prince began planning what he'd do when he succeeded to the throne. He knew, among other things, that his cousin the Baron of the Towers was capable of murder to clear his own way to the throne, and that the first to fall would be the Crown Prince, and since the Crown Prince had no interest whatever in dying, because he was having a stupendously good time and intended to go on doing so when he was emperor, and since—another of his good qualities—he wasn't an assassin or a despot and therefore didn't consider poisoning or hanging his cousin even if his cousin deserved it, he sent for the Seneschal of the Walls and informed him, in public, what he thought of him, and added that either his august cousin would depart from the capital before nightfall and go as far as he could possibly go, or the tenth person in the line of succession, Goldarab'Bar the Obese, the author, as you know, of the *First Codex of River Commerce*, would instantly become the ninth. Meabramiddir'Ven, who hadn't expected this, sought a defense, an explanation, anything, but couldn't think of anything, which suggests that he was considerably stupider than the future emperor. And the worst of it was that his illustrious cousin did not address him with indignation, nor demand justifications or avowals of innocence, but merely waited, almost smiling, arms crossed, to hear what the aspirant to regicide would say. He finally hit on a way out, not a very plausible one, but very seemly: He had no aspirations to the throne, to power, to be ruler of the Empire, oh, no no no; if he had been asking the opinion of some strategically placed persons concerning the desirability or indesirability of Heldinav'Var's succeeding to the throne, it was because he wished to prevent the vice, the shamelessness, the indecency of his cousin from being openly displayed in the person of the emperor. What would become of the Empire? What would become of its subjects, with such an example at their head? And he went on to explain how good he himself was, how honest, decent, discreet, modest, and virtuous. All the same the future emperor sent him off, because he was not only dangerous and a very poor liar, but boring. And the Baron of the Towers had nothing for it but to go, not swearing vengeance because that wouldn't have suited his role of redeemer, but declaring that he pardoned and forgave.

Since it had been made clear that he was to go as fast as possible, he set out for the mountain city. Foreseeing that he might be observed, he arrived as a redeemer, a pilgrim, on foot and poorly dressed. So much so that some gave him alms and others bowed their heads as he passed. When an ancient, poverty-stricken woman called him to come in and share her midday meal, he wouldn't sit at the table, but ate humbly crouching in the doorway. That was when he discovered that he liked this job, not as much as the job of emperor, maybe, but it was all he had. That same evening he preached for the first time.

He didn't himself know very clearly what he was preaching about, and at first he had to be careful not to get mixed up or contradict himself, but so what?—if he couldn't be an emperor he'd be a saint. Chance certainly favored him; he'd found the perfect stage for his sanctification. The city was full of petty little people who had nothing but their little jobs and their little superstitions all ready to be set in order and pigeonholed. There were the invalids, too, trying to get well or trying to die, and their relatives, hoping the invalids would get well or would die, according to the closeness of the relationship and the quantity of money involved. And all of them welcomed piety and preaching.

The emperor's cousin struck it rich. Not in gold, for as he won converts and began to believe he really was the mouthpiece of Truth and Goodness, he didn't need to fake it any longer but embraced poverty with all his heart; but in prestige, fame, respect, that's to say, in power of a certain kind. And power is what he'd been looking for. He preached in the streets, lived frugally, went barefoot, walked with his hands joined and his eyes downcast, never raised his voice or indulged himself in bad temper or anger or impatience. He wasn't a saint, but he seemed one.

Now let me tell you, sanctity is catching, much more so than vice. Obviously, Heldinav'Var never converted anybody nor even tried to, since those who succeeded in getting close to him were already convinced, but his cousin converted multitudes of unbelievers and persuaded many to pray, to live frugally and chastely, to fast and sacrifice, and other idiocies of the genre. And he induced even more to take up preaching.

A year after the precipitate departure from the capital of the Baron of the Towers, now the Servant of the Faith, the mountain city had become the most pious, holy, and overwhelmingly prayerful city the Empire had ever known. A hundred religions and a thousand sects sprouted and thrived as, in other times, painting and poetry had sprung up, or the curative waters, or the curfew, or luxury, or fortune-tellers' tents. Going out in the street you weren't pounced on by people selling baskets, jewelry, carpets, crockery, or herbs, but by people selling eternal salvation, which is a treacherous bit of merchandise, believe me, requiring wit and prudence in the handling, since even when you can sell it for a good price, once the bargain's sealed it can always turn against the seller. But like baskets, crockery, and carpets, religion offered plenty of choices. The priests revealed to the people that the roads leading to bliss were almost infinite in number and followed the most surprising routes. From frugality and abstinence to the unbridled exercise of every passion and perversion, by way of spiritual and bodily disciplines, the study of arcane texts, contemplation, renunciation, introspection, prayer, you name it, everything was a means of reaching a paradise which, according to the divinity-peddlers, could be attained by just a little effort and, of course, a little donation, usually directly proportionate to the client's—I mean the believer's—bank account.

Yet those were the years in which the face and body of the city changed the least. This really isn't surprising, given that religion doesn't take up much room; some people say it requires no room at all, at least not externally. A space about the size of a dining room was big enough for a good-sized family, with a platform or pulpit, or a column, or a niche, or a well, or some cushions, or nothing, depending upon which route to heaven was being followed. And a lot of people held their services outdoors, perhaps with the idea that without a roof to interrupt them the prayers would get aloft faster. Change, what there was of it, occurred on the roofs and rooftops and terraces, from which rose the symbols of the innumerable religions—images, stars, crosses, spheres, shafts, some of them fancy, some of them humble, all competing for the most followers in the shortest time. For there were feuds, battles, even wars between the sects, over a forgive-my-sins here or an absolve-me there, over a dozen renegades or a half-dozen apostates, over a ritual murder or a tonality in the dogma. But that brought no changes. That people were arguing over religion instead of politics or money didn't change the direction of streets or knock down old buildings or get new ones built. It merely increased the population. No longer did people come from afar seeking a cure for their ills in the water that bubbled from the depths; but they came seeking in the signs and symbols erected on the rooftops a cure for other ills, not so very different from the first ones, may I remark.

The Emperor Heldinav'Var died, and his cousin who had been Baron of the Towers and Walls died. We know who the vicious emperor's successor was, but the preacher had no successor. His sect split and split again until it was lost in the sea of creeds and soon forgotten. The city reached its apogee as a religious center, in fact, some hundred years later, under the reign of Sderemir the Borenid, a soldier of fortune in the west who, having attained the throne by unspeakable means, became a good ruler, much better than many who had royal blood and a right to sit on the throne.

To get from the western provinces to the capital, the Borenid certainly had no need to go via the city of the religions, but to understand his devious itinerary, one must remember what his intentions were. And he never forgot the generous welcome and the favors shown him, most of them quite disinterested, when he encamped at the gates of the city. So, three years later, when he took the throne of Empire, he presented the city with gifts and authorized special subsidies for it, proclaiming it Mother of True Religion.

A fine name. And a clever one. Let us recall that the Borenid, that apparently brutal man, that deceptive warrior who knew the souls of men even better than he knew swords and shields and chariots, always distrusted any power attained by inexplicable forces. Thanks to his subtlety disguised as benevolence, every creed, every church of the mountain city was convinced that it was the owner of the True Religion, and swelled up with pride, and pride is an ill counselor. Every creed and church looked down with placid condescension on its rivals. So many donations, so much official recognition could only be the perdition of the thousand sects. It's much more stimulating to be marginal, to act without recognition, than to receive public thanks; it's through struggle and polemic that the True Religions grow robust, invent new ways of drawing people, fabricate saints and prophets, apostles and popes, sharpen their wits, freshen up the merchandise and advertise it cleverly. But what do they become if all they do is repeat today and tomorrow and next year the same thing they said yesterday, the same words, the same gestures, the same expressions of piety and conviction, without risks, without competence, without ups and downs, without, in a word, martyrdom? What they become is boring. The priests got tired, the gods got tired, and the faithful got very tired. Fewer and fewer pilgrims traveled north. Since the city still had from its years as the capital all it needed to support itself without relying on goods from other places, the highways leading to it fell into disuse, got cracked, grassy, full of ant hills and badgers' holes, and the Empire, this time, really forgot it. It was remembered only by the drivers of the cargo-caravans going to and from the port, but that's very few out of the huge population of the biggest empire known in human history. At best it was a subject of a little interest to the men who drank and smoked in the bars of the seaport; to the other cities, the other ports, the other states, and the capital, it was nothing. The Borenid ruled for many years. Since he was an exceptional man, many say he was the worst emperor ever to occupy the throne and others say he was beyond all comparison the best. Be that as it may, he didn't forget the city of the true religions; they say he never forgot anything at all, and that may be true. He didn't forget the city, but he didn't worry about it either, and, without entirely neglecting it, since at least once a year he sent a confidential agent to look about and sniff the air and listen to what was going on, he classified it as a harmless place.

So it was throughout the Borenid's life and that of his sons, grandsons, and great-grandsons. The city lived on, silent, obscure, with its merchants, its rich and poor, its courts of law, its women of the streets, its officials, kids, madmen, its holidays, schools, theaters, professional societies, with everything a city should have, isolated, deaf and dumb, its back turned to the Empire, alone. Since it had been solid, rich, great, it still had the public buildings and mansions that had been built to last, but it was all getting covered with moss and lichen and vines. Abandoned pools filled up with water-lilies, wild varieties of drahilea grew in the marble hair of the statues. Everything was yielding, fleshy, full of leaves and green stalks swollen with lazy sap. Many say it had never been more beautiful, and they may be right. It was absorbed into the mountains and all that grows on the mountains, becoming part of the earth within which it had been born deep down in the caverns. Maybe it would have been all right if it had gone on that way; today it would be a vegetable city inhabited by willowmen and palmwomen, a city swaying in the wind and singing and growing in the sunlight. But human beings are incapable of being still and letting things happen without interference. Some say this is how it should be, since restlessness and dissatisfaction are the basis of progress, and that's an opinion that has to be taken into account, though it's not really worth much consideration.

To explain what happened next, we have to go back to the Borenid. That extraordinary man, strong as an ox and clever as a fox, frugal as a saint although there was nothing saintly about him at all, that conqueror risen from the mists, that king engendered in a plebeian womb by a nameless vagabond, not only knew how to keep the Empire unified and satisfied, peaceful, prosperous, active, and proud throughout his whole reign, but also managed to make his achievement last. What's more, his heirs didn't try to undo it. Generation after generation of emperors and empresses benefited from the legacy of the Borenid, and though not one, except perhaps Evviarav II, the Drakuvid, had his strength or his vision, all of them were sensible, just, and prudent. What more can one ask? Then the dynasty of the Eilaffes, also remote descendants of the Borenid, but in whom the traces of his blood were slight and dubious, came to the throne, and with them came catastrophe.

This time the South played no part. The South remained tranquil and disposed to sneer, half amused, half hopeful, at their northern brothers tearing themselves to pieces. And their northern brothers as if to please them put on a great show, violent, tumultuous, filling earth and sky with battle-cries and screams of pain. Yes—I'm talking about the Six Thousand Day War. Which didn't last six thousand days, nowhere near it, and nobody seems to know why it got called that, except some obsessive collector of historical curiosities who might explain that it took about six thousand days for the Empire to recover from the war of the three dynasties and to re-establish order, peace, and its borders. Or so say the academic historians. Maybe the true truth is something else, but I only say maybe. Maybe the true truth is that it took six thousand days, more or less, for Oddembar'Seil the Bloodthirsty to seek, locate, and exterminate the members of the other two dynasties and all their followers. What we do know is that the whole North was one great battlefield, and that since fighting was the sole occupation of the time, the northern seaport was paralyzed, and no freight-caravans passed by the mountain city. The war itself was far away; the city continued to be draped in moss and ivy, with flowers in the water tanks and on the cornices, bright-colored beetles hiding in the stone eyes of the statues and the fountains, and so it went on almost until the end, and all might have remained the same, maybe right on up to now, if Bloodthirsty, who fully deserved his appellation, hadn't been betrayed by an ambitious general.

Oddembar'Seil had to flee, but had nowhere to flee to. The South was still neutral, but not safe; the South was never safe for power-seekers. And Oddembar'Seil sought power. He fled northward. Not alone, to be sure. He divided his men into groups which blended in with the various groups fighting each other in every region they had to cross through, and pushed them on northward, far north, in a desperate and not very rational effort to reach the sea, to find ships in which they could sail down the coast on the old shipping route and disembark and attack from the east. It looked as if he might succeed. Most of his troops caught up to him in the foothills, and on a summer morning they marched off again and came to the gates of the city. I don't know, nobody knows, whether Bloodthirsty cursed or grinned; I don't know whether he looked at the unknown city with greed, or scratched his head in puzzlement. I do know he entered it peacefully, his men carrying their weapons handy but not brandishing them, and that the inhabitants of the mountain city watched him with curiosity. I know that they even approached him and offered food and shelter. He needed both, but did not accept them. I know that the enemy army caught up to him there, striking at the rear guard while it was half in the city streets, half still on the plains. Good-bye ships, good-bye shipping route and hopes of a surprise attack from the east. Everything was lost, but when you have to fight, you fight.

There have been hideous battles in the long history of the Empire. It's even possible there have been some, a few, crueler than the one that was later called the Battle of the North, as if there was only one north, one battle. But it's hard for anyone to imagine what happened, and I don't know if I can give you any idea of it. I'll try, that's all I can do. Oddembar'Seil the Bloodthirsty gave a great shout when he heard that the enemy was advancing and his men were in a vulnerable position, unready, some of them crowded into the narrow city streets and others scattered out through the fields around it. Concerning these men of his, you can say anything that's usually said about soldiers and warriors, but not that they were cowardly or undisciplined. They heard him shout and they regrouped, took arms, fell in as best they could, and tried to repel the attack. Bloodthirsty leapt across the fallen and ran to fight in the front rank, shoulder to shoulder with his men. He was no coward either.

The Battle of the North lasted exactly fifty hours. The men attacked, broke, scattered, retreated, had a bite to eat, and returned to the attack. Telling such things one is sickened by what men are. They were not men; nor were they wolves, nor hyenas, nor vultures, nor eagles. They were blind organisms, mindless, nerveless, without feeling or thought, with only the power to wound, and blood to shed. They didn't think, believe, feel, see, or hope; all they did was kill and kill again; all they did was retreat and retreat again, and attack again, and kill again. They had been born, they had worked, loved, played, grown to manhood for nothing but this, to kill in the fields of the North under the walls of a mossy, flowery city. Fifty hours after the first attack not more than a hundred men were still afoot, naked, dirty, bloody, maimed, mad. They didn't know or care who the enemy was: they went on killing, attacking, shouting with their lacerated mouths, weeping from their wounded eyes, breathing through their split nostrils, holding their weapons with what fingers they had left, returning to attack, to kill. It was then that Oddembar'Seil cut off a head that rolled on the blood-soaked ground, and on the headless body, on the filthy, hacked breastplate, flashed a collar of gold and amethysts. The future emperor shouted again, and so ended the Battle of the North: he had killed Reggnevon son of Reggnevavaun, pretender to the imperial throne.

You know how the inhabitants of the northern city and his few surviving soldiers crowned the Emperor Oddembar'Seil the Bloodthirsty on the site of his victory as he stood erect over the body of his enemy, dirty, wounded, feverish, naked, with a marble crown hacked with hammer and chisel from the head of a statue that adorned an old aristocratic garden now used for playing-fields, and how then and there he signed his first decree, declaring the city that had witnessed his triumph the capital of the Empire.

Six thousand days hadn't passed, not yet. But the war was over, and when that time really had gone by, the northern city was still capital of the Empire; and the courtiers, the functionaries, the ladies, the admirals, the judges, went to and fro by the Fountain of the Five Rivers, under the arch on which stand the mourning figures from the first mayor's tomb, through the winding, narrow streets, and sometimes stopped to drink or to wet their fingers and forehead in the alabaster basins that still ran with healing water. For the emperor had ordered that they be preserved: he never forgot that the citizens had offered him food and shelter, and he believed that this had brought him luck. He commanded that his palace be built using the walls of the Empress Sesdimillia's palace, keeping its style and plan, antiquated as they were, and he prohibited any change in the streets and buildings, the parks and fountains. The outside of houses could be repaired and painted, but not changed; the incredible staircases could not be moved; the inopportune walls could not be taken down. Building could take place outside the city limits, and did, and interiors could be remodeled, and many were, so that houses could return to what they'd been in the reign of the Listener and his heirs. And nothing more.

The six thousand days of the Emperor Oddembar'Seil the Bloodthirsty were fulfilled, and another six thousand days passed, and a bit more. His rule was harsh and violent; he was implacable with his enemies and soft with his friends. But it must be said for him that he reorganized the Empire and brought it peace, territory, and unity. He did so brutally, with more blood, more deaths, with woe and mourning, but Reggnevaun would have been no more merciful, nor can we know what might have happened if the Six Thousand Day War hadn't been fought. A stroke finished him in the midst of a banquet, and the tears shed for him were few and false.

Many years have passed and many emperors have lived and reigned, but the mountain city is still the capital of the Empire. Toadies and social climbers invent poetical names and illustrious origins for it, and Drauwdo the Brawny is a mere character in bedtime tales for children who don't want to go to sleep yet, but the Bloodthirsty was perhaps the first who understood it, and made his understanding clear when he ordered that it not be touched or changed. And those who came after him must have guessed the profound wisdom in this order, which seemed so little in accord with the spirit of the times, since they too enforced it. Here it stands, as in the years of the healing waters, of the gods, of the musicians, of the battles. It looked like a dense mesh of gold, with tiny, irregular openings, pulled tight, stretched across the mountains. It's grown on the farther side, of course, and seven more roads have been added to the one that ran to it; all eight are wide and well-paved as royal roads should be, and swarm with travelers and traffic. It turned its back on the plain that was a desert, a garden, a battlefield; the new mansions, the rich houses, the palaces of the nobility, are to the north, on the road that leads to the distant port. It shines at night, and the light on the peaks never goes out, only dimming in the dawn, as when the painters and poets used to talk and drink in the cafes. It prospers and thrives as it did when the healing water welled up out of the ground. It's a splendid capital, beautiful, mysterious, charming, old as the capital of an old Empire should be, solid, wealthy, built to last thousands and thousands of years. And yet I wonder. . . .

BOOK TWO

THE GREATEST EMPIRE

PORTRAIT
OF
THE
EMPRESS

Yes, said the storyteller, I knew the Great Empress, and having known her, I can tell you that of all of the people who praise her, weep for her, write about her life and deeds, make up songs about her, not one of them does her justice. And probably they never will, because she was greater than any poem or elegy or chapter in a history book. She wasn't young or beautiful or learned; she wasn't good-natured; she was rude, harsh, and pigheaded. But I know what made her great. It was the wisdom that lies in seeing things in a different way and using knowledge in a different way. It's not something anybody ever taught her. Abderjhalda didn't get her education in palace schoolrooms or exclusive colleges for children of the nobility, but in the streets. And when I say streets I mean miserable hovels, crowded holes, tenements, I mean little shops with filthy windows and furtive customers, cafés where no sensible person would ask for a glass of water, lousy hotels with people crammed into the rooms, where if you dug around in the basement you'd probably turn up a corpse or two that happened to have had its throat cut. There she was born, there she grew up, there she got her education, in what may be the best school of government. Notice I say government, not power. Power, bah! she'd say, looking disillusioned. Only if you forget about power can you govern well, she'd say. And it was true. She forgot about the power she had, which was immense, and so power, ignored and disdained, courted her, trotted after her, like a prostitute fawning on a good-looking wealthy man. But she despised it utterly and made it wait like a beggar at the palace gates. Anybody could approach her, anybody could come into the palace and talk to her, for not depending on power, she had no fear, and dispensed with protocol and ceremony. She was the first person on the imperial throne for centuries and centuries who kept no bodyguards, the first to go down into the streets unprotected, without armed men surrounding her, carried in a sedan chair like any rich woman, or on foot like any workman's or tradesman's wife. So it was that I knew her.

I was a very young man then, scarcely more than a boy, and I was just beginning to tell stories in the squares and streetcorners of the capital. Nobody knew me, nobody had offered me so much as a booth in the outskirts of the city where I could tell my stories. I had no visions of the future, I wasn't aspiring to be where I am now, sitting on cushions on carpets on a marble floor, gazing at stained-glass windows, drapes and crystal lamps while I recall my tale. I wasn't greeted with the bows and murmurs that meet me now when I enter the Great Tent. I told stories in the streets, that was all. Every day, to be sure, more people gathered round to hear me, and the more people there were the better I spoke, the happier and surer of myself I felt, the more colors, scenes, characters, landscapes, and battles filled my tales. And next day there were more people, and the day after still more, and when the police finally got around to objecting because people couldn't get through the streets where I was telling my stories, I had to move to Northern Domains Square, and soon after to the Market Place. I was still three years short of twenty when one day a coach stopped alongside the square. I didn't notice it. I was already used to officials, officers, great ladies, whole families arriving in coaches to join the circle sitting around me. A woman got out. I didn't even look at her, but went on speaking. I was telling the history, the true history, not the fabrication that got made up later, of the Curse of Ervolgerd IV, that emperor of the Vlajanis dynasty who after his death protected his friends and took atrocious vengeance on his enemies, driving his assassin mad and forcing him to mutilate himself at the palace gates under the horrified eyes of the crowd drawn there by his delirious screams. I was describing the first public appearance of the dead emperor when the woman sat down among the people listening to me and listened to me with them. It was a cold day, a cutting wind blowing down from the north, the sky grey. People had brought braziers to the Market Place and heated pots of chocolate on the coals, or spiced wine, or thick soup. Some of them had cloaks, others held their heads down and hid their hands in their sleeves. Somebody offered the woman a steaming cup and she said thanks and drank it. And for several hours, until I finished my tale, saying: *And Ervolgerd the Corpse never returned again to walk among the living,* she and a wrinkled old woman and her grandson, who'd both been there since the start of the story, shared a tattered cloak that had been washed so often it was threadbare. I ate the food the audience offered me, took the money they gave me, and stayed a while listening to what people had to say about what they'd heard, for I was young then, weak, the fruits of vanity still tempted me. Finally I got up, stamped on the ground to warm up and get the pins and needles out of my feet, and left. Three streets away, the coach caught up with me. The coachman told me to get in. I said no, of course. A storyteller knows from the start the risks he runs, and if he's a real storyteller he avoids them with care, using violence if he has to. I carried no weapon, I never had one and have never needed one; I just said no and went on walking. The woman who'd been in my audience wrapped up in an old cloak with an old woman and her grandson leaned out the coach window: "Come on, you stupid kid!" she shouted. "The empress orders you to obey!"

I'd never seen the Great Empress. How could I have? I lived in a humble house in a humble district, like most people of my profession I had few friends and those few were as poor and obscure as I was, and obviously storytellers don't enter the imperial palace. If one of them does he isn't a storyteller, he's a poet. And yet I entered the imperial palace. I wasn't a poet, I'm not a poet, I never will be, yet I entered the imperial palace. I'd never seen the Great Empress, never heard her speak, didn't know her face, but the instant I heard her shout at me I knew it was her, and if they'd tortured me to make me deny it, I couldn't have, I would have gone on saying, yes, that's her!

The coach had stopped. I got in and sat down beside her. She asked my name and how old I was, and I told her. She didn't ask or say anything else till we arrived at the palace about an hour later. At first I was afraid. This is the great lady who rules the hugest empire ever known—what does she want with me? Does she want to kill me? Lock me up in a cell? Kidnap me? Make me her gigolo? Turn me into a servant, a eunuch, an ass-licking courtier? Of course I was afraid, but she was so quiet and natural, taking everything so easy, the grey day, me sitting by her, the bumping and swaying of the coach, that my fear wore off and in fact I got rather sleepy.

"You're going to sit here and you're going to tell me the lives of all the emperors who preceded me," she said.

"What?"

"You heard me, you aren't deaf."

"Your Imperial Majesty is crazy," I said.

She burst out laughing. She put her hands on her hips and laughed like a washerwoman.

We were in a palace room that looked out onto a palace garden. There was a fireplace with a fire burning in it and carpets and a piece of gilt furniture with a round mirror in the middle and flowers all over the place and a gaudy parrot swinging on a ring hung from the ceiling.

"All right," she said, "what's this about me being crazy?"

"I hope Your Imperial Majesty will find it possible to pardon me," I said, "but if Your Imperial Majesty thinks one life is long enough to recount the deeds of the rulers of the Empire, it means Your Imperial Majesty doesn't know anything about history, or is crazy, or both."

She sat down in a very high-backed, straight chair. "I'm going to tell you three things," she said. "First, I couldn't be more sane. Second, I really don't know anything about the history of the Empire, or a lot of other things. And third, if you say Your Imperial Majesty one more time I'm going to knock you into the middle of that garden."

From then on I called her ma'am, since that's what she liked to be called, like the ancient empresses of the heroic times or the fragile secret women of the dynasties of the third Middle Empire. Every day, for years, I sat down in that same room at nightfall, and told the empress all I knew, all I could, about the emperors and the empire. I made two conditions, one of them silly, the other serious: that she'd have that malevolent and presumptuous bird removed, and that nobody should know I came to the imperial palace. It didn't matter about the parrot, it may have tickled her, or was of no importance to her. But she wanted to know why I wanted my visits to the palace kept secret. I had to explain to her that a storyteller is something more than a man who recounts things for the pleasure and instruction of the crowd. I had to tell her that a storyteller obeys certain rules and accepts certain ways of living that aren't laid out in any treatise but that are as important or more important than the words he uses to make his sentences. And I told her that no storyteller ever bows down to power, and I would not. If she, the empress, knew nothing about the empire, I could teach her, and it was my duty to do so, serving not the throne but the people who upheld the throne; but nobody else should know about it, because although I didn't need to make any profit from what I was doing there, still I didn't want people saying that I hadn't been paid anything, not a coin or a shoebuckle or a grain of rice, for the same stories I told in the streets and squares. Other people, I told her, officials, captains, bureaucrats, servants, can enter the palace without risk, because they have nothing to lose. And a poet can, if he's the real thing, because being beyond power he can't lose. But a storyteller is no more than a free man, and being a free man is a dangerous business. I told her this, and she understood. She never said a word about my presence there, and I never met anybody on my way to and from the side door that led to the room that looked out on the garden. There she'd be waiting for me, and there she'd listen to me, attentive, very rarely asking me a question or two.

Through the years she had left to live, which were many, though not enough, I spoke to her of the Empire, and I'm happy to say that she understood the meaning of what I told her and knew the difference between models to imitate, adapting them to the times, and examples to reject or forget or avoid with care. I began with the obscure eras of the Divided States, from which no chronicles or even names remain. I went on to the Chiefs, to the Lords, to the Little Kingdoms, mentioning here and there a warrior, a battle, a *coup d'etat*, a conquest. And after a few months I got to the first emperor, the one who called himself the Emperor Without Empire, who built a palace in the middle of a desert, had a huge gold throne made, sat down on it, and said: I am the emperor. I told her that on that day the Empire was born. And I told her about the dynasty that followed, the first, during which the Empire began to grow and find its strength. By the time I got to the Kao'dao, those rageful and visionary emperors who made the first code of law and moved the throne from the desert to the cities, two years had passed, and I was no longer telling my stories outdoors in the squares, in rain or cold or heat or snow. I told them in a pavilion of silk and wood at the end of an avenue of sycamores that no longer exists, a pavilion constructed especially for me by the Tea-Shredders Guild. But I didn't talk about such matters to the Great Empress, and though she saw I had better clothes and shoes now, she asked me nothing. She went on listening. And now and then she'd speak about herself, when I'd finished with the mad kings, or the wise ones, or the sick or saintly or warlike or ambitious ones, for every kind of man or woman has managed to fit their buttocks onto the imperial throne.

"Yes," the empress said, "new blood's always needed, wherever and whenever, on the throne. More than ever in these times. But of course no such disinterested thought inspired my wish to climb up here and sit on the golden seat. To tell you the truth, I took my first step in this direction so that old Dudu could have somewhere to die. I didn't want him dying in the street, where the sweepers would find his body in the gutter and dump it in the ditch along with spoiled food and dead cats and bits and scraps of stuff even beggars can't use. I wanted him to die in a bed with a blanket over him and his head on a pillow. I wanted him buried in a hole dug in the earth and covered over, and then a stone put there, with his name, which wasn't Dudu but something a lot more complicated. But of course I haven't even told you who he was. He's worth remembering because it's worth remembering every- thing you meet in life, just for its own sake. He called himself a juggler, but fumbling with plates and balls and worn-out hats in a dump where they sell bad liquor doesn't make a man a juggler. He was a fat, lazy, lascivious old drunk, and that's the best I can say about him. When the waters of the Great Flood began lapping at the mud and wattle huts on the edge of town, the woman who maybe was my mother told me to stay put, keep still, be quiet, and she'd try to get out and come back to get me. I didn't believe her, I didn't have any reason to believe her, but I kept still and quiet because at ten years old I'd already learned quite a lot. Only after hours had gone by I started crying because I was cold and scared. Plop, clop, plop, clop went old Dudu's cartwheels in the water that had started rushing down the alley. But I howled louder than the water and the wheels, and the plop, clop halted, and the old man pulled away the boards that closed the doorway and said, 'Aha, a kid!' He took me up into his little wagon, he handed me the traces and told me to drive. I cried and drove and the old man went ahead singing—

> Ladies and gentlemen, here's the rain,
> it breeds weasels and toads,
> the old whore, the rain,
> it gets into your bones
> and rots out your braaaaaain!

"But when he was dying (she said), he wasn't fat any more. He was a grey skeleton lying in the rags on the wagon. He wasn't drunk any more because the tumors that were growing all over inside him were in his throat too and he couldn't drink alcohol or anything else. He wasn't lascivious any more, he didn't have the strength to move his eyes even to look at a woman let alone jump on her, and he had only the shadow of the thing he'd used so often to get wine without paying for it from the women in the bars, and to rape me in the half-ruined houses the flood had left empty, and to keep warm with smuggled liquor in a brothel, winter nights. It wasn't because I was generous that I wanted him to die in bed not in a ditch. Just the opposite. If the old man died in the street I'd be taken up, no matter what, being so young, and the police would have free use of me till some bureaucrat stuck a seal on a paper saying that the old man died from natural causes and they could dump the half-rotten body into the ditch. Then they'd let me go again, onto the streets, without the wagon, without anything, worse than before. So I drove the wagon around with the old man on it, dying. He couldn't sing his dirty song they'd nicknamed him for any more, 'Du-du mama, du-du baby,' but I sang at the top of my voice:

> Ladies and gentlemen, this is love,
> so sweet it makes you quiver,
> like wind, it can blow you apart
> and send shivers up your liver,
> but it soothes your heaaaaaaart!

"I had three possibilities in mind (she went on), but I confess that I never really expected that the trader would be the one to look after me in the end. Thank goodness he decided to wait for me, at night, hidden in the gap between two houses, and asked me what my song meant, proposed that I come with him, and listened to my conditions, which were so modest that he had to smile. Thank goodness, because the other two, an ex-servant who sold herbs and syrups on the street and a tinsmith, were both married, and their wives would have made my life impossible for sure. All three had houses, which is why they interested me, but the trader's was the best. It had two whole windows. His name was Boroimar. He used to stick an apostrophe in front of the last syllable to make it look like he came from a noble family, and he told a lot of stories about past grandeurs that nobody believed, or maybe some people did, but not me.

"Old Dudu was fat, Boroimar was skinny; the beggar was a drunk, the trader never drank anything but fruit juice or milk; the old goat would sleep with any woman anyhow anywhere, but the other one was scared to death of women and the only thing he wanted of them was to look and look and look till he got up courage enough to do a little pawing. The old guy who died had had something fairly efficient between his legs, but the man with the house with two windows—who was dying too—had a shapeless sort of object that couldn't stand up for anything. The old guy, in his day, assaulted and exploited and enjoyed, but this one hesitated and held back and was never satisfied. He'd look, and sniff, and touch, and slobber, and wet himself and sob, and five minutes later he'd start all over. I'd been through a lot of physical pain from the old guy and I didn't feel like learning a whole new range of tortures. The old guy died in a soft bed with sheets and blankets, his head on a pillow, trying to hum *du-du mama, du-du baby,* with a real doctor looking after him, not some filthy witch-doctor, and we buried him in a hole in the ground under a stone with his real name on it. The trader stayed alive for a while, and I smiled and did everything he asked, thinking about the solid walls of his house, the wood floors, the windows looking out on the street, dreaming that I'd get hold of it all and wouldn't ever have to live in the street again. I smiled, I sang to him, I brought him his food, I even washed him, perfumed him, stroked his head, which was getting bald. And I dreamed so hard that I convinced him my indifference was kindness, and he had a public scribe draw up a document saying that, having no children or wife or brothers, he left me everything he had. And a week later he died of food poisoning. No, I didn't kill him. I didn't kill him because it didn't occur to me. If it had, who knows? Now that I'd had a taste of house, shelter, bed, hot soup every day, I might have killed him. But he went off to have dinner with a little fellow who came every so often to sell him goods, probably stolen, since it was all done in secret and the stuff was stored a long time before it was put up for sale, and they ate baked fish in an eating-house by the river and next morning they were dead, both of them and a lot of other people who'd eaten there. The police rounded up the restaurant owner and his employees and didn't bother with me, as they hadn't bothered with me when old Dudu died. When I'd got Boroimar buried, I took over his business. I was fifteen.

"When I was seventeen I was living with a lieutenant who'd come to my place to sell a ring to pay a gambling debt, so he said. I gave him a lot less than the ring was worth and a lot less than he needed, because I was already good at doing business and knew when a man wanted more than he said he wanted. And I knew that men don't think. No, don't laugh. They don't think. Now and then one of them thinks, sure, and says what he thought, or writes it down, and that's so unusual that nobody forgets it. People stick these bits that other men have thought together as best they can, sometimes in appropriate ways and sometimes in really silly ways, they repeat a set of other people's disconnected thoughts for one situation and another set just as disconnected for another situation and believe they're thinking. The man who can remember the most thoughts somebody else thought and twist them around to adapt to the most situations passes for the most intelligent, and the others all admire him. Somebody else shows up who can think, and speaks or writes, and people say he's crazy, and they may even stone him, but his ideas remain and the nonthinkers eventually get hold of them. And so other people's ideas, which get used like handkerchiefs or scarves, keep getting more numerous, and this is called progress. I was seventeen, I couldn't read or write, I didn't know mineralogy or chemistry or geography or theology; but I made the lieutenant into a captain and the captain into a colonel by the simple process of rejecting what people said they thought, and trying to find a new idea. I found two. One of them turns on the second one, a very old one, that says that we're all made of the same clay. We'll talk about the first one later.

"The colonel got married, because I told him he ought to. His wife was very rich and had a large, well-connected family. He used to meet me in a stone house in the woods, on beyond the country houses of the nobles and the magistrates. I'd sold the business for a good sum, not out of need, having in mind that idea about the clay we're all made

of, telling a couple of gossips that I wasn't thinking of selling, sacrific-
ing a few things so that the buyers I had my eye on would think I was
inexperienced and didn't know the value of the stuff I had there; and
here I was now, living in a stone house with six windows and a balcony
on the upper floor and six windows and a double door on the lower
floor. I was getting bored, and so I had time to find a second idea. I
thought: *I can.*

"You realize that's a new idea, right? It's something that comes a
little, a very little, from outside, but mostly from inside. Maybe the
words and the order they're said in are old; that's true enough; I'd
almost say it's a good thing. New words in a new order can be alarming, since mostly they just hide frivolity or nothingness. But if the old
words name another way of seeing, then you've thought of a new idea,
and that's not something easy to do, believe me. I did it. I thought: *I
can.* And when I'd thought it, I joined it to the other idea, and looked
around me, and saw all the other people not thinking. I didn't go on
and discover another thought, but I decided something. So I pressured
the colonel a bit. The poor guy was getting tired of me, or maybe not,
maybe it was just that I was an inconvenience to him in his new position with his new responsibilities: but since he wasn't a bad fellow, he
felt grateful to me and wasn't going to drop me. I used what he
thought were ideas he'd thought, and we parted in tears. I assure you
his tears were real. I left that house among the trees with a coach-load
of clothes, tableware, jewels, perfumes, linens, furs, and money.

"Those were hard times. But I ask you, what times aren't hard?
They suited me: people coming and going, the social classes mixing
together, no questions asked, everybody preoccupied with something
or other. Anybody could say her family papers had been lost, or talk
about treason, catastrophes, ruin, or say she'd come from a long way
off. I paid bottom price for a very fine house in an elegant neighborhood. It had belonged to a merchant who went bankrupt. I furnished

it and fancied it up, making sure that the facade and the gardens stayed as impressive as they'd been when the merchant lived there and his wife gave parties and his sons put on hunts and excursions thanks to the stupidity of those who'll pay a thousand for stuff not worth ten which the merchant, count on it, had bought for two. I wore black. I hired servants. Very little was left of the money I'd had from the sale of the business and from the colonel. So what did I do? Did I go out looking for money and security? No, no, of course not. Just the opposite. Within a few days all the rich men that lived in that rich neighborhood had been told by their servants, who'd been told by my servants, that a young widow was living in that house there, who wouldn't go out, or receive company, or see anyone . . ."

Yes, said the storyteller, she herself told me the story we all know, which goes on changing and gets embellished little by little; and long years from now, when not her children but her grandchildren's grandchildren rule, it will have become something as untrue and incoherent as the false history of Ervolgerd the Dead or the false tales about the empresses from beyond the desert. And so storytellers will have to sit in their tents to tell the truth, and if anybody still trusts them, somebody will believe them.

Now, I was no longer a humble boy telling stories in the squares. I was a young man for whom special tents were set up so he could sit in them to speak and people could come to listen from far away. At the time, I thought I'd achieved wisdom: I lived in the same little house in the same poor neighborhood, and had only added a few things to it, stoves to keep me warm in winter, dishes, a carpet for the spare room, lamps in every room. I still had few friends, pretty much the same ones as before; I didn't travel by coach but on foot, as before, as I still did until just recently, when rheumatism, not vanity, has obliged me to use a sedan chair instead of my legs. And I went on going to the palace in secret, to the room that looked out on a garden, where I told the Great Empress the lives of the Lords of the Empire. She listened, attentive, serious, taking in everything I said in silence except for an occasional question. They weren't the stupid, shrill questions idle women ask, but thoughtful and concrete, like the questions humble women ask softly and timidly. The Great Empress asked them with an imperative curiosity, as if they mattered, and not only to her, which they did. And now and then it was she who talked. Always for a reason, and never in arrogance, which she had none of. Something I'd mentioned would remind her of a person or an event in her life, and then she'd talk. Or perhaps she needed someone to listen to her when her solitude filled her with words. It was thus that I learned the story of the tricobezoar. Plenty of foolish, banal tales are told about this event; I want to tell how it happened that the wife of Mr. Ereddam'Ghcen, who after all was a mere rich man, a very rich man to be sure but not a nobleman, merely the master of immense plantations of rice and innumerable mills, was able to approach the emperor. The truth is, the emperor approached her. He called her to his side, inaugurating with a simple message of politeness one of the most peaceful eras the Empire ever enjoyed, and luckily still enjoys.

Do you know what a tricobezoar is? Animals are shorthaired or longhaired. All female animals lick their young, and most animals lick themselves or their herdmates. And at certain times of the year they shed. Some of them swallow a good deal of hair during their long or short lives, and this hair is indigestible and difficult to eliminate; it gets deposited in a nook or cranny of the stomach, where food and digestive acids work on it, forming a ball that gets bigger and harder as time goes on. It doesn't kill the animal, but when people butcher a dead animal, occasionally, rarely, they come on a tricobezoar, or bezoar-stone. And you can bet they fight fiercely for the possession of this gut-grown jewel, because it's supposed to have curative and magical powers. Maybe it does, maybe; even I don't know. The emperor's physician, in any case, said that he did know, and the emperor believed him.

Idraüsse IV was on the throne. A lot of you lived under his rule and know what kind of emperor he was—a good man, an unhappy man, too mild, too easily influenced. It might have been a good period for the people, but they were chaotic, contradictory years. Idraüsse trusted everything and everyone, believing everyone around him had good intentions and wanted what he wanted, the well-being of his subjects. But those closest to an emperor aren't always honest men; if they were they'd be doing honest work and wouldn't have time to machinate and conspire to get the protection of power or commit the iniquities they commit to get the throne to listen to them. What's more, the emperor was a sick man. Anything made him bleed, even the rubbing of heavy clothing; his knees, his ankles, his elbows would swell up with huge blood-blisters that had to be pierced to keep him from howling in pain and becoming a complete invalid, and then he'd bleed and bleed no matter what they did; his legs and arms were twisted up in grotesque positions, and although his face was quite beautiful, his body could inspire disgust and horror. The doctors straightened his limbs with gentle exercises and tended his sores, but then there'd be a new attack and they'd have to begin all over again. He'd married a beautiful young noblewoman, strong and healthy, the Empress Kremmennah, in order to give the Empire a healthy heir, not a bleeder like himself. We know how cruel the destiny of men and countries can be. His illness allowed him to approach the empress only twice, and neither time bore fruit; and then, one night, the strong, healthy young empress caught her foot in the hem of a dress, fell down a marble staircase, and broke her neck. Idraüsse wept for her and interpreted her death as a sign: the dynasty of the Elkerides would die with him. He was, as it happened, wrong.

"Yes," the empress said, "I was married to Ereddam'Ghcen, the very rich man with a great house with a garden that backed onto mine, the man who, having seen me a couple of times up on my balcony, insisted that one of his daughters pay a neighborly visit to the sorrowful young widow. He was a widower. His children were all married and he was lonely. He was a good man, not too bright. He did think, though he hadn't selected the best from other people's thoughts, only the most inoffensive. He didn't believe, for instance, that the South should be laid waste with fire and sword, or that everybody around him was out to cheat him, or that money was going to save him from death or misfortune, or that he ought to maltreat people who worked for him, or that what he didn't know was dangerous. Ours was a peaceful marriage. And a good bargain for us all: his children didn't fret themselves wondering who'd look after their father till he died, he'd found somebody to look after him and keep him company, I had more money than I'd ever thought it possible to have, and his fortune was so huge that his sons and daughters-in-law and sons-in-law didn't see me as robbing them of anything. The imperial palace was a long way off. I didn't think about going that far, why should I? It seemed to me that I was doing fine, I couldn't do better. I could consider myself satisfied. And when the time came I'd bury my husband and live a nice life with no shocks or surprises, eating all I liked, going to the theater, doling out charity, occasionally having a reception in the drawing rooms of the house, strolling in gardens and along avenues with some woman friend as agreeable and placid as myself. How I could have imagined myself as agreeable and placid, I'll never know. Maybe because my childhood had been poor and violent, so that I associated wealth with peace, which is false, and even if it were true it wouldn't apply to people. Still, I should have known better, because sometimes I felt very uneasy, almost angry: looking after my husband, running the house, receiving a few guests and making a few visits, embroidering by the window—it wasn't enough. So I'd undertake to change things, refurnish a room, think up new ways to lay out the garden, have a pergola built or a pool put in, and supervise the work myself. I even took an interest in Mr. Ereddam'Ghcen's business and suggested a few innovations which, to his great satisfaction, and mine, were highly successful. I tried to think my own thoughts about my restlessness and my bursts of activity, and saw that I had too much energy and needed something to spend it on. What could I do, what more was there to do? I did everything that was at hand to do. But night would come and we'd sit in the sitting room talking about little daily things and I wouldn't feel tired, I'd feel angry. I hid the anger, and it grew. We'd talk, too, about what people in the streets were saying, in the Chamber of Commerce, in the squares, the clubs, the cafés: rumors about the new bridge, or some municipal ordinance, or the arrangements for some public festival, and I'd say what I'd have done if I'd been one of the engineers or the town councillors. My husband would be amazed, his daughters would shake their heads and say women shouldn't meddle in such matters, and one of his sons might look at me curiously or say that it seemed to him I was right. And we'd talk about the emperor, about his illness, his doctors. So we learned that they were trying out a new cure, and so I learned that in the name of the Emperor Idraüsse IV the doctors were asking anybody who found a tricobezoar to bring it to the palace to help stop the sick man's hemorrhages. What's a tricobezoar? I asked. And when they told me, I remembered that old Dudu had had what he called three magic stones, and that I still had them, along with a worked silver tea-stirrer. Tripestone, hiddenstone, bilestone, he called the three. Remembering that, I seemed to see the old man, the deepset, red-veined eyes, the unsteady mouth, the tortoise neck, the wine-swollen belly, the stained fingers, and the dirty palm on which lay three stones:

"'You'll never see the like of these, kid, no way. This is a tripestone, this is a hiddenstone, this is a bilestone, and they're all magic. Tripestone makes hair grow, strengthens the kidneys, whitens the teeth. Hiddenstone enriches the blood, cures eye disease, takes off smallpox scars, and heals broken bones. Bilestone cures jaundice, stops vomiting, and drives away nightmares and madness.' He'd laugh and close up his hand. 'And the three together give a man what he needs to satisfy every woman he meets, and keep death away.'

"The tripestone was greyish brown, opaque, wrinkled; the hiddenstone was darker, almost black, and smooth, soft to the touch; the bilestone was greenish, with brighter, yellowish veins. The hiddenstone was the tricobezoar.

"I hadn't looked at them since the day he was buried, when I'd dumped out what was in the leather bag he always kept with him and in the heap of filthy stuff found them and the silver tea-stirrer, which I kept. I didn't believe in magic but still I kept the three stones because how can you not believe in magic? I don't say it doesn't exist, all I say is I wouldn't trust one minute of my life to it.

"So I went to the palace. I could have sent a servant with the stones, but I was curious to see the house of power. It didn't impress me, maybe because I was prepared to be astonished and diminished by the magnificence and pomp. Magnificence was there, wealth, luxury, and power, but no beauty, no interest, or passion, or intelligence. It was just a big business office where everybody worked very hard. I showed my three stones to a bureaucrat who examined them and gave me back the two that couldn't help the emperor. Then he thanked me, praised my generosity, and asked me very pleasantly what my name was and where I lived. And I went back to my house which was quite beautiful, sufficiently luxurious, very small compared to the palace, and more and more boring.

"A month after that the imperial messenger came.

"My husband, his children, his sons-in-law and daughters-in-law got all excited and kept asking me questions. I told them about the tricobezoar, saying that when I was a little girl I'd been given it by a servant in my parents' country house, because I'd never told them the truth about my childhood—why should I? And I told the messenger that I was quite willing to go to the palace next day to see the emperor.

"I wasn't the only one. Twenty-three people had given their hidden-stones to prevent the emperor's hemorrhages, and he called them in one by one and thanked them, because it had now been many days since he'd had bleeding or swellings in his joints. My husband's daughters and daughters-in-law wanted me to wear every jewel I had; they wanted their father to buy me a new gown and coat and shoes and gloves and fan and hairdo; they wanted me to shadow my eyelids and pluck my eyebrows and paint my cheeks and mouth. I said no. With a smile, because they were good girls and terribly upset, but I said no. Next day the poor things were almost in tears seeing me put on a simple blue dress, shoes that were nice but not new and not particularly showy, plain blue gloves, and no jewels, none at all. You can't, you just can't! they said. At least wear this gold chain, or a pearl necklace, or your diamond ring, something, a jeweled belt, a pin . . . The carriage came. I kissed my husband and the girls and went to the palace.

"The emperor didn't much impress me either, since I'd seen sick men before, past hope, near death, past relief and remedy. He received me very simply, looked at me attentively, smiled, and said he was extremely grateful. And the doctors and counselors around him looked at me with curiosity. I held up my head and looked right back at them, one by one, without the slightest timidity, and not with curiosity but with such cold lack of interest that one of them nearly said something but didn't, and another flinched as if I'd threatened him. I did it deliberately, of course. And then I ceased to look at them, as if they weren't there. Nor did I raise my eyes when they all left the room at a sign from the emperor. He told me to sit beside him and asked my name, though he certainly already knew it, and what my husband did, and if I had children, and how I had come by the hiddenstone.

"Magic can't be trusted, I assure you; what's useful is quickness and certainty in making up one's mind. And that's not magic even if it looks like it, because you can only do it when you've learned to think your own thoughts. In those few minutes I had realized that the emperor was dying, that some of the people around him were fakes and the rest incompetents, and that here, at the throne, I could find a use for the energy I wasted moving furniture around my house, building pergolas in my garden, studying budgets and markets in my husband's office. Once I knew that and knew I knew it and discussed it with myself and accepted it, when the emperor asked how I'd come by the stone, I told him the truth and added, truthfully, that he and I alone knew it. Then he asked me—what could he ask me? come on, that one's easy—a man who ruled the world, sick, exhausted, smothered in praise and adulation, disappointed, disillusioned—what could he ask me? Why I'd told him what I told him. And this time I didn't answer with the truth. Of course not. I told him that my secret weighed upon me, not always but sometimes, which wasn't true. I told him that when I felt especially happy or unhappy my secret weighed most heavily and was hardest to bear. And, of course, he asked me whether at the moment I was happy or unhappy, and I said: Both. In short, I drew him deeper into the informality that he had chosen for these meetings with people who'd parted with their hiddenstones for his sake. And by giving a personal tone to what was said I confused him, so that I could reassure him immediately, as if he was the one doing me a favor. He found this all so unexpected that I was the only one of the twenty-three who spent the whole afternoon with the emperor. And the only one who came back, once and again."

Yes, said the storyteller: her influence in the imperial government began long before she became the Great Empress, long before she ascended to the throne. She was still the wife of the rich landowner and flour and grain merchant, she had no position, no official designation, but the emperor listened to her. At first he didn't follow her advice, or not always, and didn't base his decisions on her opinions; but the woman disconcerted him because she showed him things in another light, from different angles, turned them into something very different from what they'd seemed, and at the same time explained to him how he could understand how a minister felt, an employee, a rich man, a poor laborer, a fisherman, a nobleman, a bureaucrat, a soldier: in a word, how to make governing not a heavy legacy but a vocation, an adventure. For the first time in years, perhaps in his whole life, the emperor was happy; no less ill for that, but happy and serene. And the people felt the same. It was thanks to her, to give just one example, that the stevedores' strike was settled, which had threatened to become a bloody struggle. On the advice of a couple of rapacious little men, the emperor was about to order the army to intervene, when Abderjhalda spoke up, and we know now what that means. While the emperor was reading the decree before signing it, she was drinking tea, looking out the window, very interested in what she saw out there, beyond the palace walls. And as if she wasn't talking to him, and as if it didn't matter at all to her what he was doing and was about to do, she said:

"There was a doctor that looked after a rich man who had a chronic illness. One day the sick man had a very serious attack, painful, cruel, and his children asked the doctor not to try and prolong his life, since death would free him from all suffering. 'Yes, that's true,' the doctor thought, 'they're right: the sick man will rest at last, I'll be well paid both for doctoring him and setting him free from his torment, and I won't have to go on year after year, day after day, night after night, vainly rushing here to give the poor man some useless medicine; and the children will inherit, and won't suffer because their father's in pain, and they'll remember him fondly.' But before he quite resolved to suspend treatment, he looked into their eyes, those children of his patient. And he looked into the sick man's eyes. And he looked at himself in a mirror on the wall across the room. The children's eyes were bright; the sick man's eyes were opaque; and on the day, not far off now, when death came at last, women would drape black cloth across the mirror. He saw another solution, then, which would do as much good as the first one to the sick man and to himself, though not to the children; but it would be much fairer to them all."

The Emperor Idraüsse IV looked at the mirrors of his salon and said, "I understand."

The soldiers stayed shut up in their quarters waiting for an order which didn't come. Three days later the stevedores marched in front of the palace shouting hurray for the emperor, and the day after that they went back to work.

The members of the council, the ministers, and the secretaries all hated her, of course, but she didn't oppose them, or sneer at them, or try to win them over; she ignored them. They didn't exist, she didn't see or hear them, didn't know they were there. One of them tried to put a stop to her visits to the palace, but his machinations were so clumsy that they resulted in his being exiled to Lemnarabad. Another tried to collude with her, another made an attempt on her life, and so on, until, defeated though they didn't want to admit it, they agreed the best thing to do was wait till her influence over the emperor waned and ceased, as had happened before. A vain hope, and in their hearts they knew it, but what else could they do?

Mr. Ereddam'Ghcen died of a sudden pneumonia, and she buried him with pomp and ceremony, wept for him, and wore mourning for him. When she began to go out again, she went to the palace, sat down with the emperor, and explained to him, clearly, mildly, firmly, what would become of the Empire if he died a childless widower; and then she explained what would become of the Empire while he lived and when he died, if he married her. A year later the Emperor Idraüsse IV, ninth ruler of the dynasty of the Elkerides, married Abderjhalda and crowned her empress.

The whole Empire looked with distrust on this woman of whom little was known and much spoken, young, not beautiful, not an aristocrat, a rich merchant's widow, hard, not delicately educated nor marvelously elegant, and they asked what disasters she'd cause, how many of her relatives she'd make ministers and generals, what luxuries or vices she'd spend money on, how much longer the sick emperor would live now. The whole Empire was mistaken. There were no new ministers or generals, no wild orgies, no lovers, no poison in the emperor's soup. Everything went on as before, or at least seemed to. At first the empress was no more than she'd been before, a confidante or counselor. She sat on the throne beside the emperor; she came to his bed sometimes, though the disease in his blood kept him from doing anything but talking with her or sleeping by her side, so that it appeared that he would indeed die childless and his dynasty would end with him; she appeared at official ceremonies; and that was all. She began by employing her energy for herself: she learned to read and write, to speak all the dialects of the Empire, she learned law, economics, mathematics, though she didn't want to hear anything about chemistry or astronomy; she learned geography and strategy, and summoned a storyteller, a young man who'd recently begun practicing his trade in the streets and squares, to tell her about those who had sat before her on the Golden Throne.

At the end of two or three years, Abderjhalda knew a great deal, the people were already calling her the Great Empress, and the emperor left the government in her hands while his illness slowly grew worse. The time came when he was rarely able to get up, dress, walk, or eat without help. Yet he lived several years more. The Great Empress looked after him herself: she chose his doctors and attendants, checked that his medicines were given, that he ate as he should and received the injections and cauteries and treatments for his twisted limbs whenever it was necessary. This was why he had some good spells, when he felt almost like a well man who can sign a document or lean out a window or stop in the middle of a walk to ask a question, bow, look at the west, go on walking. . . . This was why he was able at last, twice, painfully, perilously, to have relations with the empress; and though he considered it a miracle, or to be precise two miracles, because he didn't think that he'd fully and totally played his part on either of those two sad nights, this was why the empress bore two sons, Eggrizen and Fenabber. The elder, Eggrizen, is our present emperor, Idraüsse V.

"Yes," the empress said, "that was one of the reasons, of course it was. I didn't pick you just because you were a good storyteller, though that was part of it. But there were other good storytellers, cleverer, wiser, more famous, and I could have chosen any one of them, except that the reason they were cleverer and wiser was that they were older, sometimes a lot older. Maybe you'll be like them one day, and even greater than they. I believe you will. I had to be able to believe it, because my sons, who are going to sit on the throne of Empire, have to be not just strong and healthy and handsome, they have to have that vein of madness and passion that lets a man or a woman see the other world which is the shadow of this one, and of which this world is the shadow. And now, good-bye till tomorrow."

Yes, said the storyteller, the emperor died not long after, when Prince Eggrizen was playing in the palace gardens and his teachers were getting ready to teach him to read, to ride, to command, and when Prince Fenabber was beginning to walk and babble. There'd be no more princes of the Elkerides, to be sure, but the succession was assured, a great relief to many who had feared new struggles for power. And they could rest easy, as it was clear that the Great Empress was strong enough to put down any attempt to prevent her sons from inheriting the throne. And the people loved her: neither she nor her boys needed watchmen or guards, for only a madman or an idiot, seeing her in danger, would have gone on sitting on the doorstep in the sun and not rushed to defend her with their life. She arranged the strangest burial ever heard of for the dead emperor. It was as splendid as most imperial funerals, but an edict prohibited gifts and requested music and flowers. And whoever wished, man, woman, or child, noble or commoner, soldier or beggar, could enter the palace mortuary, at any time, without precedencies or protocols, and say farewell to their emperor. The most skillful embalmers had hurried from Irbandil and worked so swiftly, using all their craft and knowledge, that the emperor lay now, serene and beautiful, his troubled blood at peace at last, a smile on his pale lips, among brocaded silks and down cushions, and his subjects came by him and some paused and raised a hand to touch his forehead or cheek or the fringe of his garments. And they all felt, faintly or deeply according to their capacity to feel, the sadness of ending, of knowing this was the end, that never again would Idraüsse sit on the golden seat of the Lords of the Empire, or open his eyes to the morning, or even feel pain, that he'd never talk to his children, never put on the soft slippers that didn't hurt his feet, that his rings and his dreams and his clothes and his thoughts and his pain were useless, empty, and that even if someone else used them they wouldn't be the same. For thirty days the viewing went on, then he was buried. During those thirty days I didn't go to the palace and didn't see the empress or her sons. Afterwards I kept on going there to tell her the history of the emperors. And while I told my tales, secretly in the palace and openly in tents that kept getting bigger and fancier, the Empire prospered, grew rich and peaceful. Now and then there was a commotion, naturally; people got restless. But then they found there was no reason for it, and with the passage of years the subjects of the Empire learned to replace restlessness by an expectancy that easily became enthusiasm, whether they understood the cause of it or not. For example: a year after

Idraüsse's death the empress named as Finance Minister a Southerner, a self-taught man with no pompous titles from the Imperial Academies, and she awarded the Imperial Prize of Art to a Southern painter, a scruffy, mannerless fellow who, in a miserable cane shack beside the marshes, had painted cruel, masterful works satirizing the government and blaming it for the poverty and backwardness of his land. The Empire feared the worst. But Clabb-lar-Klabbe was the best finance minister the Empire had had for millennia, and you know I'm not exaggerating, you know there was and still is and will be for years to come enough money for universities and hospitals, for aid to the sick and the poor and the handicapped, for helping those who can't help themselves, for restorations and conservation and embellishment, for better roads and ports, for building museums and schools, for making sure everybody has light, heat, and food. And you know that she didn't confront the South with weapons, or decrees, or disdain, as so many emperors had done, but tried to understand, and did. Maybe she discovered new thoughts, I don't know. She understood that the transformation of the South would come, if ever, from its own marshes, its intransigent tribes, its forest towns and lake cities, not from the throne. She understood that such a transformation might not be pleasant or convenient, and that the best she could do was to keep the South at peace, without violence. Hence, she put up no resistance: she recognized the existence of the South, removed all military garrisons from the borders, had the fences and barriers and barbed wire cleared away, encouraged and even flattered the rebels, gave in on a lot of little points of which she exaggerated the importance and held firm on a few big issues which she played down. And the Southern rebels began doing business with the northern lands, visited the cities, toured the palace, smiled, and fell asleep.

When the Great Empress prohibited all private transportation by wheeled vehicles, many people said she was crazy. Even I, who knew her well by then, looked at her in astonishment and asked her what could be the use of so absurd a measure.

"They increase delinquency," she answered. "They've increased divorces and confinements for mental instability."

"I confess I don't understand you, ma'am," I said. "What have wheeled vehicles got to do with all that? What you ought to do, surely, is institute measures against delinquency, divorces, and insanity."

"And increase the size of the police force and extend their powers?" said she. "Make it even harder for people to get a divorce? Encourage doctors to study and treat the mad? How stupid. You wouldn't be a good ruler, my dear friend, though I hope my sons will be. All we'd get by that would be more policemen full of pride and brutality, more lawyers full of red tape, more doctors full of fatuity, and hence more criminal assaults, more divorces, and more nut cases."

"And by prohibiting private transportation—?" I inquired.

"We'll see," she told me.

She was right, of course. Cars and private planes disappeared. Only those who absolutely had to travel more than twenty kilometers were allowed to use public transportation on wheels. Most people walked, or rode donkeys, or, if they were wealthy, had themselves carried in litters. Life slowed down. People didn't get anxious, because it wasn't any use. The big centers of buying and selling and banking and industry disappeared, where everybody used to crowd in and push each other and get cross and curse each other out, and small shops opened, little places in every neighborhood where every merchant and banker and businessman knew his customers and their families. The big hospitals that used to serve a whole city or even several cities all disappeared, since an injured person or a woman in childbirth couldn't travel a long way quickly any more, and little health centers opened that people could walk to and where every doctor knew her patients and had time to chat with them about how the weather was, how the river was rising, how the kids were growing, and even how they felt. The big schools disappeared, where the students were only a number on a form; now the teachers knew why their students were the way they were, and the kids got up without a big rush, walked hand in hand a few blocks without anybody having to escort them, and got to class in plenty of time. People stopped taking tranquilizers, husbands didn't yell at their wives or wives at their husbands, and nobody knocked the kids around. And bad feelings cooled down, and instead of getting a weapon in order to take money off somebody else, people used their time for something other than hatred and meanwhile began to work to change things, now that there were no rapid vehicles and distances had grown longer. Even the cities changed. The huge cities where a person felt solitary and abandoned came apart, every neighborhood separating itself off into little centers, each one almost a city, self-sufficient, with its schools and hospitals and museums and markets and no more than two or three bored, sleepy policemen sitting in the sun and sipping a lemonade with an old neighbor retired from business. The little cities didn't grow and didn't feel any need to increase their area and population, but along the long road that separated one from the next new towns grew up, just as small, just as quiet, full of gardens and orchards and the low houses of people who knew each other and teachers and doctors and storytellers and good-natured policemen. The roads got narrower and better and along them rolled the only busses that were permitted, which were free, but which you couldn't use unless you were going to visit your old aunt who lived more than twenty kilos away, or were transporting foodstuff from one city to another, or going to a party given by a distant friend. I won't say there were no more crimes, failed marriages, or insanity. There were, there still are, but few, so few that each one has plenty of people paying attention to it, worrying about it, trying to help, so that criminal tendencies, divorce, and insanity are a misfortune nowadays only for the individuals who suffer from them. And the Great Empress smiled in satisfaction and I admitted to her she'd been right and told her the history of Sderemir the Borenid.

"Yes," she said, "I know a lot of people say the world is complicated. The ones who say so are the ones who are kept anxious all the time by their work or their family, by a move or an illness, a storm, anything unexpected, anything at all; and then they make bad choices and when things turn out badly they blame it on the world for being complicated and not on their own low and imperfect standards. Why don't they go further? Why say 'the world is so complicated' and stop there? I say the world is complicated, but not incomprehensible. Only, you have to look at it steadily. Isn't it true a person's shoulder hurts sometimes because they've got a disorder in their stomach? And then what does a stupid doctor do? Orders massage of the shoulder. What does a wise doctor do? He takes time to think about it, watches the patient carefully, gives him some medicine for his stomach, and the pain in his shoulder goes away. Better yet, he explains to his patients what they have to do to keep their stomach from getting out of order. One day his patient's going to get old and die, just like himself, just like us, and one day, incredible as it may seem, the Empire's going to die, and how foolish people are who whine about it, and whine about how complicated the world is. A seamstress's room is complicated too, but even at night, with the lights out, she can reach out in the darkness and find the yellow thread, the needles, the pincushion. We couldn't, because we don't know the order things are in, in the seamstress's room. And we can't see the order the world is in. But all the same it's there, right under our eyes."

Yes, said the storyteller, the Empire will die, like her, but it will die remembering her. Idraüsse V is a good emperor, as good as other emperors the Empire loved and respected. There will be others, I don't say there won't be, and young storytellers will recount their deeds and words. And there will be wise, kind empresses, who will stand on the palace balcony and make people weep for love of them. But there couldn't be a second empress capable of pacifying and enriching the greatest Empire mankind has ever known, capable of despising power, of walking the streets unprotected, of secretly summoning a young storyteller to her rooms so he can teach her what she doesn't know, of founding a sound, strong, wise dynasty.

"Yes," said the empress, "I never get angry any more, and when night comes I'm tired out. No more foolish talk now. Good night."

AND
THE
STREETS
DESERTED

The storyteller said: The emperor decreed that a city be founded. There were countless cities in the Empire: sacred cities, industrial cities, warrior cities, forbidden cities, wise ones, monstrous ones, maritime, ruined, hidden, licentious, stinking, forgotten, nascent, damned, peaceable, and dangerous cities. But the emperor, fourth of the Kiautonor dynasty, was a lascivious and ostentatious man. Recently he had purchased, in a town on the border of the Southern lands, some went so far as to say in a village on an island deep in the heart of the South, this last being improbable for reasons known to all, a new concubine. An Assistant (Third Class) of the Inner Chamber reported, before they pulled out his teeth, cut off his tongue, and sent him to beg in the streets of the port as a traitor, that the girl was very young girl, dark, thin, and that she was shut up in a window-less, lampless building in an hexagonal pavilion in the Garden of the Three Black Tyrants, and given nothing to eat but wild joca meat and chopped rafilia stalks to keep her lively and ardent. People believed him because nobody had seen her, although everybody heard her screams, night after night and sometimes in daytime, which confirmed the rumor, already become legend, concerning the immense size of the emperor's member, and the other rumor that never did become a legend concerning the almost abnormal smallness of the girl. And the emperor, fourth of the Kiautonor dynasty, decided one day to leave the Empire a monument to this acquisition which had given him so much pleasure, and so decreed that a city be founded. He called into his presence one autumn morning a certain minister, to whom, scorning protocol and hierarchies, he gave the order, talked a bit about beauty, briefly, since he wasn't familiar with the subject, described more by gestures than by words how monumental and imposing it was to be, sent the functionary off, and almost immediately forgot about the city which didn't yet exist.

The functionary, a nobleman, a hard worker, a widower, an unbeliever, aged by attacks of Ohmaz's Disease, was the Minister of Aerial Cults as well as being temporarily in charge of the Rites of the Flame since the death of the Priestess, possibly by suicide. His name was Senoeb'Diaül, and he knew nothing about cities. For which reason he brought together in his office an architect, an engineer, a sculptor, a geographer, a painter, an astronomer, a mathematician, a storyteller, a general, and a priest, and told them what their job was: By summer, the city must be built, resplendent, magnificent, and inhabited.

We will not go into details (said the storyteller) about the preparatory work, which like any project in its first stages was confused and uncertain, so that reading the reports aggravated the illness of the nobleman Senoeb'Diaül, each attack becoming longer and more frequent. We will say only that on the first morning of winter the expedition set off to found and build the city that would bear the name of the little, young, dark-skinned concubine, who by the way was already dead, destroyed by fever and injuries. The long, slow-moving procession of vehicles, animals, men, and machinery departed at dawn from the imperial capital, and nobody saw it go save a beggar and a prostitute or two and a suicide perched on the cupola of the central tower of the Chamber of Foreign Commerce.

The journey was difficult. They had to cross three provinces, one deep in snow, the next storm-beaten, and the next ever hotter, passing through eight cities, twenty-five towns, and three military posts. They arrived at last, on the thirty-seventh day of winter, at the Valley of Loôc. The location was not only adequate, it was ideal. So much so that the nobleman promised to recommend that the emperor give the geographer, the astronomer, and the architect to the emperor a seat in their respective Academies and a medal with at least three ogives. The Edibu River thundered down out of the Twin Peaks, reaching the valley with only a pleasant murmur, and ran shining through the green plain in a curve that touched the valley's rim. The sea wind lingered on the slopes and let warm rains fall, and then the sun would rise, to set very late in the far gap between two mountains.

And so, after a moment of astonishment, the nobleman Senoeb'Diaül ordered that the ceremony commence. The priest intoned the prayer, the Office for the Seventh Day of the Ascension of Queiah, in honor of the minister:

"We are those who have remained," he said, "and those who shall not follow Thee on the ways of the wind that is born in the mouths of Thy sons, for the twelve chains of guilt prevent our movement. When Thy widowed wives have given birth and Thou arrivest at the Precincts, send ozone, O Queiah, to Thine acolytes that they may set us free, O Queiah, to follow Thy footsteps, O Queiah!"

With the final invocation, the engineer gave the nobleman the golden pikestaff, which he stuck into the soft earth. From the top of it flamed the ferocious banner of the Empire. The city had been founded.

During the rest of winter and all spring the stonecutters and masons worked ceaselessly; the architect emended plans, the priest offered prayers, the engineer and the mathematician calculated, the storyteller summed up, the astronomer studied, the sculptor carved, the geographer measured, the painter ground his colors, the general kept watch, and Senoeb'Diaül suffered. Every fortnight a messenger left for the imperial capital with a memorandum for the emperor. At the palace he was given a recompense and a day off, and the memorandum was read by the Second Secretary of the Assistant (Fourth Class) of the Sub-Manager of the Maintenance Section of the Ministry of Southern Provincial Affairs and carefully filed under the letter H. The emperor presided at the festival commemorating the Treaty of Hondarrán, planned a punitive expedition to be sent against the Southern nations, invented new titles for his first-born son, hunted with prohibited weapons in the woods of Jiznerr, and had no idea that in the Loôc Valley a city was growing.

The city stretched out to cover the plain on both sides of the Edibu River. It was built of pink marble and yellow wood with blue windows. Six avenues crossed it, three running north-south and three east-west; all the other streets were semicircular, following the curve of the river. In the intersections of the avenues stood statues of white stone, each symbolizing a victory of the Empire, and where the curved streets met the avenues, onyx fountains bearing figures of small girls in bronze and gold shot up sprays of cold water from the deep wells. There was a stadium, seven temples, a library, two theaters, three inns for travelers, a hospital, nine schools, ten restaurants, and a cemetery. Outside the walls on the south side was the red light district, and inside the walls on the north side, the military barracks. Along the river-banks ran two esplanades joined by a bridge every three blocks. The houses were low, and looking in through the deep doorways one saw at the end of the dark corridor the inner garden and the slender pillars of the balconies. Flowers grew on roofs and vines festooned the walls. The heart of the city was a great open square flanked by the houses and official buildings of the city government, the museum, the archives, and the court house. In the middle towered a bronze effigy of the emperor standing on a slain tiger, his brow lifted to heaven, sword and scepter in his hands. Around it was a garden of exotic plants, with stone benches and sunshades of particolored silk.

On the first day of summer, the nobleman Senoeb'Diaül moved into the mayor's apartments, and that night for the first time in a long time he slept easy, the first time since that autumn morning when he had bowed before the emperor.

And now certain personages appear who heretofore seemed to have nothing to do with our story: the empress, for example, and one of her sons, and the suicide on the tower of the Chamber of Foreign Commerce, and some others, as we shall see.

The empress had been very pretty, very delicate, and very stupid. The years had given her beauty, strength, and sagacity, three virtues of which the last was the most valuable. She had come to the palace very young, with many other girls of the nobility, and had been chosen by the old empress to be the prince's wife. She had borne sons and daughters, she had put on the crown in a ceremony that she then had thought moving and that now seemed to her, at most, a bore. She never raised her voice, and had seen to it, first by instinct, then by intention, that the emperor knew nothing about her. The emperor had long ago deserted her, for which she thanked several obscure gods, in order to dedicate himself to annexing territories, hunting, and buying new women. They saw each other only at certain official functions. The empress felt no pity for the emperor's concubines because she could not and would not feel pity, and because in her youth she had suffered the same torments they did, and if she had had any pleasure, denied it now. But the affair of the thin dark girl, and the founding of a city to celebrate this scandal of screams and frenzy, had turned her indifference to scorn. The girl was dead and forgotten, yes, but the city lived.

The empress had tried once to kill it before it was born, but the attempt miscarried because her chosen instrument, the man to whom the girl's father had promised her before he sold her at a better price to the envoys of the emperor, turned out to be a weakling, and instead of doing what he was supposed to do, in the darkness, quickly and mercilessly, as he might have done, he climbed up onto the cupola and threw himself off and died shattered at the foot of the tower of the Chamber of Foreign Commerce on the first morning of winter. She had ninety-two icy days, then, to think of another solution. When spring came she sent for her younger son and walked with him in a garden of silver palm trees and metal birds.

The younger son was called Yveldiva'Ad and had only one title, Prince of Innieris. Innieris was a district that had been eliminated seven generations ago and currently was part of Subsandas, a poor maritime province rendered wretched by inordinately long winters, by the ghosts of those who perished at sea, and by desperate invasions of invalids and exiles from the island of Obuer. Nobody held Yveldiva'Ad in much account—fourth in the line of succession to the throne, he was morose, sickly, and unpredictable, and always seemed to know more than anybody ought to know, whether it concerned mathematics, botany, metallurgy, silk painting, prosody, or the propensities and behavior of everybody living in the palace—nobody except his mother the empress. I'm sure I don't need to remind you that Yveldiva'Ad was the fifth emperor of the Kiautonor dynasty, and that he governed fairly well, though his subjects didn't love him, but we all know that the love of their people matters little to emperors, and even less to the Kiautonors.

Yveldiva'Ad, Prince of Innieris, had one leg shorter than the other and a twisted back, was color-blind, couldn't stand cold, and couldn't swallow solid food. He loved music, power, sunlight, cats, the poems of the Saga of Ferel'Da, and gold. And he loved his mother.

So, three days after that meeting in the garden among the silver palm trees, in which many things were decided, including vengeance and the succession to the Golden Throne, there departed from the west gate of the imperial capital an itinerant priest accompanied by five acolytes and sixteen disciples. Although the priest could pass for a holy man, with his crippled body, his lame walk, his lowered eyes, his body muffled in cloaks despite the mildness of the season, the acolytes and disciples all looked strangely alike, tough, hefty, and impassive, walking stiff and soldierly, surrounding the deformed man; but they had gold enough to close the watchful eyes of the guards inspecting their equipment and the trappings of bright metal that could be seen under their clothing. Once away from the capital, before they started around towards the southern sea, they waited for a carriage escorted by fifty more men.

A bulletin from the personal doctor of the Prince of Innieris informed the court that the young lord was keeping to his bed and had been prescribed complete rest, due to liver trouble complicated by a skin condition which, though not serious, might be contagious, so that it was not recommended that visits be paid to his apartments.

In the new city of the Loôc Valley, near the end of spring, the general spoke one night with the nobleman Senoeb'Diaül. That infirm gentleman did not share the soldier's anxiety. He saw nothing alarming about the rustic settlement discovered by patrols on the other side of the Twin Peaks. The general, however, insisted that nobody had been living there when the region was inspected a few days before their arrival in the valley. Well, said the nobleman, that doesn't signify; harmless nomads looking for forage, peasants whose farms were drowned out by the spring floods, fugitives looking for a hideout where they'll be forgotten, it's unimportant; anyhow, they might be useful if they're looking for work. Next day the nobleman was further reassured when the general brought him the report of a closer inspection of the settlement: mostly women, few men, no children, two or three old people, a crippled, semi-invalid priest. They said they'd come from a town decimated by bandits and cattle thieves, who'd killed almost all the men and all the children. But the general was a cruel, mistrustful man: that was why he had attained his rank. He didn't like the women who had welcomed him, too amiable, too well dressed. He distrusted the men, in whom he sniffed the familiar stink of soldier, not peasant sweat. He didn't believe that mountain bandits, more fighters than murderers, would kill all the children of a town. He wondered how the priest of a village that lived by herding cattle and sowing grain could be so richly fitted out. And finally he had noticed that these people had more houses than they could occupy, and that in the empty houses were traces of life, tools, arms, crumpled cloaks, clothing, even the sheath of a sword under a bench. He made up his mind, behind Senoeb'Diaül's back, to fall on them, cut the men's throats, hand the dark-skinned women over to his soldiers, maybe torture the priest, who didn't look strong and who if he survived might tell him the real explanation for the existence of this settlement, and finally set fire to the buildings of wood and hide.

But the suspiciousness that had made him a general drove him to plan his operation meticulously, and thus too slowly, thinking about the men who would no doubt be hidden on the hill slopes among the trees, and so came the first day of summer, that night when everybody slept in the new houses of stone and marble and yellow wood and blue glass in the city by the river.

Two days later, three inhabitants of the suspect village on the other side of the Twin Peaks, two women and an elderly man, asked to speak to the nobleman Senoeb'Diaül. We're strong, healthy, hard workers, they said. We don't have a home any more, this city is new, we could be of use here. The last of the messengers to the capital had already left carrying the final report, with a request for functionaries and citizens for the city, and it had been four days and nights since the nobleman had suffered an attack of his disease. The Edibu River sang beneath the balconies of the mayor's house, the pink marble grew warm in the sun, the particolored sunshades twinkled in the central square, and the general unfortunately changed his plans.

In the imperial capital, in an office of the Ministry of Southern Provincial Affairs, the new message, the last, was read by an impatient bureaucrat who for two weeks, ever since the death of his superior, had been thinking about nothing but a raise in rank and pay. It was archived under the letter H. The emperor was vacationing in his summer villa; his elder son was meeting every other day with ministers, preparing himself for a throne he would never occupy; and the empress was waiting.

Many years afterward, one night, alone, as he had always been since his mother's death, in a room of the palace that opened on a garden of palm trees, the fifth emperor of the Kiautonor dynasty remembered that there was a dead city in the Loôc Valley. And since it was summer and he heard frogs croaking, he wondered what wild things slithered on the pink marble, and what creatures splashed in the fountains. He imagined the wind slipping along the passageways and the rain falling on the cracked tiles of the roofs, the statues, the tatters of colored silk sunshades. He said to himself that maybe the ghosts of the dead walked the empty streets and entered the houses and sat down at the tables, and this made him remember the banquet celebrated on the night after the nomads had been allowed to move into the city, the banquet over which he had presided as priest. He recalled how the men who had built the city came, drawn by curiosity and by idleness and by the scent of the dark-skinned women; he recalled the sleeping potion in the red wine and the cheerful slaughter executed by the women in the name of their sister who died in the imperial capital, prisoner of the man who was his father, the slaughter which his confidential agents watched to make sure that nobody survived it, the slaughter which was his shortcut to the throne. The first to die were the soldiers, who were on leave that night because the general had postponed his plan, hoping to catch the men he'd never seen and who were there, in the darkness under the walls, outside the gates. Then came the turn of the plumbers, the masons, the glaziers, who died more slowly because they had gathered and prepared the materials from which the city was born. The women shrieked, red with blood up to the elbows, barefoot, intoxicated. The men finished off the job when the wounds were insufficient, and he walked among the bodies looking at open mouths and glazed eyes and the oozing lips of wounds, reciting it all to himself so he wouldn't forget it when he next met his mother the empress. While the geographer, the architect, the storyteller, the mathematician, the painter, the engineer, were dying, the women sang a love song that told about a maiden who called her lover every night imitating the song of the nocturnal grosbeak and how the lover, hearing it, left the pleasures of the table and gambling and friendship and ran to meet her in a forest hut, while their knives stabbed, cut, sliced, and they gouged out eyes and tore out fingernails. The heart of the nobleman Seneob'Diaül gave out before they got to him, but the women talked it over and decided to cut his body to bits as they would have liked to do with the body of the emperor and throw the pieces over the walls. And yet the wrinkled skin chapped by disease, the withered fingers, the toothless gums not only revolted them but resisted the sharpness of their knives, so they soaked him, dead, in the blood of the other dead, and thus managed to hide his ugliness, and their knifeblades slipped in easily and cut through the thin, hard flesh to the bone. Then they looked for the general. There was a fight, but a short one: the five sentinels who had remained in the barracks died at the hands of the prince's men, and the women caught the general at the point of driving his sword into his breast and danced with him and forced him to sing the love song with them and stripped him and cut him into pieces as they had done with the nobleman who had been Minister of Aerial Cults, but the heart of the general, who did not suffer from Ohmaz's Disease, kept beating while the dark-skinned women labored joyfully over his body.

That night, as the silver palm trees rustled in the garden, Yveldiva'Ad, Fifth Emperor of the Dynasty of the Kiautonor, wondered if the unburied dead had been turned into shades so they could gather up their bodies and watch them rot and dry in the summer sun, and if since then they met to shriek and moan in the curved avenues and the squares of Hadremaür, the dead city of Loôc Valley. It was a pointless question, since the emperor did not believe in ghosts.

The emperor lay down in his bed that was too wide, too high and, as he did every night, tossed and turned, sleepless and exasperated, till dawn. When he slept at last, the sunlight of another summer shone yellow on the palm trees of the garden of guilt.

THE
POOL

To Hugo Padeletti

The storyteller said: People choose strange professions, don't you agree? I'm not talking about picturesque or unusual jobs, but about people who don't live in order to be or try to be the best persons possible, but only to add titles to their name, empty, hollow, resounding titles, false, useless trappings that weigh them down and suck them dry and end up by replacing them altogether. This all has to do what I'm about to tell you.

There was a man who lived in a house in a city that was the capital of the Empire, many, many years ago. Not that that matters: it could have happened yesterday, it could happen tomorrow, or some day next year.

But the Empire then wasn't what it is today. It hadn't achieved what is now proudly called Progress, though perhaps it was on the way to it. The capital was a mess of a place where, as always, wise emperors succeeded stupid ones and vice versa. In the days I'm telling you about, the ruling emperor was of the dynasty of the Chaixis, Chaloumell the Bald, not altogether a bad man, but one who loved wealth and power too well, so that if he wasn't quite a disaster for the people, neither was he a blessing.

He wasn't one of the emperors that everybody loves or everybody hates. Some adulated him, some conspired against him, as usual. Powerful families and those who aspired to power supported and upheld and defended him while they fought among themselves for the best places near the throne. Simple folk got along as best they could. And some people met in secret places to plan the downfall and death of the Lord of the Golden Throne.

On a day in early spring the Emperor Chaloumell was informed by one of his ministers that a faction, who called themselves by the name of a wildflower that his gardeners had never let grow in the palace grounds, were rapidly gaining followers, arming themselves one way and another, and preparing for rebellion. The emperor was alarmed. So, that very night, the Imperial Guard swept through the city and surprised a meeting of the Borkhausis. Almost all the conspirators died cruelly, but among those who escaped was a girl called Veevil.

Well, now, in a tree-lined street, a very quiet, out-of-the-way street far from the city center and the public buildings, there stood a white house with a big front door that always stood ajar. The oldest neighbors said their grandparents had told them it used to be an asylum, a brothel, a school, a rest-house for pilgrims, and that a treasure was buried in the courtyard. It didn't look to be any of those things. It just looked like a house. It had a lot of rooms with high ceilings and windows with wooden shutters opening onto the courtyard; in the garden behind it were trees, a fountain, and a pool; in the hot weather it stayed cool inside the thick walls and you could hear the sound of water and the voices of the birds in the leaves. It smelled like stored grain, damp earth, and spices. Anyone passing by could come in, out of curiosity or out of need. In fact, many people came through that door. Those who came out of curiosity crossed the courtyard, wet their hands in the water of the fountain, and strolled a bit under the trees; the boldest peeked into the rooms. Then they went off to tell their friends and relatives, for days after, what they'd seen. Those who came out of need crossed the courtyard, went through an arcade almost hidden by vines, and knocked on a half-closed door that was on the right if you were going to the garden behind the house. From inside the room someone would answer, telling them to wait or to come in.

The bald emperor, fifteenth of the Chaixis dynasty, was not a well man. He had sick fits and fainting fits, blood ran from his nose sometimes and his hands trembled. Sometimes his knees grew weak and he had to sit down and breathe through his mouth while the nausea kept growing.

"His Imperial Majesty would be well advised to see a doctor," said the courtiers.

"Doctors are all asses," said the emperor.

The empress said nothing because she cared nothing about her husband's health: she had given him six sons, she had a lover, and she liked emeralds, thick sweet liqueurs, parties, and very young girls.

"I will not permit those dirty ignorant little men to go poking about inside me," said the emperor.

But he had a fainting fit one day that lasted hours, and when he woke he felt that he couldn't breathe and death must be near. He gave in. When he had breath enough, he ordered that a doctor be sent for. There was none in the palace, but somebody said, "In Whiterose Street there's an old doctor. They say he knows a lot and cures the most desperate cases."

The Duke of Asfiddes, who for years had aspired to a ministry and had never achieved it because he was too rich and his wife was too beautiful, entered the half-open front door. Accustomed to being received everywhere with great ceremony, he was disconcerted by the silence and the lack of syrupy voices and curtseys. After feeling disconcerted he got angry. With great strides he stormed around opening doors and sticking his head into rooms. He saw many things he did not expect to see, and when he came to the vine-covered door farthest down the arcade and opened it, he found himself facing a man who sat cross-legged on the mat on the stone floor.

"Good day," the man said.

"I am the Duke of Asfiddes, sent in search of a doctor by His Imperial Majesty Chaloumell VII!"

"Good day," the man said.

"Good day," said the duke.

When the duke returned to the palace, furious with himself, the doctor, His Imperial Majesty, and everything else, the emperor was having another spell of shortness of breath and was seeing death in every corner.

"Where's the doctor?" they asked the duke, and he had to confess, "He says he isn't going to come. He says sick people have to come to his house. He does his curing there."

The emperor was too busy breathing to hear this, but one of the ministers sent for the captain of the Guard and ordered him to go to the white house in Whiterose Street and fetch the man by force.

The duke summoned the captain before he left and described the doctor to him. The captain listened attentively and went to get his men. But when the duke arrived at the palace gates to wait for the Guards, a tall man with greying hair, wearing a linen tunic, barefoot, was talking with the soldiers on duty.

The duke came up to him. "You came," he said.

"Yes."

"You did well to do so. The Guards were going to your house to fetch you away by force."

"I had to go out to look for ambalias," the doctor said, "and in the Silversmiths' Quarter I saw the old women who make the fasteners for necklaces, so I thought that perhaps emperors fall ill of other illnesses than commoners do. So I came."

The duke sent a soldier to call off the captain. The captain was annoyed: he enjoyed fetching people away by force.

The doctor was brought before the emperor and the courtiers talked hopefully of a cure. But the emperor got no better. Not only that, he got worse, and so went on saying doctors were asses and never again would he let one be brought to the palace even if his fainting fits lasted hours or days and the shortness of breath brought him to the brink of death clothed in the red of the blood that ran from his nose and pounded in the veins of his neck and temple.

If anybody tried to defend physicians, Chaloumell told them that the only one he had allowed into the palace hadn't examined him carefully nor shown respect for him, for him, the emperor: that he hadn't palpated nor ausculted, and had said nothing except that he shouldn't go on sleeping in that room, that he should learn to play the serel, should not travel in the mountains, and should eat only white foods.

"A lot of asses," said the emperor, breathing heavily and clutching the arms of his chair to keep his hands from trembling, "and he was the most asinine of the lot. Steamed fish, potatoes, tubelid roots, bah!"

When Veevil fled from the house where the Imperial Guardsmen were cutting the conspirators' throats, her only thought was to get out of the capital that night. She ran and ran, crossing streets and parks, her hand over her mouth so that nobody could hear her sobbing. All at once she stopped, sat down on the doorstep of a house, and thought. Why was she on the run? Nobody knew her name, any more than she knew the names of the other members of the group. So nobody was going to denounce her, even if some had been saved from the slaughter to be tortured. What's more, others might have got away as she had. What she had to do was stay in the capital, wait a while, try to find others who had escaped, and with them reorganize the rebellion to bring down this emperor who cared nothing for his people. She got up from the doorstep and, walking tranquilly, not sobbing, swinging her arms like any carefree young woman, went home. Her parents and brothers were asleep. She went up the stairs quietly and to her room. She didn't light the lights, she got undressed, opened the balcony door that looked out to the back, and smiled to see in the big house across the gardens a light still burning: the old doctor was studying. Or sitting by a sick person, or meditating, or whatever. She got into bed and fell asleep.

Some days went by, maybe some weeks. The empress was in a vile humor. So was the captain of the Guards. The emperor didn't see death waiting but his hands trembled and he felt shooting pains in the nape of his neck. People went into the white house on the tree-lined street and Veevil greeted the old doctor from her balcony when she saw him walk in the garden and sit by the pool, and he smiled at her. Sometimes he raised his hand in a gesture of salute and sat watching her, thinking how beautiful she was.

In the middle of spring a square, solid, serious man came in the front door. Passing through the courtyard where the buried treasure was said to be, near the gurgling fountain, under the trees whose leaves moved with a sound of silky paper and the birds swelled out their chests calling to one another, he made no wrong turns and did not lose his temper as the Duke of Asfiddes had. He waited a moment and looked about, and then clapped his hands and cried, "Hey! Anybody here?"

His voice rang out and was amplified as it struck the white walls and came back to him as if from a secret grotto beyond the inhabited parts of the house. But nobody answered. He returned to the court-yard, and as the duke had done, opened several doors. And going from one door to the next he saw the arcade almost hidden by creepers and went along it and came to the vine-hidden door, approached it, opened it. The man sitting cross-legged on the mat on the stone floor opened his eyes. "Good day," he said.

"Ah, good day," said the other. "I'm looking for the doctor."

"That's me."

"May I come in?"

"Yes."

So he entered the room and glanced round, looking for a chair, a bench, something to sit down on, and for medical instruments and bottles of medicines, and saw nothing. Accordingly he took two steps and sat down on the mat.

"I'm ill," he said.

"Hmm," the doctor said, "yes, but it's not serious."

The man was silent a moment looking at him.

"How can you possibly know? I haven't been in this room five seconds."

"If it was serious, your body would force you to feel some kind of fear. And all fears are exclusive: yours wouldn't have allowed you to take any interest in what you found in the room."

"Good," the man said, "good. You may be right."

"What is your work?"

"I'm a merchant," the man said. "I deal in glass. Glass goods."

"What need is there to lie?"

"Eh?"

"Selling glass doesn't lead to callused hands, or a straight spine with the shoulders back."

The man turned his head and let his gaze wander over the walls and the window that gave on the garden. He finally looked again at the doctor. "Actually," he said, "I was a dealer in glass and crystal a long time ago, and I'd like to do that again, but at present I'm a workman."

"You are?"

"Yes, I am."

"And what is it that makes you feel sick?"

"It hurts here."

"Did you go to school when you were a boy?"

"Yes," the man said.

"What did you like best to study?"

"Nothing. I hated studying."

"Ah," said the doctor.

"Sometimes I feel a burning cold that rises from my stomach into my throat."

"Ah," the doctor said again. "And if now you had the time and money for studying, which would you prefer, mathematics or music?"

The man thought it over. "Mathematics," he said, opening his eyes wide.

"Why?"

"It's more useful. I don't say I don't enjoy music, but if you want music you hire a musician."

"Possibly," said the doctor. "Have you ever had the impression of having known for a long time a person you've just met?"

"I don't know," the man said. "Maybe so, I don't remember, one of those notions you have when you're very young."

"Is there a very deep wardrobe in your bedroom?"

"No. There's a wardrobe, but it's not very deep."

Then the doctor leaned over and touched the side of the neck of the man who called himself a workman, laying one finger under the earlobe. "Does that hurt?"

"No."

The doctor withdrew his hand, sat up very straight again, and said, "No, it's not serious. You'll be well soon."

"What must I do?"

"I'll prepare a medicine for you to take. That will require several days. Meanwhile, every evening, as the sun begins to set, you're going to stop your work in the shop for a moment."

"Where?"

"In the workshop. And you're going to sit down on the ground facing a low table on which is a sheet of white paper, a pen, and green ink, and you're going to draw a tree."

"A tree?"

"Yes."

"What tree?"

"Any tree. It could be a sycamore, a plane, a linden, whatever. It could be a palm tree. Even a bush."

"The same tree every day?"

"That's not indispensable," the doctor said, "but it would be preferable. Still, if you have a yen to change trees, there's no reason not to."

"And when you give me the medicine, I'll leave off drawing the tree?"

"Ah, no. But you might draw a different one."

The man sighed. "All right," he said. "What do I owe you?"

"Nothing."

"But how's that? Don't your patients pay you?"

"In a sense they do."

"Green ink," the man said, "good, good. And white paper. When should I come back?"

"Day after tomorrow."

"Should I bring the trees I draw?"

"Yes," said the doctor.

"Good. Good-bye," the man said, and left.

The doctor closed his eyes. Not for long, for that morning a woman came with her son, and a man with lung disease, and a gardener who had cut his left hand with the pruning shears, and an ancient man wheeled in a handbarrow by two of his grandsons, and a boy who wanted to learn the names of the flowers that grow on the cold mountains of the North.

When the sun was halfway across the sky, the doctor went to the kitchen and ate a red fruit and a crusty roll. And then he went into the garden and sat down at the edge of the pool, in the shadow of the great ferns growing among the stones.

"Hi! Isn't it too hot there?" Veevil called from her balcony.

He looked at her and shook his head and said to himself again that she was very beautiful, and she laughed and disappeared into her house. The doctor closed his eyes and thought about the pool. He opened them and saw that the girl was climbing the fence. She let herself drop down into his garden.

"What do you mean it's not hot?" Veevil said and sat down. "It's extremely hot. And I want to ask you three things: Do you like sitting by the pool a lot? Do medicinal herbs grow here? Are there a lot of sick people?"

"Yes, yes, and yes," said the doctor.

"Oh, come on, is that all?"

"Didn't I answer?"

"Yes, but I don't like answers. What I want is a conversation."

"Ah," said he.

"Or am I wasting your time?"

"No, no. Don't leave."

"Good, I'll stay. So, why are there so many sick people?"

"Because it's easier to get sick than to look for one's right place in the world."

"Explain, explain."

"Yes," said the doctor. "We keep adding needless things, false things to ourselves, till we can't see ourselves and forget what our true shape is. And if we've forgotten what shape we are, how can we find the right place to be? And who dares pull away the falsities that are stuck to his eyelids, his fingernails, his heels? So then something goes wrong in the house and in the world, and we get sick."

"Ah," said she. "Like the caloco fruit, that has five rinds."

"Yes."

"And we all have false things stuck to us?"

"Almost all."

They sat silent a while.

"What's serious isn't having them," said the doctor. "What's serious is loving them."

"What false things could I pull off myself?"

"I don't know," he said. "I don't know you."

After two days, the man who said he was a workman who had dealt in glasswares came back and showed the doctor two trees drawn in green ink on two sheets of white paper.

"I think they're snowtrees," he said, "but I'm not sure. In any case they're very old."

"Snowtrees live hundreds of years," said the doctor, and bent over to touch the side of the sick man's neck with one finger. "Does that hurt?"

"No."

"In two days I'll have your medicine ready. Is your bed in the center of the room?"

"No, it's in a corner. Why? Should I move it?"

"No, but you're to take away all the furniture between the bed and the door."

"Good," the man said, and stood up. "Do I go on drawing trees?"

"Yes."

That night there was a great storm and the doctor got almost no sleep, looking after the sick people who temporarily occupied several of the rooms of the house. One of them woke at daybreak, when the thunder and lightning had died down but it was raining hard, and told him that he felt he was going to die that night.

"That's good," the doctor said. "Death too is necessary. And fitting. If it seems to you that you're going to die, so it will be. Every one feels his death come, sees it, smells it, hears it."

"It's raining," the sick man said.

"Yes, but that doesn't matter to Lady Death."

"To me neither," said the sick man. "What matters to me is having a lathe."

"You could send to ask your wife to buy you one."

"When it stops raining and the sun comes out," said the man in bed, "I'm going to live on the banks of Singkaló where the earth is red and fertile. And I'm going to make myself a lathe."

"And Lady Death?"

"Bah," said the sick man. "She can have all that stuff, the house, the carriages, the children we had, the silverware in silverware chests." And he went to sleep.

The Emperor Chaloumell VII, fifteenth of the House of the Chaixis, felt bad on stormy days and worse on stormy nights, so next morning his royal garments were spotted with the blood that dripped from his nose, thick, dark, evil-smelling blood.

"Don't talk to me about doctors," he gasped.

Next day the sun came out, and the next day, and Veevil popped out on her bedroom balcony. The man who drew trees came at noon to get his medicine.

"Yesterday I drew a broom-palm," he said.

"Broom-palms are handsome and majestic," said the doctor.

"I don't know," the man said. "I don't like them much. But I drew one."

"You're to take sixteen drops of this medicine, sixteen," the doctor said, "when you wake up, before getting out of bed, each day for three days, and then come see me."

"Do I go on drawing trees?"

"Yes."

The doctor was left alone, looking at the vine-wreathed door and thinking that if this man drew another broom-palm, and then one more, he might arrive at admitting what his real profession was. Rapid steps were heard, and the door was flung open with such force that it struck the wall like an explosion.

"What have you done?" Veevil shouted. "What have you done?"

"I haven't done anything," said the doctor.

"Oh, no? You haven't done anything? So why does Zigud-da come to see you, hah? Why?"

"Oh, so he's called Zigud-da. I didn't know. He comes to see me because he's sick, but what he's got isn't serious."

"Damn you," said she, "damn you. Damn you and your mother and your grandmother and your children and your children's children, damn you and I hope you die choking in your own blood."

"Veevil," the doctor said.

The girl leaned towards him and looked into his eyes: "Yes," she said, "damn you, and I hope you die and I can dance on your body."

She straightened up, turned, and left leaving the door open. The doctor closed his eyes and looked within himself and breathed seventy times with his attention on the air passing in and out, each time deeper, each time more peaceful.

That evening Veevil went to Nevviasoria Square and sat down among the people listening to a storyteller. The people listened, she did not. She sat very quiet, her eyes fixed on the man who was speaking and her hands crossed on her lap. She had been there a good while when somebody sat down next to her, leaning forward as if to hear better. One of Veevil's hands moved and touched the ground, and when it returned to her lap, somebody's hand was in that same place hiding a folded piece of paper.

That evening Zigud-da drew in green ink another broom-palm, looked at it with a certain satisfaction, and lifted his hand to the side of his neck and pressed, asking himself, "Why's he looking for a pain in my neck when what hurts is my belly?"

That night the empress gave a party and the emperor stayed in his room and ate venison with murcula sauce and drank wine while thinking about the suitability of bringing the settlers of Sid-Ballein, who had had the insolence to rebel against an unimportant tax, to work on the renovation and enlargement of the palace. He would tell the foremen to treat them well, however. He wouldn't forget that, the Emperor Chaloumell the Bald, who wanted his subjects to think well of him when he was dead.

Two days later, Veevil went to the doctor's house, but without running and slamming doors. She climbed over the dividing wall as usual and walked through the garden, which was growing dark, to the edge of the pool.

"Where's my friend Mr. Doctor?" she crooned.

But no one heard her except an owl who couldn't tell her, and she went to the kitchen, where a lamp was burning.

"Good evening," she said.

"Good evening, Veevil. I thought you'd come, because in this bowl here, see? I've got currant pudding."

"I don't like sweet things," she said.

"No?"

"Not much."

The doctor handed her a wooden spoon and the girl sat down on a bench at the white table and ate currant pudding, and he ate dark bread, and neither of the two said anything for a long time.

"That man," she said at last.

The doctor didn't answer. She waited while he chewed a piece of dark bread and then tore off another piece with his fingers, silent.

"I wonder if you're aware of what's going on around you," the girl said.

"I am aware."

"That man is the captain of the Imperial Palace Guard."

"I know."

"You knew?"

"No, but he drew another broom-palm, so that now I know."

"I don't understand you, I really don't understand you. You know so much, you guess so much, why do you stay hidden away here in this house making poultices and mixing cough syrup instead of making people do what you want?"

The doctor smiled at her. "Oh, Veevil," he said, "if I was in that business how could I know anything or see anything? See, not guess."

Again there was silence until she said, "The Chaixis dynasty has got to be done away with."

"Isn't that what Zigud-da intends to do?"

"Then you knew!"

"No," the doctor said.

"But you said it!"

"It wasn't I that said it. Veevil and Zigud-da are saying it."

"Don't say my name with that hyena's."

"Is the currant pudding good?"

"I don't care about currant pudding! Yes, it's good. Thanks. I want to talk about something different. I want to talk about Zigud-da's death."

"Not the emperor's death?"

"Once the emperor's down nobody will defend him, he can just be sent into exile." She ate another spoonful of currant pudding. "We Borkhausis want a man on the throne who'll look after the wellbeing of the people, not a monster of cowardice and egoism like Chaloumell. But the Imperial Guards have their eyes on the Golden Throne too. And the Guards are strong, they have money and arms, they have men in every strategic point of the Empire. If a man of the Imperial Guard comes to the throne, it will be a tragedy for the people."

"And if one of the Borkhausis does, it won't?"

"No, of course it won't, how could you think so? The Guards are despotic, rigid, ambitious, almost worse than the Chaixis. We're going to be just, we're going to bring the people justice and freedom."

"Those are two very beautiful words, Veevil. And big words. Big enough that they shouldn't leave room for a man's death."

"Zigud-da has to die," she said. "Is he very ill?"

"No."

"Then something has to be done to make him get very ill and die. If we kill him, the Imperial Guards will suspect us and come after us and kill us like cockroaches. Zigud-da has to die, don't you see that? We have to keep these brainless, remorseless brutes in uniform from the path to the throne. And the captain's right in the middle of that path."

"He's nearly cured," said the doctor.

"You're sure?"

"Yes. He drew the seeds of the broom-palm at the foot of the trunk. And he jumped when I put my finger on the side of his neck and pressed, here."

"He has to die. He has to get sick and die," the girl said.

"No."

"But don't you see that this man is evil?"

"He may be."

"Don't doctors fight against evil? Don't they want to do good?"

"Yes."

"So? What does he have to draw, or think, or eat, that will make him ill?"

"My teacher taught me many things," the doctor said. "But the day I left my house to go live in his, that day I learned to wash the pots and pans in the kitchen and how to tell a spider who's going to lay eggs from a spider going hunting."

"I don't see what that has to do with Zigud-da's death."

"Yes, you do, Veevil. With a very little effort, you do see. Even if maybe you don't want to see it."

"If Zigud-da gets sick and dies, I'll leave my house and come to yours forever."

The doctor felt a piercing pain in his chest.

"I can learn to wash pots and pans," she said, "and all about spiders and herbs. And I can help you with your patients and keep you company and keep the house clean and give you lovely strong healthy children."

"And what would the two of us talk about on winter nights, Veevil, when we were alone, in the lamp light, in the kitchen?"

"Does that mean you won't make him get sick and die?"

"I don't know," the doctor said.

She stood up and looked at the clay bowl. She reached out, took the wooden spoon, and buried it in the thick, shiny pudding.

"I'll come back tomorrow," she said, "if you'll think about everything I said."

"Yes."

The old doctor, who had been alone all his life, as other men with other jobs are alone all their lives, poets, twentiers, storytellers—the old doctor slept alone that night in his narrow bed, a restless and unquiet sleep. Twice he woke for no reason, and twice got up and went to look at his patients. It seemed to him, while he was putting a pitcher of fresh water by the bedside of one of them, a boy with an authoritarian father and a throat condition, it seemed to him that Veevil had not left but was still there with him in the white house.

But the girl was in fact off in an abandoned warehouse near the river, speaking low and fast, surrounded by people listening to her; and when she left there very late, almost at daybreak, she had hidden in a pocket of her coat a little silver box in which was a fine white powder.

Since the emperor loved his palace, that morning he sent for the captain of the Imperial Guard and held a long conversation with him.

"If His Imperial Majesty approves," said Zigud-da, "we shall set off this afternoon. We shall camp at Tusugga and make a surprise attack on Sid-Ballein tomorrow at noon when the inhabitants are eating or resting."

The emperor approved. Zigud-da gave orders to his men, then left the palace and went to the house in Whiterose Street. He had to wait under the vines because, in the room with the mat-covered stone floor, the doctor was talking with someone. What the captain of the Guard thought as he waited is something no one will ever know. But the probability is that he was impatient; and since he was no longer ill, it's also probable that he had forgotten about the broom-palms and instead of the green leaves swaying in the wind and shining in the sun he remembered a game he used to play as a child in the dusty streets of Eriamod or the skills he'd had to demonstrate to be admitted into the Imperial Guard. What we do know is that when a fat woman came out of the room, wobbling over the flagstones with unsteady steps, he went on waiting for the doctor to call him, and hearing nothing for a long while, approached the door and went in.

"Good day," said the doctor.

"Good day," and he sat down.

"You're not sick any more."

"No," Zigud-da said, "I don't have any pain here and the cold burning doesn't come up from my stomach."

As the doctor said nothing, the captain of the Imperial Guard went on: "What should I do now? Should I go on drawing trees?"

"Would you like to?"

"No. It takes too much time. And later today I have to do some traveling."

"No more sketches, then. And your bedroom furniture can go back where it was. Don't take any more of the medicine I gave you. What you can do is look closely at the trees you see along the way as you travel. And for three days, take this other medicine I've prepared for you."

The doctor got up, left the captain alone, and went to a room that opened on the courtyard of the fountain, facing the rooms where his patients were. There he chose a flask, went out and recrossed the courtyard. But before he came to the vine-wreathed arcade , the sunlight shone on the glass flask and the liquid in it, and the doctor stopped. For a moment he felt again the sharp pain he felt last night in the kitchen facing Veevil. He clenched his hand on the flask, went into the room and sat down on the mat. He said to the man who was waiting there, "No, don't take anything. It will be better."

"But what if I get sick again?"

"That is possible. All of us could take ill at any moment. All the same I think that you won't get sick again for a long time; there are other ways of preventing the illness you had. While you're traveling you'll feel well, and when you come back you're going to buy some sessely seeds, dry them in the sun, grind them and keep them in a cool dry place, and use them once a month to season your food."

The man stood up. "Nothing else?"

"Nothing else."

"Good. What do I owe you?"

"At the moment, nothing. If it ever occurs to you that you're in my debt, then you'll know what to bring me."

"And if it doesn't occur to me?"

"Then we'll see," said the doctor.

"Goodbye," said Captain Zigud-da, and left.

Perhaps the story of the man who lived in a house on Whiterose Street with the door always ajar, which people said used to be a brothel and a pilgrims' inn, and which had a buried treasure hidden in the courtyard, ought to end here. I ask myself if that would not be the most fitting. But the most fitting isn't always what we like best, and sometimes we storytellers find it hard to finish, to be done with a story. So I'll go on and tell you that the old doctor buried in the garden, in a deep hole, the flask that should have held a clear transparent liquid and which held instead a thick liquid full of sediment. And that same night he told Veevil two things: that what is called evil is also necessary, and that the world is immensely rich and varied yet is one and the same because the most disparate things are brothers and the things farthest apart are equivalent. What the girl replied to this doesn't matter; she left, and never jumped over the garden wall again.

I'll also tell you that Chaloumell the Bald died soon after, passing from one of his fainting fits to death with only a shudder and a cry, but that the Chaixis dynasty didn't end with him. His eldest son ascended to the throne, Cheirantes III, known to history by the disrespectful nickname Mad Horse, who married the second daughter of the Duke of N'Cevvilea but almost immediately took as his concubine one of the girls from Sid-Ballein who was working on the new additions to the palace. This was the pretext for an uprising of the Imperial Guard, who declared it unfitting that a prisoner whom they had brought as a slave from afar should be given a high position at court. Mad Horse pretended to be cowed by the rebellion, promised to surrender, and asked for a secret meeting with the ringleaders to plead for his life. The meeting was to be in a pavilion near the palace, but none of the leaders of the uprising got that far. They fell into a deep pit dug in the woods surrounding the pavilion built by the second Chaixis emperor for one of his mistresses, and the brilliant Lord of the Golden Throne entertained himself by cutting their throats until his arm got tired, and left the rest there in the pit to die of hunger and thirst. The girl from Sid-Ballein bore the emperor the only son he had, since the empress never conceived, some said because she was barren, others, because the emperor never lay with her. And this only son of the Mad Horse was the Emperor Cheanoth I, whom the Empire will not soon forget, for of all the wise, just men who have sat on the Golden Throne, he was one of the best.

And one day that boy who wanted to learn the names of the flowers that grow in the cold mountains of the North came back to the house in Whiterose Street, and didn't leave it again, but stayed as apprentice. And when his master died, he, being then a man grown, went on practicing medicine and watching the world, sitting in the evening beside the pool that reflected the treasure buried in the courtyard and the limitless boundaries of the house.

BASIC
WEAPONS

The storyteller said: But if we want to understand, really understand, the history of the Emperor Horhórides III, seventh ruler of the House of the Jénningses, we must pause to recall that the years he lived in were hardly peaceful ones. All the Jénningses emperors had turbulent souls and contorted minds, and turbulent and contorted was the age when they occupied the Golden Throne. Horhórides III's period was less troubled, perhaps, but even more extravagant. There was no war, no famine, no plague: but vice flourished, as did smuggling, assassination, greed, hypocrisy, and the arts of the hideous. In short, there was no happiness, no innocence. Maybe the plague would have been preferable. And to demonstrate this, I leave the emperor for a little while to tell you a brief story; for a good story saves long explanations, and I, who have told so many, assure you that this is a good one.

Master Bramaltariq had seventeen horses, nine wives, and three bearskin cloaks, one dyed green, one purple, and one blue. In the wretched alley called The Eagle was a shop of curiosities, and curiosities was certainly the word for them, whose owner was named Drondlann: he had a round bald head, a short neck, long powerful arms, and a massive body without an ounce of fat on it. He had no legs, but an ingenious harness attached two wheels to him, which he pushed with his arms, thus propelling himself quickly and silently. Nobody knew how he had lost his legs: if in a fight, or an accident, or if he'd been born so.

When Master Bramaltariq passed through the High Street with his cortege, Drondlann gave a push to his wheels and left his den to go hide among the trees bordering the avenue and watch. Master Bramaltariq's wives were very white and very plump, and sat on gilt pillows with colored tassels. He hired out his stallions to country folk who had only mares; he kept the colts. He lived in a big stone house built in the middle of a lake of black water; it had verandas of carved wood, mirrors in the ceilings, curtains in the windows, and torch-lit hidey-holes mined with traps. Drondlann had no horses nor bearskin cloaks; all he had was the curiosity shop and his two wheels and a plant of hatred in his belly which he watered carefully every day. He watched Master Bramaltariq go by with his wives and servants, and the plant thrust its flowers into his throat and wrists. He told himself that he was as good a man as that soft fatty, and better, recalling how when he made a lucky sale, he'd go find a certain dark, thin, weatherbeaten prostitute, a bit of scum from the dregs of the slums, who'd leave next morning with a small share of the money and two bruised furrows in her thighs.

Nobody knew anything for sure about where Drondlann got his merchandise. But it was known that it was Grugroul who brought him the blond boy. Around then the sale of dwarfs had fallen off; they were a drug on the market when, only two seasons back, everybody was mad to have at least one dwarf chained at the street door or in a cage hung from the drawing room ceiling. About the time Master Bramaltariq acquired his ninth wife, Drondlann began to stop doing business with the people who came to Eagle Alley to sell dwarfs.

"I don't want dwarfs," he told them, "they're not selling."

"Giants," one of these disappointed salesmen proposed, "giants, huh? What do you think? If dwarfs aren't selling, giants will, huh? Because a giant's the opposite of a dwarf, right, huh?"

Drondlann didn't kick the stupid man out the door, though he considered it carefully and thoroughly, as he considered everything.

"No," he said finally, "no, no giants. Out. Out of here, and don't come back. Unless," and he smiled, "unless you bring me something really out of the ordinary."

The cripple of Eagle Alley was hoping that somebody would bring him something rare enough to justify the long trip to the bridge that ran from the lakeshore to the stone house on the islet, so that he could offer it to Master Bramaltariq. He wanted to hear the stallions neighing and see the plump women reclining on wrinkled silken carpets. He wanted to smell the incense burning in niches and look up to see his own reflection in the mirrored ceilings. He wanted to look at the black lake from the house, roll along the polished floors, spy, and water the plant in his belly.

The salesman told somebody what the dealer wanted, and that somebody told another somebody, and so on until it got to Grugroul.

A few days later a winged fetus was brought to Eagle Alley. It was unfortunately dead. But Drondlann paid a few coins for it and promptly, before it began to rot, sold it to a man in a hood who said he wanted it for his master, a sufficiently dubious claim. Drondlann assured him that since the creature had a leathery skin it would last a good while. The hooded man never came back. Then a six-legged dragon was brought to him. He could neither sell it nor feed it. The animal refused rats, tender shoots, birds, mushrooms, spiders, and hot coals, and so died of starvation. The dealer thought that he'd been most unwise not to ask the seller what six-legged dragons ate, having simply assumed that it ate what four-legged ones did. Another day he was offered a white snake with gills and antennae, but, recalling the dragon, he refused it. He bought a hermaphrodite and two children without ears or eyes and sold all three at a good price, even though one of the kids did nothing but moan and sob, but sad to say, there are people who like things like that. He also bought a blond dragonfly that lived on filth and excrement. He clipped her fore-wings to prevent her escaping and so let her loose in the shop much of the time. He tried to have sex with her and she offered no resistance, but when he saw what her belly ended in between the hindmost legs, he withdrew, feeling rather sick. She did not appear to be offended. She wasn't easy to sell, but he didn't worry about it since not only did it cost nothing to feed her but she disposed of all kinds of filth and nasty stuff, and he had a kind of fondness for her. In the end he put her at half price, a real steal for anybody who wanted a blond dragonfly in the house, and The Riuder of the Water Pyramid bought her, conveniently preventing people from saying Drondlann had unsaleable items in his shop. And so with other things, nothing extraordinary, nothing he could go offer at the house on the lake, till the day Grugroul came with the boy. The owner of the curiosity shop thought the boy belonged to the salesman and didn't look at him.

"I'll sell him to you," Grugroul said.

Drondlann didn't bother to turn his head; he was astute enough to have learned not to examine the merchandise, whatever it might be. If there was nothing special about the boy, as he thought, it wasn't worth the trouble to twist his neck, and if there was, to show interest might be counterproductive.

"Not interested," he said.

Grugroul smiled. "You're going to miss something exceptional," he said.

So then the merchant of Eagle Alley turned his head slowly, very slowly, and looked at the merchandise. He shrugged. "Why would I want that?"

For he saw a boy, just a boy—complete, nothing missing, nothing added. Blond, two bright eyes, two ears, a nose, a mouth, teeth, two arms, two hands, body, two legs, two feet. Drondlann turned his back and began to clean the cages.

"He doesn't talk," Grugroul said.

"Big deal."

He opened the door of the cage that held the giant bat that a young scholar who didn't wish to give his name had promised to come for tomorrow, and took out the bowl to change the water.

"He knows how to dance," Grugroul persisted.

Now this did surprise the dealer. The word echoed in his head: dance, dance.

"Dance," he repeated. "What's that?"

He hadn't forgotten his caution; but he had, now and then, encountered and sold an article that seemed commonplace but wasn't. The Dame of the Hill, for instance, widow of The Jungaï of the Silos, had gone mad, or so it was said though nobody was sure, after keeping in her house for a month an old man she'd bought from him to feed her birds. Since the old man didn't live at the same time as the Dame but a few minutes ahead of her, he answered her questions before she asked them, or talked about things that began happening as he was finishing his sentence. And Adanssanto of the Tunnels had killed his adopted son, a newborn infant that Drondlann had fetched from the marshes of the South, because he claimed the infant produced dreams. Or a dream. At any rate he was declared not guilty, because the infant came, after all, from the South. But the whole affair had been a bother and a waste of time, and Adanssanto of the Tunnels had never fully recovered.

"What's dancing?" he repeated in surprise, holding the dirty water dish in his hand.

Grugroul, who was no fool either, saw the dealer in curiosities was interested, intrigued.

"You'll see," he said. "This boy moves his body not only the way we do to walk or bathe or get into a cart, but in a special way: he puts it in an infinite number of positions, each lasting a few seconds or fractions of a second, and all the positions are different, or are repeated in long series. And he goes on doing it till he's ordered to stop."

Drondlann of the Wheels lost all interest. This dancing business sounded stupid. He plunged the dirty dish into the water bucket. This time, though he still didn't know it, he had behaved stupidly. Grugroul clapped his hands. He cried, "Tattoot! Dance!"

Then the boy did what the salesman had described: he danced. He moved first without changing place, both feet as if fixed to the ground. He waved his arms, lifted them, held them out; he swayed, and he made circles with his body, twisting his waist, and with his head, that seemed to turn freely at the end of his long neck. Then he leapt, without ceasing to sway the rest of his body. He spun on one foot, on the other, bowed down, swept the ground with his hands, straightened up, ran two steps to one side, three to the other, his arms held high, his head fallen back. Grugroul had stepped aside and turned his back, looking out into the alley through the shop window. And the dealer? He had felt the world begin to spin quicker than it had ever done, more dizzily than when it was an incandescent lump of rock trailing gases and gathering dust under the attentive eye of God. The dealer had seen the dead risen from their graves, had smelled all the odors earth exhaled, from the deserts to the orchards, had seen a black army march across a petrified sea, had picked the flowers of childhood running barefoot, had ridden in golden armor across a golden field pursuing golden women, had been drunken with liquors distilled deep in hidden caves, and when the sky began to come collapsing down on his shoulders, the water dish dropped from his hands and smashed to bits, and the giant bat gave a croak.

"Enough!" Drondlann yelled.

Grugroul clapped his hands. The boy stood still. Only then did Grugroul turn round. "What do you think?" he said.

Caution abandoned the dealer of Eagle Alley. Master Bramaltariq was old, fat, hairy, soft, and weak. He had nine young wives. He had swollen veins in his legs, he had protruding eyes from labored breathing and sluggish digestion.

"How much?"

Till noon they sat haggling over the boy. At noon, exhausted, each torn between the conviction he'd been swindled and the hope he'd swindled the other, they parted. Grugroul went back to his inn and by evening was on his way south, and Drondlann found another water dish for the bat, cleaned the cages, swept up, and spent most of the afternoon thinking.

The water of the lake was black and very still. No fishermen or boatmen worked out that way. The dealer in curiosities arrived in his donkey-cart, and two servants carried him upstairs. They were getting to the top, only three steps to go, two, one, they were almost there, when in the distance the seventeen horses neighed. Drondlann's hands clenched behind the servants' necks and his whole body became tense and hard as he said to himself that he was an idiot, and in that moment between one step and the next he changed the plan that had brought him there.

"No, I won't sell him to you," he said to Master Bramaltariq after describing the boy. "I wouldn't sell him for all the gold in the world. Never. He's like my own flesh and blood. I've had him by my side since he was born and he's like my own son now, and I love him as such. I swear by all that's sacred that it destroys my soul to have to do this. But times are hard, misery is knocking at my door. I'll rent him to you."

"What's that, have to see, how's that," muttered the old man, distrustful like all old men.

"I'll rent him to you," repeated Drondlann. "You'll give me money, not to keep him, but to see him. I bring him one day, you watch him dance, I get my money, I take him away. Another day I bring him, you see him dance."

"Who'll feed him?" the master interrupted.

Drondlann was not looking at the women reclining on pillows and carpets. He tried to keep his eyes on the face of the old man, and saw him agitated, moving restlessly, his little sharp eyes shifting, his lips half open.

"I will," he said.

The fat man thought the bargain was good and the dealer a fool. He accepted.

Five times after that the dealer in curiosities came from Eagle Alley to Master Bramaltariq's stone house on the lake. The first time was at evening. The sky was red, the horses were silent, the water looked still and black as a sheet of cast iron.

"Dance, Tattoot!" he cried.

The dealer knew the boy never repeated the patterns he made with his body; he knew it because he had watched him secretly in the house in Eagle Alley, making him dance once and again. But here, in the stone house on the lake, he did not watch him. He knew that if he himself fell into the trap, he'd lose everything. So the blond boy danced in the high salon and Drondlann kept his eyes on Master Bramaltariq and the women. The plump white women tried to stand up, opened their mouths, wept, moved their heads, stretched out their hands, groaned, screamed. But none of this affected fat Master Bramaltariq: he was rigid, desperate, staring at the boy. His face seemed to swell, the features trembling and melting like those of a corpse hanged a long time ago. And the arms and legs of the boy went on filling the room with flights, ciphers, dreams, memories, guilt, hunger, fever. Two of the women were crawling on the floor, another fell back on the cushions with her eyes closed and her tongue hanging out. Master Bramaltariq was apoplectic. The dealer clapped his hands, motioned to the boy to follow him, and left.

The second time he insisted that the women not be present.

"They take half your pleasure from you," he said to Master Bramaltariq. "They breathe it in from you, drink it, devour it. You'll watch better alone."

The fat man assented, quickly, anxiously. He had the wives shut up in the next room, and they snivelled and scrabbled at the door in vain all evening. Drondlann clapped his hands and gave the command. The boy danced.

Dance: a word easily spoken. At that time an unknown word, which the dealer in curiosities thought Grugroul had invented, for the art of dancing had been lost; a word which to him, since he had heard it and learned to say it in secret, seemed to slide off his lips almost without the need to use his mouth. That is what the boy did: dance, dance. And Drondlann did not watch him, and outside it was already night. On the other hand Master Bramaltariq, who despite his wives, cloaks, wealth, and horses was a fool, followed with staring, reddened eyes every movement of that body passing and repassing through the air of the room. The veins of his neck and temples stood out like stretched cords; he breathed with increasing difficulty and made senseless gestures as if trying to restrain the dancer, or help him, or kill him. But the master of the dance was the other man, the merchant, who was not a fool. The fat master of the stone house fell back in his chair. Drondlann clapped his hands. The boy stood still. The owner of the lands, waters, farms, and souls of Bramaltariquenländ had his eyes open and was still trying to wave his hands: the fingers stretched and contracted, buried in the fur of the blue bearskin cloak. Drondlann smiled at him, spoke to him the way merchants and priests speak, promising marvels, and helped him to sit up.

"Tomorrow," the fat old man managed to say.

The other frowned and proposed a day of rest.

"Tomorrow," the old man insisted. "Tomorrow. Tomorrow."

The dealer said certainly, of course, tomorrow. And the next day he went again with the boy and met Master Bramaltariq full of impatience. Drondlann thought it a pity that the fat man was too foolish even to realize he was near death, for he would have enjoyed seeing terror in those piggy eyes buried in the fat face. Nobody else was in the room and no women whimpered behind the closed doors. It was possible that death would not yet enter through one of those doors: that depended on his skill.

It was stormy, and the boy smiled; he liked rain and lightning. There was a thunderclap, and without waiting for the handclap the boy began to dance. The dealer had to make a great effort to keep from watching him: he heard the galloping of the golden steeds, he longed for the deserts and the fiery liquors and the petrified seas and his childhood. But he got hold of himself and made himself think about his shop in Eagle Alley, the cages, the sharp stink, the visits by buyers and sellers, the shadows, the dim windows that looked on the street. He hated it, but he was going to miss it.

And at another thunderclap Master Bramaltariq got up from his chair. The dealer watched him stand there, trembling, bloated, unsteady; he saw him reach out his arm as if he wanted to touch the dancer. Then that short, fat arm in its bejeweled, gold-fringed silk sleeve began to move, up, down, right, left, and the other arm was moving too, and the round head was swaying. He made two steps heavy enough to collapse the floor of the room and lifted one leg. Drondlann realized that the fat man was trying to dance, and broke out laughing. The shopkeeper of Eagle Alley roared with laughter at Master Bramaltariq, and the thunder boomed outdoors, and indoors the boy moved swiftly through the room taking various poses, and the dying old man sweated in his heavy clothing trying to imitate that white shape that intoxicated his blood and senses. But no one heard, no one knew anything. Drondlann clapped his hands and stopped the dance and left. Master Bramaltariq did not notice: he was in the middle of the room turning slowly about with one hand on his breast and the other held up towards the stormclouds.

Drondlann let several days pass, waiting till the master summoned him. Again it was evening, but the sky was clear. He wondered if there were black, quiet fish in that lake. The boy danced.

The shopkeeper of Eagle Alley had seen madness and death. Years ago, many years ago, astride a horse, hearing laughing trumpets blow the call to arms and the charge, he had seen men around him go mad and die. He himself had gone into madness and death and had returned to life: he had brandished a sword, raised a shield, borne a severed head aloft on a lance. And what was his life, now, in the shop in the alley?

He stopped the dance one moment before Master Bramaltariq plunged into delirium. He went to him and talked to him slowly, softly, gently. He told him that this dance had been the last. Yes, the last unless . . . But the precautions, the circumlocutions, were useless. The old gentleman did not hear him. So Drondlann took from his pocket the document and the stiletto, pricked the old man's right index finger, and had him sign the bottom of the page in blood. That was all, and the sky was still bright when the servants carried him down the staircase.

That night he hid the document under a loose board in the floor of the shop, and could not sleep.

Next day he took it from its hiding place and went with the boy to the house on the lake. Master Bramaltariq was no longer speaking, he who had given commands, issued judgments, ordered punishments. He was so mute that Drondlann thought he could take him back to the shop in Eagle Alley and sell him cheap. He clapped his hands.

He had no more than looked at the old man when he had the pleasure of seeing him die. He did not die like a warrior. He was no longer powerful, no longer imposing, not even fat. His reddish face had turned grey and the knotted veins were dark and swollen. He was not sweating: he was dried up, withered, feeble. But he wanted to go on watching the boy's mobile body, go on watching till death. And he died mad, gasping like one of the black lake fish, sprawled across what had been his treasures and luxuries.

Drondlann clapped his hands and the boy stopped dancing. He called the servants and the wives, he joined them in the funeral laments, howled, struck his clenched fists on his breast, bowed down to earth keening.

And after what he thought a decent interval, after the fat man was buried and the stupefaction of death had passed, when everybody was asking what would become of those vast properties and immense riches, the dealer in curiosities called for a lawyer and showed him the document.

It was beautiful, that house of stone and wood in the middle of the lake, so beautiful that he never once went back to the shop in Eagle Alley. When the stink there became insupportable the neighbors dragged off the corpses of the curiosities, shared out the cages and furniture, sealed up the doors and windows. The ex-dealer remained quite untroubled and went on living peacefully, never clapping his hands. The blond boy got fat: he ate too much and lazed through the days, looked after by the wives and servants. Sometimes thunder made him start. Drondlann had twenty-three stallions, eleven wives, three short cloaks of green, purple, and blue bearskin; he was no longer Drondlann but Master Bramaltariq, and sometimes he dreamed of a white form that moved dancing through the rooms of the house on the lake, in the years of the reign of Emperor Horhórides III, of the dynasty of the Jénningses.

"DOWN
THERE
IN THE
SOUTH"

Vast is the Empire, said the storyteller, so vast that a man can't cross it in his lifetime. You might be born in Lyumba-Lavior and start traveling and never stop and when death came, however long in coming, you might not even have reached Gim-Ghimlassa. Life can be lived anywhere, an ancient poet is said to have said, and if you meditate on that you'll see it's a noble thought. You can live in the great, handsome cities of the North, the white capitals with sonorous names or the grey fortress-cities or the beach-side resort towns full of music. You can live in tents in the desert following the oases that shift with the seasons. You can live on the rivers in houseboats, fishing, doing laundry, scrubbing the deck, watching people and houses and fields go by, making love in a hammock and bargaining with different people every day. You can live in a log cabin near the mountain peaks, in a marble palace, in a fetid slum, a convent, a school, a tower, a brothel. And also you can live in the South.

Yes, yes, my good people, I do believe it: you can live in the South. And die there. And can get born, grow, learn, kill, suffer in the South. Do you know the South? Have you been to that forbidden, tempting land? Have you gone to that paradise of monsters, cave of the assassins, realm of barbarity? Do you know the people of the South? Have you bedded their women, got drunk with their men, listened to their old people? It's cold here now in the North; for months now the cold hasn't let up, and this morning we got up in the dark and blew on our fingers and froze our feet on the floor and lighted the hearthfire and the stoves. Poor folk knocked the ashes off yesterday's embers and rich folk ordered servants to stoke the furnace fires in the basements of their great houses. We've drunk hot chocolate and wrapped up warm and at midmorning we've gone into a bar for a hot punch. Some vagabonds have died in the snowy fields and no bird sings and the ice thaws on windows and drips from the stone rosettes of balconies, and tonight there will be stars in a clear sky, and tomorrow we'll be colder than we were today.

And it's warm, now, down South. The days are long and pitiless. A white sun breeds clouds of mist on the lagoons in the marshland. People walk barefoot on the ground and the grass, half naked; they wake early, very early; they sleep through the midday and get up again when the sun sinks purple behind the tops of the huge trees. That's how it is down there in the South, green, suffocating, humid, full of violence and somnolence. Men and women don't gather around a fire but under palm trees that shoot up tall to escape the ferns that fasten on their trunks. And they don't listen to storytellers tell the deeds of the Empire, because the South refuses to admit that it's part of the Empire. They listen, sure enough, but they listen to something different: something that I've thought might be a treasure as great as the history of the greatest, most powerful empire known to man, or might be that same story told differently: they listen to the voices of the damp, warm earth, the sounds of the wind, the song of rivers, and what the leaves, the air, the animals are saying.

Yes, and it's always been that way, always. There've been emperors who dreamed of subjugating the South. There've been emperors who tried it, and some thought they'd done it. But with what? I ask, with what? With power, weapons, armies, fire, terror? Useless, all that, completely useless: all power can do is silence people, keep them from singing, arguing, dancing, talking, brawling, making speeches and composing music. That's all. That's a lot, you may say, but I tell you it's not enough. For what power can keep the earth from speaking to people? What weapons can keep water from running and stones from rolling? What artillery can keep a storm from crouching on the horizon, ready to burst? That's something no emperor has managed yet. On the contrary, not seldom, when they wanted silence, quiet, submission from the South, what they got was the tumult of war and rebellion.

It was thus, trying to subdue the South, that the Emperor Sebbredel IV died, eleventh ruler of the House of the Bbredasoës, mediocre rulers all of them, all forgotten but two: the founder of the dynasty, Babbabed the Silent, and the last, Sebbredel IV, famed and remembered not for his own merits but for those of a fugitive, an adventurer, on whom fate played a dirty trick.

Who was Liel-Andranassder, are we going to find out? Yes, yes, I know what you're going to say, and even if you're right, and I tell you that you're right, yet I also tell you that you're wrong. A life, like a story, has many parts, and each part is made of other ever smaller parts; for, however small and banal it may be, part of a story is a story, and part of a life is a life. You're going to tell me about the man who changed an Empire and altered the course of history, and that's the truth. And I'm going to tell you, and it's the truth too, about a young man, son of a bankrupt noble family, who'd lived surrounded by luxury and every amenity, and couldn't resign himself to poverty when it came. His parents took him with them to the modest country house which was all they had left, but at twenty Liel-Andranassder left that life, which he considered contemptible and despicable, and came to the capital. I won't tell you all he did for eight long years, but I can tell you that he went through real humiliation and shame, that he endured the unendurable, lost what innocence he'd had, got fat, turned lazy, lascivious, and fawning. But he also got what he wanted: a lot of money. Easy money, that ran quickly through his pale hands in a senseless, hopeless chase after respectability and honor, though he didn't then know the meaning of those words. And when he got to the end of the money he'd go back to the gaming houses, to usury, to sycophancy, and for a while he'd have plenty again. Until one night he killed a man who accused him of rigging the game.

His clothes smeared with blood, trembling, stammering, all he could do was vomit near the corpse: till then he'd only seen respectable corpses, with powerful relatives, for whom he had to weep and mourn convincingly. But to his own surprise he recovered quickly, put horror aside, washed his face and hands, and scattered a bit of gold here and there among the croupiers and managers and waiters. He persuaded himself that the people of the casino would dispose of the body in gratitude for his gifts and to avoid a scandal; and he went home. He told himself he was safe.

He didn't sleep much that night. To tell the truth, he didn't sleep at all. He tried to think, is what he did. But he was so full of alcohol and confusion that all he could bring to mind was the dead man's face, the insult, the wounds, the horrified eyes of the owner of the casino. And he told himself that it was unimportant; he was a gentleman, obliged to kill to defend his honor, everybody knew him and would protect him, nothing would happen, the other man was a rustic, a nobody, with no connections, no influence.

Now here is a little detail that doesn't show up in the great chronicles and history books but only in a letter or a little-known account here and there, and that we'd even prefer to forget: Liel-Andranassder had, in fact, rigged the game. How could he not, when it was his principal source of income? Everybody knew he cheated, so that recently he'd only been able to play against out-of-towners, people who didn't know him. And he knew perfectly well, how could he not know it, that he'd cheated the dead man. But so what? He was a notable person, member of an ancient, distinguished noble family; his grandfathers had been generals of the Empire; his grandmothers had been presented at court; he himself had once been invited to a palace reception and had seen, from a distance, the Emperor Sebbredel IV.

Another detail, and this one does show up in the history books and folios of chronicles, the sagas and the popular songs: the dead man was not a nobody.

It was near dawn when Liel-Andranassder heard steps in his anteroom. He jumped out of bed and got dressed in a hurry. He decided he ought to leave the city for a few days, go visit his parents in the country till the police stopped asking questions or the dead man's relations stopped looking for him. That's what he'd do, sure enough, he'd tell the servants to get the carriage ready right away.

What happened next has been very badly misinterpreted. The legend has it that his loyal and devoted servants warned him of the danger he was in so that he could escape. My dear friends, when you hear people say that, hasten to deny it, to say that's not quite how it was, and if they don't believe you, tell them it was I who told you so. Liel-Andranassder did escape, that's true, and did so thanks to one of his servants, that's true: but it wasn't loyalty or affection, but rancor, that moved the man to go that morning to his master's bedroom and say, "Police. Looks like they're coming here."

"The police?" he said, trying to make it look as if he wasn't interested, and failing totally.

"Yes. Yes sir, that's it. The police. About a hundred of them. Sent by the Duke of Sandemoross."

"What?" he squealed.

"Yes," said the servant, happy to see this master who paid him poorly and treated him worse tied up in knots with fear, "and the Chief of the Imperial Police in person is in charge of them. It seems that last night somebody with a dagger killed the emperor's stepbrother, the Governor of Abbel-Kammir, who was in the capital incognito."

And so Liel-Andranassder made his getaway. He sent the servant off, locked his door, thought of suicide a moment and ruled it out, not because he was a coward, you have to admit he wasn't that, but because he had a wild hope of escape, and jumped out the window. And from here on the legends tell the truth: he had incredible good luck. It was just dawn. The Duke of Sandemoross, nephew of the empress, was entering the street door as the master of the house ran out the tradesmen's gate behind the house.

Five minutes later the duke, roaring with fury, ordered that the house be sacked and burned.

Five minutes later Liel-Andranassder was walking slowly through the market place like an idle gentleman who'd got up unusually early and come out to see at what was for sale in the stalls. He stopped here and there, asked the price of a buckle, praised a length of velvet, examined some engravings, tested the edge of a dagger, and went on his way. He couldn't have bought anything since he hadn't a penny on him, but he needed to think, he wanted to gain time, to try to work out a plan, and above all he wanted to hear what was being said. He knew the market is the city's soundbox. So he learned that they were looking for him, and thought again of suicide and again refused the thought. He went back across the market place and came to the river, and there a prostitute saved him.

When the duke's men got to the riverbank, not because they knew he was there but because they were looking everywhere, he was sleeping in a rather dirty bed aboard one of those barges where you can gamble and buy women, and the prostitute was combing her hair in front of the mirror and looking at the gold ring glittering on the middle finger of her left hand, more than satisfied by this unexpected client who hadn't even wanted much from her. The barge was sailing upstream towards Durbbafal because its master didn't like policemen and, finding that a search was going on throughout the city, came back to his boat almost on Liel-Andranassder's heels without stopping to find out who or what the police were looking for. That day the search for the assassin was limited to the capital and its environs, and only late that night did the duke admit that the criminal might have left the city, and began to think of extending the hunt. And so when the Imperial Police reached Durbbafal, the assassin was no longer there.

He was on his way south. He hadn't chosen to hide in the South; as a Northerner he feared and despised those unknown provinces. But at the moment he had no choice. He had hopes, oh, yes, he still had real hopes of escaping. In an inn he had traded his elegant clothes for something to eat and a cotton tunic, and put on sandals instead of heeled shoes. He wasn't walking alone, but he meant to abandon his companions whenever and wherever he could safely do so. And furthermore, for the moment at least, he was safe, because he wore pinned on his chest the badge of the Imperial Police, and walked among men who also wore the badge of the Imperial Police, under the command of a sergeant, a veteran of the Selbic Wars, who'd served twelve years in the troop of the Duke of Sandemoross.

This too is on record in the chronicles: how Liel-Andranassder, the ruined nobleman, gambler and cheat, hunted as an assassin, got drunk in the inn with a couple of vagabonds, and how the police came on them along the road from Durbbafal to Laprac-Lennut and took them to the nearest police post. Hearing talk there of the assassination of the emperor's stepbrother, and desperate to evade suspicion, he'd started talking too, telling with drunken enjoyment what he'd do to that assassin if he met him.

"That fat fellow might be useful," said the sergeant, who was an imbecile, and whose orders were to recruit as many men as he could to hunt the criminal throughout the Empire.

They stuck the drunk's head in a basin of cold water, let him sleep on a bench, and when he woke up gave him coffee and asked his name.

"Andronessio," he said.

"Your papers."

"I haven't got any," he stammered.

"You let them get stolen, stupid," said the sergeant. "Make him out some temporary papers. You're in the police now, got it?"

"Yessir."

"And if you disobey an order or make a mistake, just once, I'll have you stuck in jail for the rest of your life, which will be extremely short, got it?"

"Yessir."

"I wonder if he'll be any use," the sergeant sighed, and paid him no more attention.

So all of a sudden he was a policeman, had papers of identity, and was going away from the capital. Those were days of weariness, hunger, hardship; his feet were cut and bruised, he lost weight, his skin was chafed by the roughness of common clothing, his fingernails got dirty, his hair long and wild. He missed his house, his money, his servants, his carriage, his soft bed, his polished floors, and gambling, and the vile society he knew so well. But they hadn't caught him. Not yet.

And so he marched for three months, sleeping in the rain, living on bits and scraps, helping arrest and punish poor devils, vagabonds, whores, thieves. Until in a town near the border of Brusta-Dzan province he realized that he had become somebody else.

"How come they call you Fatty?" the innkeeper asked.

"Me?"

"Hey, Andronessio, it's on account of you used to be fat," one of the policemen said.

The others laughed.

"Yes," said Andronessio, "guess I was. A long time ago."

And he got up to look at himself in a dim mirror near the stairs. The man looking back from the spotted quicksilver was not Liel-Andranassder. Nor was he Fatty. Nor was he Andronessio the policeman. Who would he be now? Who could he be?

"I'm me," he said to himself, but he still didn't know who he was.

Twelve leagues farther on, learning they'd been ordered to take another road that led northward and would bring them back to the capital, he ran off one night, barefoot, without the badge of the Imperial Police, leaving his mates asleep and the improvised camp without a guard. This time it was his own decision to go south. He was resolved to keep clear away from the emperor, the duke, the capital, the Imperial Police, and danger, and he didn't have anywhere else to go. Death was waiting for him in the North as a murderer and now as a deserter. He knew it was waiting for him in the South too, but maybe there it wouldn't take so long to come.

There is a border between the North and the South, we all know that. But if in a lot of places the border is definite, visible, firmly under the control of the bureaucracy, in a lot of other place it isn't. It's as if it wasn't there. So one day he crossed the border without knowing it. All he knew was that the weather kept getting hotter, that he was hungry and thirsty all the time, that his wounds and cuts had scarred over, and that he had very few memories left of houses with servants and soft beds, of men with knives at the exit of a gambling-den, of police and manhunts.

One night he fell asleep more heavily than usual and when the sun rose he struggled to wake but could not. He went on sleeping and dreamed. I can't tell you what he dreamed, but I imagine there were faces, many faces, and running blood. I imagine also that he was afraid, that he sweat cold and tossed and moaned, even cried out aloud, but could not wake.

Many days later he opened his eyes and saw a straw roof. He fell asleep again and opened his eye again and saw a window. After sleeping dreamlessly some hours more he woke. It was night. Someone asked him his name.

"I don't know," he said.

He was given water. Where did he come from? somebody asked.

"I don't know," he said, and slept, and did not dream.

Next morning he heard noises and voices before he opened his eyes; he stayed still, feeling his body heavy and aching. He was hungry.

"I'm hungry," he said.

"Good," somebody said.

A woman gave him food. During that day two or three men came and stood around looking at him and one of them talked to the woman. But it was a long time before he could get up and walk.

The woman's name was Rammsa. She had five children. Her eldest son was one of the men who had showed up the first day to look at him. "You drank poisonous water from the Tigers' Well," he said.

"Ah. I didn't know it was poisonous."

"How could anyone not know that?" asked Orgammbm, son of Rammsa. "How could anyone not know so many things? Your name, for instance. Have you forgotten it?"

"No, it's not that," he said, "not that. I know I had many names."

"Many names," said Orgammbm, and stopped, and stared at him.

"Yes."

He ate and drank in the mud hut where Rammsa lived with her three youngest children. During the day he sat under the trees or watched the river run, and one day he asked Genna, Orgammbm's youngest sister, to teach him to braid leather, because he wanted to make himself sandals.

"Women don't braid leather," Genna said, looking at him wonderingly, "that's men's work."

He laughed because Genna wasn't a woman but a child who scarcely reached his shoulder, and she said she'd call one of her brothers to teach him.

"And what do women do, Genna?" he asked, before she'd gone far.

She turned around and stood looking at him in silence, as if asking herself whether or not to answer him. Finally she decided it was worth the trouble, and she began to sing softly:

> *The world is nothing and nothing*
> *You have to sit and think*
> *Shut your eyes and think*
> *Hold out your hand and think*
> *Breathe deep and think*
> *Move your feet and think*
> *And then the world is nothing and is*
> *The kitchen of your house*

"And what does that mean?" he asked.

"What it means," said Genna, and went to find her brother.

He learned to braid leather and made himself two pair of sandals and a belt, which he showed to Orgammbm. Rammsa's eldest son told him that they were well made, almost as if by a craftsman; and showed them to his mother, saying, "He says he remembers having many names but doesn't know his name."

Rammsa looked at the two young men sitting on her house-mat, her son who was like all men, a bit stupid, very vulnerable, and very valiant, and the other, the stranger, who was not like all men. She had said, "Give him to me, he'll live," when the men had brought him in dying, struggling, convulsing, lips swollen, gasping for breath, nose and mouth full of dried blood. And she, who had washed him and cared for him, had forced him to swallow green mandremillia seeds and made him lie face down so that he wouldn't choke and had cleaned up the vomit and the blood, she was ready to smile, to give hopeful approval, to speak. But because she had suffered, had had a hard life and learned prudence, she said only, "Good," and looked out the window at the river. "Good," she said again, "it might or might not mean anything. We don't even know where he comes from. And he doesn't know, either, does he?"

He did remember where he came from, of course he did, though sometimes it seemed to him that these memories were dreams born of the poison, or belonged to somebody else; but as he was becoming prudent, like Rammsa, he said, "That's it. I don't know. I don't know where I come from or who I am."

"No," said Rammsa, "that's foolishness. Everybody is who he is."

"But the world is nothing and nothing," he said, not knowing why he said it, only because he thought that what the mother had said was a good way to end the daughter's song.

Rammsa started, she who was always so calm. "Who told you that?"

"Genna, Rammsa's daughter."

Nobody said anything more. Orgammbm lowered his eyes and looked again at the sandals and belt, and Rammsa did nothing: she just sat there, serene, with them. And in the quiet and silence he thought how almost always Rammsa seemed to be doing nothing, but that might not be so, for an idle or useless woman couldn't be as important as he felt her to be.

A few days later they told him to go. They didn't kick him out, but told him he had to go. At that moment, with his burden of memories, his own or somebody else's, it occurred to him that the Imperial Police were coming and the inhabitants of the city, town, whatever this was he was living in, were trying to save him. If he'd gone on being the man who fled the capital after stabbing the emperor's stepbrother to death, he surely would have thought differently: that they hated him, were driving him away, resented him because in the convalescent wanderer they'd guessed the Northerner used to luxuries and conveniences they'd never known. But even if he no longer was that man, he kept some trace of him, and so he did think about danger. Perhaps Rammsa saw it in his eyes, for she smiled and said, "Nothing bad is going to happen to you, son, unless you want it to. But you're going to have to go."

His alarm passed. But not because Rammsa said that, not because he realized that his pursuers were far away, but because his talk with the woman had convinced him that the things he'd considered important weren't so important, and that the empty place he'd always filled up with all the stuff he had valued so much was indeed empty, empty and open, waiting for what was to come to fill its positions, its ranks, waiting for clear light to fall on clear shapes, and clear spaces to waken clear echoes.

"Why?" he asked the woman.

"Because that is how it is," she said, "and we have to do a thing so that it can be as it is. Because we were made to know, not to submit."

And she spoke with such haughty certainty and finality that he could ask no more.

He said nothing and set to shaping a walking stick, but Rammsa's response had made him think of the song sung him by Genna, the child not as tall as his shoulder, and so he worked away without paying much heed to what he was doing, hoping to see or hear the little girl. Orgammbm came by instead, with one of his younger brothers.

"You're going to need a knife," he said, offering him one with a broad, strong blade and an antler haft.

Perhaps he felt once more how the flesh of the man had given to the knife, there in the cobbled street near the door of the gaming house. Or perhaps not, perhaps he felt nothing of the sort and what happened was because the voices of the earth and water are so strong in the South that even a man coming from luxury and corruption can hear them. I don't know, and there's nobody who can find out for me; it's not in words, written or sung, and nobody can tell us. I only know that he answered, "No. I don't want a knife. I don't want weapons."

"You don't?" Orgammbm's younger brother asked. "You really don't? A spear, bow and arrows? Nothing?"

"No. Nothing."

"How are you going to hunt, then?"

"I'm not going to hunt."

And yet he had hunted when he lived in the cities of the North, all rigged out with fine leather boots and costly, well-oiled weapons, in a cavalcade under the crowns of the autumn trees on the country estate of some nobleman who hadn't been able to get out of inviting him. But now, no, now he didn't want to hunt: let tigers poison the wells, let his guts knot up with hunger, but he wasn't going to hunt.

"Very well," said Orgammbm, "very well, but you'll want something to fish with."

"I don't know," he said. "A net, maybe."

And next morning he left. But before he left, in the night, two things happened to him: he saw the townsmen dance, only the men, naked, shining, grave, all the men of the village, between the houses and the riverbank; and he spoke with Genna.

"What are they doing?" he asked the girl.

"Dancing, don't you see?"

"Yes, but why?"

"What a question," she said condescendingly.

"I mean is it a religious occasion, or are they celebrating something?"

"I don't understand," she said, and went on watching the men dance.

"It's I who don't understand," he said.

"That's true," said the girl.

They stayed side by side, watching. He saw the bare feet fall and rise, the heels strike and slide, the toes grip the hard earth, the bodies arch, the heads turn, the half-closed eyes, the open mouths.

"What are they dancing?" he asked.

"Ah!" said she. "Finally you understand. It's the Twenty-Fourth Dance. It's called Seven Shells."

And next morning he left, as he had said he would. He took his two pair of sandals, his belt, a bag of provisions, and a net. It was hot. The sky was cloudy but the sun's so strong there in the South that it heated up everything from above the heavy clouds. And there's so much water there, the rivers run and leap and overflow their channels, marshes spread out and lakes fill the low places, so that the world is green and golden and everything grows and sings. He had to keep off the insects that flew and crawled and dropped from branches, but his sandals protected the soles of his feet, and in the morning he'd pick damp tiaulana leaves, squeeze them with his fingers, and cover his body, face, arms and shoulders with the whitish juice. He lived on fruit and spinner-bird eggs and sometimes eggs of the little zedanna bird who leaves them to keep warm in the sun and goes off pecking up bugs by the water and only returns to them at evening; and he drank nothing but running water which was not stagnant, or dirty, or thick. He slept in the fork of a big tree when he found one, and if he didn't find one he didn't sleep but walked on, always farther south.

He was going upstream along a large river, trying to keep close to its course, walking towards its springs. In places the river formed meanders and swamps, where the water seemed not to come from sources far to the south, but to well up endlessly out of the ground. He rested when the morning was getting on and the heat grew almost unbearable: he cleared the ground about the trunk of some high-topped tree not overgrown with ferns and creepers, and sat down there, not leaning back, his arms loose on his lifted knees, his stick within reach of his hand, and dozed. But his eyes were not always shut: he gazed now and then at the water or the green shadow, or watched small shy animals peep from the mouths of their burrows.

He soon noticed that in the South the air was not that inert space he had known in parks, the suffocating perfumed mantle of bedrooms, the weary, stale atmosphere of casinos. The air he breathed here was as thick and fertile as the earth and water. The earth sustained everything and under it was the water; but the water rose up too and covered the earth, and the air that was above them both extended down into the earth enriched by the water, silent or noisy, and a white-gold dust floated and drifted around still things and among the insects with transparent wings and the greedy birds darting among fleshy leaves. And this joyous commotion went on all the time, everywhere, and he had to take part in it.

One evening he heard someone singing, another evening he saw a hanged man.

He was so tired when he first heard the singing that he thought he'd fallen asleep and was dreaming. But that couldn't be: he was awake, walking, going forward, slowly but with a goal, that of finding a safe place to sleep. He wasn't dreaming, for sure: somebody was singing. It might have been a man, for the voice was deep, opaque, almost harsh; but he was sure it was a woman, though he didn't know why. It's occurred to me that since Genna had hinted to him that there were things women did, and since it had been she who sang for him, he thought that in the South women did the singing as men did the dancing. He wasn't entirely mistaken about this, I can tell you, not entirely. He stopped and listened. It wasn't the best place to be standing, since the big, white, blind ants, which the North knows only as traveller's tales, roamed there, quick, insatiable insects that feed on living wood and destroy tree-roots and soften the ground till it turns to a kind of ash that would give way under a rat's weight let alone a man's, but he stood still, because whether or not he sank into the ground was less important than listening to the song. And the song was very simple, almost foolish, almost nonsense like the songs happy kids make up while they're hopping on one foot or walking where they're not supposed to.

The man with the spear goes running, running, the song went. And it went on:

> *The rush-mat woman speaks, she speaks and says.*
> *There's a child in the hammock.*
> *There's a tree by the river.*
> *There's a fish in the basket.*
> *And we're still waiting, we're still waiting.*

After that came a long silence, and when he was thinking about going on, not sure whether to look for the singer or for a place to sleep, the voice was heard again: *there's a child in the hammock, there's a tree by the river,* and so on to the end. This time he stayed still for a long time, but though he stood alert, hearing all the sounds of the forest, the song was done, and he went on his way, and despite weariness and sleepiness did not sleep for hours yet to come.

Day after day he went on through the humid wilderness, alert to great and lesser perils, the needs of his body and those of the unknown world he was crossing. For though he tried to find what to eat when he was hungry and where to rest when he felt he couldn't go on, he also did his best not to cut young branches that barred his way, not to destroy the shoots of the great trees or the pale buds that put forth from the branches, and he walked mindfully, as if he and the earth and the things that grew in it and walked on it were brothers, each life dependent on the others' lives. When his solitude weighed on him he thought about Rammsa, her children, the men who danced the dance called Seven Shells, and was comforted. And sometimes he thought, but indifferently, with no change in his state of mind, about the men and women of the North, the salons, the parks, the festivals, the marble statues and the still air; about luxury, servants, gold, and power. And so he came to know his name.

And he went on day after day, he didn't know how many days because he had no way to count them and had no desire to, and one morning suddenly the river ran out into marshlands and the marshes vanished into solid ground and he thought the river was gone. It wasn't, of course; never have I heard of a river vanishing like a magician at the fair, finished like a piece of bread. It hadn't disappeared, and after one more day's walk across the soft muddy land swarming with aquatic larvae and shoots of wetland plants he found it again, only now it was a little thread of water, a brook that didn't seem remotely related to the mighty torrent he'd been following. But he went on following it, since it was all he had to keep him from walking in circles without ever getting anywhere.

The brook ran from a lake. And in the lake, as wide as a sea, a city was built on wooden pilings, greenish and eaten away by the years and the water, but more durable than the hardest stone. Boats carved from hollowed tree-trunks rocked, moored to the pilings, and in the boats were oars painted in bright colors, nets, baskets, fishing gear. He spent a whole day looking at the lake town from a distance, and the next day he walked down to the shore of the lake, before the men came down to the boats and unmoored them and went fishing. He spoke with them, and spoke with the women; children came up and touched his stiffened tunic and leather belt and took hold of his walking stick and looked at him with wide eyes.

That day the men didn't go out fishing. The people of the lake town asked him his name and he told them. They offered him food and drink and took him to one of the houses and told him he could rest there. They told him, too, that he could stay with them as long as he liked before he went on his way.

"They're waiting for you," said one of the women, who was called Selldae. "They're waiting for you somewhere else."

"Yes," said an old man, who was missing some fingers of his left hand, "and they know you're going to come."

"Where?" he asked.

"Oh, over there," said the old man, waving with his good hand, a gesture that included everything on the far side of the lake. "Over there."

"Where you go," said Selldae's sister, who looked like her but was fatter, heavier, sadder, "there they'll be waiting for you."

"And you?" he asked. "Were you waiting for me too?"

Yes, they told him. And they told him that not everything was said and that the man who has come must go, and that he who has come and gone must always come back, some day.

He might have asked what that meant, or not asked but assumed that it was some legend or tradition of the South, but he did neither, now that he knew his name, and accepted and was silent, knowing, as they knew, that he must go and must return. He stayed six days in the village on the lake, a far shorter stay than he had made in Rammsa's village, but after all he was not ill now. He slept in a tiny, very high house over the water; he ate, sometimes with the women in one or another house, most often in Selldae's sister's house, or with the old man with the mutilated hand and his grandsons, or with other men; he went fishing before sunrise with the youngest men and one or two hardy old ones; he helped repair the roofs of some houses after a storm and dived into the dark waters of the lake with the fishermen to inspect the pilings planted down in the lake-bottom. One night he heard a young girl singing, who lived with Selldae though she didn't seem to be one of her daughters; she sang:

The water is a burnt body
that goes by;
the song the color of earth
rules your house and your belly
and doesn't go by;
you won't see the world
that is green;
the earth is the body of the man
who comes back.

And one evening he saved a little child who'd just begun to walk and fell into the lake from the platform of his mother's house. The mother was a tiny, serious young woman who adorned her hair with yellow flowers at night, and three days later gave birth to her fourth child. She received her sodden, bawling son, who clung to her neck, and said that she had never thought that her boy was going to be one of those who come back from death. He was on the point of telling her that in fact the child hadn't been dead, that he'd caught him a second before he went down and was drowned, but he said nothing to her, and instead of talking, which might be useless, thought that in these matters of death a second counts for nothing and that maybe the child was in fact dead when he fell into the water, before he fell, when he was born, before he was born, like us all. She said no more to him either, did not cry, did not thank him, and went off with the little boy who went on bawling and hanging on to her neck, leaving a trail of drops of lake water on the weathered boards of the platform.

He left the village at dawn of the seventh day. He carried a pouch full of provisions and had a new walking stick, stronger, better made, and a tunic of newly woven cotton, shorter and more comfortable than the old one. Some of the men, almost all of them actually, went with him in their boats to the far side of the lake.

"Over there," they told him when they landed, "are the sources of the river."

"And over there," another man said, "the foothills of the Drambulnyarad. And over that way, the Bogs of Nan, and there, you have to be careful about quicksand."

"Good," he said, "farewell," and then stopped. "What is that music?"

"That's the Sixth Dance," said one of the fishermen. "The one called The Lamp and the Cauldron."

Then he asked, "How many dances are there?"

"Thirty-seven," they replied. "For a long, long time there have been thirty-seven dances."

He did not go towards Drambulnyarad nor towards the Bogs of Nan but went on in search of the springs of the river. Now he went far more quickly; he had learned to follow the tracks of the big rodents that go along clearing and beating a path that's almost invisible because though their paws and teeth leave the ground bare, they don't harm the tender little branches growing across it that hide it; he had learned you can't walk far or easily when the sun falls straight down on the earth, nor when it's very red or very white around the horizon; that you have to drink by day, very early or very late, never at midday or in the middle of the night, and always in places where the earth shows the tracks of many different kinds of animals; that you have to walk first and eat after, and after eating walk slowly a very short way and then sleep; that you can walk far and eat little so long as you drink enough; that it doesn't work to eat much and walk much; and that it's dangerous to eat much and walk little.

Coming to a clearing made by man and not by fire or water or animals, on a stormy evening, he thought he was near a settlement and decided to rest where he was that night and come among people next day. He studied the ground, selected a place, and sat down. Very soon rain began to fall. There was a great bolt of lightning, and before the thunder sounded he glimpsed a man turning slowly around, as if to look at him, across the clearing. In what light was left he looked at the man again and saw he kept turning and as if wavering in the wind. He got up, went over, and spoke; but the man's feet did not touch the ground: he was hanging by the neck on a rope tied to a branch not far up the tree, he was blindfolded and his hands were tied behind his back; his lips were purple, his torso naked, his chest laid open with the point of a knife or spear, a wound that had bled when the executed man was still alive. Now that he knew how to read the earth, the plants, and even the air and water, now that he knew the smells, and the tips of his fingers had grown as sensitive as the palms of his hands had grown hard and callused, he knew that five men had brought this one by force, and behind them had come a woman; he knew that they had struggled a little, not much, with the prisoner, and that they had hanged him after marking his chest, had waited for him to die, had peeled and eaten some fruit while they waited, and had gone, the woman ahead, the men following, this time slowly, peacefully.

A dead man should be buried—in the South, in the North, anywhere, everywhere. He stayed near the hanged man and waited till the earth grew soft under the rain, and when he felt the mud yielding and with a little effort could push his feet into it, he used a dead branch and a stone to dig a grave at the foot of the gallows tree.

The storm passed; like a wrathful woman who yells and breaks all the plates and bowls in the cupboard and goes off to stay in her mother's house or with her elder sister, it went away muttering between its teeth and sobbing, and left silence and fallen twigs and puddles and bent trees and the moon away up there in the black sky.

Next day he went on walking but found no settlement, nor on the next day or the next. He ate little, slept, drank, walked and walked, and thought about the hanged man, about death, vengeance, justice. He heard no singing, but talk of justice; he was in a courtroom.

He had carefully avoided courts, up there in the North, I tell you that, for this man who walked through the green and rancorous South no longer thought about the rich provinces where dry judges consult dusty papers before choosing life or death for an accused man whom they know nothing about, but even if he'd frequented courtrooms assiduously he wouldn't have been able to identify what he saw now as a place and ceremony where it was decided what was just and what was not.

He saw no drapes of black and purple velvet, no balustrades of marble and bronze, no uniforms or robes. The judge was not a thin, bilious man, nor a greasy, sleepy, fat one, but a dark-eyed, middle-aged woman. There were no prosecutors, no defenders, and a lot of people were there to see judgment done. And there was an old woman, a very old woman, who had been carried there on a litter, probably because she could no longer travel a long way through trees and ferns, ford rivers, or cross rope bridges, sitting behind the stump that served as the judge's seat. Now and then she spoke to the woman who was the judge, only to her, never to anyone else, reminding her of similar cases or giving her advice.

He saw two men absolved and two men and a woman condemned. He heard laughter and saw a defendant and a claimant noisily settle their difference, but he also saw tears and lamentation and heard groans and complaints. The condemned woman screamed insults and tried to kill the judge, and one of the guilty men sat down on the ground and wept.

He asked how it was that there were no guards nor prison cells nor police.

"How can you not know that?" they asked him, and he remembered Ramma's children.

They told him that there were prisons, and that some people were foolish enough to escape or resist, but that everybody knew what was in store for people who didn't submit to village law.

"The judge may be a bad person," they said to him, "and the sentence may be wrong, but justice is justice."

Then he spoke of the hanged man, and they said that there are crimes that are punished by death and that death can be the best thing that can happen to a woman or a man.

"If they're driven out," they said, "if they can't find shelter or protection anywhere. Do you think anybody could survive, alone, in the wilderness?"

"I do," he said. "I've been surviving."

"That's different," they answered.

"And I buried the hanged man."

"Good," they said. "Why not?"

"Compassion isn't a crime," the judge said.

"Anybody who comes by can bury a criminal's body," said a man, "if he's listened to the women and knows how long a moment is."

"Of course," he said, and told them his name and where he was going.

But he did not go to their town. He accepted some provisions and took his leave of them.

"You must keep watch for your brother," the very old woman told him.

"Farewell," he said.

Next day it was very hot, so that he didn't go as far as on the previous days, and saw water evaporating from the broad leaves and the river-mist rising till it was almost opaque by noon. He wondered how it was that the whole forest wasn't baked crisp under the white sun, and rested for hours sitting under a giant tree with dense foliage. But in the North it was very cold, a malign and cutting cold that froze nostrils and fingertips, breath and heart. The Emperor Sebbredel IV, eleventh of the dynasty of the Bbredasoës, listened to his ministers and got more and more uneasy. Why did these things have to happen to him? What kind of useless people did he have serving him? Why didn't these imbeciles do their duty? Weren't they paid well so that the emperor could sleep sound and wake cheerful, looking forward to festivals, tourneys, willing and pretty women, a boring meeting or two with functionaries, of course, but all the luxury and satisfactions proper to the life of the most powerful man in the world? And now this? Now, as in his grandfather's grandfather's time, he had to think about a punitive expedition against the Southern Provinces? Oh, no, he wasn't going to subject himself to the discomforts of military life, he wasn't going to put his royal person in danger far from the palace, the capital, the court, floundering in swamps, driven mad by insects, to kill some evil-smelling rebellious little men whose wives weren't even acceptable as loot since they smelled just as bad, and besides he'd heard they were all witches. In a word, Sebbredel IV was scared.

It's fortunate that we citizens of the Empire can, at such times, remember brave and generous emperors such as Atelmaneth III, the Red, or Yhsberaduïn the Eaglet, or Rivvner I, who founded the Vnerádir dynasty; or brave and pitiless emperors like Ssulmenit VI, or Biriandirn II, or Dalmauster the Stormy; or brave, mad emperors like the Ferret; or empresses who left the silks and jewels and gratifications of their rank and boldly led armies, like Ysadellma, or Esseriantha the Beautiful, or Mitrria, or Dejsjarbaïl. It's fortunate, I say, because the mere existence of such men as Sebbredel IV is a disgrace to the Empire, and the history of their governments plagued by vacillation, weakness, and petty egoism is enough to disillusion people; and a disillusioned people is the hardest to govern.

"Who is this man? What's his name? Where did he come from?" the emperor demanded.

"We don't know, my Lord," said the minister of the interior.

"What do you mean, Lord Minister, we don't know? Have we run out of spies? Don't we spend good money from the treasury so that informers and provocateurs do their work and don't come to us with vague guesses? Don't we train clever youngsters to mix with those damned rebels and send us detailed reports so we can crush them before they threaten our power?"

"Yes, my Lord," said the minister of finance.

"Yes, my Lord," said the minister of war, "but . . ."

"But what?" demanded the emperor.

The minister of war took out a paper with a long list of names. "My Lord, our agents in the South have gone silent. Some are dead," he said hurriedly, "and we know perfectly how and when they died. Rebald'Dizzdan, known in the South as Ganngraamm, for instance, drowned a little over five months ago in Lake Fviagga, near Drambulnyarad. Addroë, known as The Black, fell from a cliff in the Hotspring Mountains. Rubvian'Daur died in a knife fight about four and a half months ago in the Five Goats Range. Drrambinia'Sdar, one of our most effective spies, was found strangled to death in—"

"Enough!" said the emperor. "I am not interested."

There was a silence in the great throne room. The ministers waited for the emperor to speak, and the emperor tapped his right-hand fingers on the arm of the throne.

"They're all dead?" he asked.

"No, my Lord," said the minister of the interior, "but a good many. Those who remain have informed us that this situation may be regarded as an emergency."

"Who is this man?" the emperor asked again.

"No one knows, Sire," the ministers said again.

"What does he want? What is he up to? Is he inciting rebellion? Has he declared war on the North? Does he aspire to the throne? Or can he be bought off?"

"It appears that for now he simply travels around the country, and that alone causes a certain dangerous unrest."

"But why? What do the stupid reports say?"

"The reports, my Lord," said the minister of war, "say that a man is preparing to raise the South against the Imperial throne. The people of the rebel provinces call him The Man, or The One Coming. Some say he was born in the South and grew up and lives alone deep in the wilderness, which is clearly impossible. Others say he came from the North originally, and some of them even think he was an important man, a nobleman connected to the court. And they say he has had many names, doubtless to elude pursuit."

"There is no physical description, my Lord," the minister of the interior put in, "that we can use to identify him. Some say he's young, others that he's old. It appears that he's dark, but in the South of course most people are unpleasantly dark-skinned. And that he has light eyes like a Northerner, which seems improbable, though it does undeniably occur. And that he's extremely tall and thin, and if Your Supreme Majesty will permit, I will say that this last may be the only certain fact, but it's useless, because all those Southerners eat badly and are riddled with chronic ailments and deficiencies of all sorts. For the same reason I am of the opinion that he cannot be as tall as they say."

"Where is he?"

"At the present moment, my Lord, this is not known, but we have documented his passage through the following towns."

"The towns don't matter," said the emperor. "What I want to know is what this individual intends to do and what forces he has."

"The reports, my Lord, are incomplete and inconclusive on those points."

Angélica Gorodischer

The emperor went into a fit of rage. When he calmed down, red-faced and shaky, and let his ministers go on talking, all he could find out was that the South was not disturbed, but rather too quiet; that of the thousands of spies sent into the South perhaps half a dozen remained alive, and those few had escaped and were in the capital, rendered useless by terror, bewitched perhaps, hidden, writing reports and collecting wages; that the Southerners were moving about from town to town with unusual frequency; that they had no organized army, and that the whole South was repeating one phrase, a watch-word no doubt, though it wasn't changed daily as was proper: *It hasn't all been said.*

"It means revolution, no doubt of it," said the minister of war.

"I realize that, Lord Minister, I am not an idiot," said the emperor, who perhaps was not such an idiot but who did not realize anything.

Never before had the North marched against the South without cause. Well, this time, they did.

While orders went out from the capital to all the Northern camps and garrisons, the people in the Southern towns waited for the man who was going to come. If in some village some kid asked who and how and why and where from and what for, his parents, his grandparents, his uncles if he'd lost his parents, answered: "He who went away has returned."

The littlest ones or the most innocent ones persisted: "And is he going to come stay with us?"

And the older people smiled and said, "He went away and has returned, and he goes and returns, and will go and will return."

"But why?"

"Because it hasn't all been said."

About the time the fatuous emperor ordered fine embroidered robes to wear over his armor, the man who was walking through the hot green South and who had now known lake cities and tree cities and secret cities underground, in hollow trees and hidden by poisonous plants and giant ant hills, took his way almost to the limit which very few have ever reached if in truth anyone ever reached it, and turned back in the other direction, and talked with men, and women talked to him, and he saw the Twenty-Ninth Dance, which is called Before Waking, and the Twelfth, Mastery of Ignorance, and the Second, Complications of a Hand, and the Eleventh, An Oil Lamp is not a Cowbell, and the Seventeenth, The Place, and much more. About the time the armies were gathered and the generals getting impatient and the emperor was seeking a pretext for delaying departure even if only for a day, just one more day, he came to a silent town. It hadn't rained for a long time in that region, and everything seemed covered with dust and ash. Only as he entered the place did he realize he was in a dead city.

In the North, in the rich elegant capital, in the marble palace with blue translucent roofs and domes of copper and gold, the Emperor Sebbredel IV said at last, "Tomorrow. Tomorrow at daybreak."

And in the South, in the dead city, a man entered the houses of wood and straw, frightened off the carrion-eaters with a stick, and, sorehearted and weary, buried the dead under the sheltering trees. In the North the eleventh ruler of the House of the Bbredasoës put on his armor and over it a robe of blue velvet embroidered with pearls and silver thread, and in the South the man who came and went away gave water to the sole survivor of the plague.

The North threw flowers before the Imperial armies and Sebbredel IV became increasingly cheerful. His armor was heavy and awkward, to be sure, but it gave him the comforting sense of being invulnerable, almost immortal, as an emperor beloved by his people should be. What could a few ragged, sick, superstitious tramps do against the most powerful army led to certain victory by the most powerful ruler of the greatest empire known to man? We'll destroy them in the first encounter, the minister of war assured him. The Department of Revenues is going to ask Your Supreme Highness's approval of new taxes to cover the costs of the expedition without burdening the Treasury, said the minister of finance. And the emperor said to himself that as soon as they got back he would bestow new titles on these capable and loyal officials.

The two men on foot entered the village at midday, and people came to welcome them. Maannda told of the plague and how he had returned from death. That night they were eating under the eaves of a house and in front of them sat a woman of the South, a dark woman, big, ponderous, getting old, who walked very erect and spoke in a soft voice. "They say armed men are coming, a lot of them, from up there, from the house of power," she said.

He went on eating, but Maannda set his bowl on the ground. "Again?"

"What do you mean, 'again,' little man?" said the woman. "Maybe you've seen armed men from the North before?"

"Not I," Maannda said, "but my grandfather's grandfather saw them."

"This time is different," the woman said. "This time we aren't going to die, but to fight. This time the one who had to come has come."

He looked up then. He said, "I'm not going to fight."

"No?" said she.

"How can you not fight?" Maannda asked. "You buried the dead, you listened to the women, you held up the roof of the house, I was dead and you brought me back."

"You weren't dead," he said.

"Yes I was," Maannda insisted, "I was dead, I'm the one who knows that best, aren't I? And you came and you went and you refused weapons and you forgot your names and you knew your name—how can you not fight?"

And a young girl, not young enough to hum like Genna and not old enough to sit in judgment, left the villagers who surrounded them, and came up to where he sat with Maannda and the blind woman, and everyone was silent and listened.

"But all has not been said," she said, "for words are the shadow and the light of things and things are only what is being born and being;

And so when there is no bread we need only sit and await the new day, and the new day will bring us bread;

In the heart of the hungry man despair lays its traps and the man weeps and curses;

But all is not said,

And a man does ill to weep and curse when to sit and hope is well;

For as bread comes, comes one who does not know his name yet knows he is called by many names;

One to whom women speak, telling the secrets of women and those of the house and village;

And he who is to come depends on no one, has no one, has nothing: he must make his sandals and his pouches and weave his clothing and braid his belts;

For this he must find for himself food and drink and sleep and shelter and guard himself from the perils of solitude;

And he who is to come must go, always, for there is no whole or true coming or arrival without leaving and departure;

But all is not said, for he goes and comes and goes again;

And he who is to come will be unarmed and will refuse arms though they are made and adorned for him;

And he who is to come will be he who secures the roofs and foundations of your house, he who draws from death and the depths those who are all but lost, he who sees your city and your house because he can see the world, he who knows nothing and knows all, he who from the heart of your earth rises up and may be seen by all for what he is;

For all is not said because night follows day and the wise man sleeps until sunrise;

But the brave man's eyes are open and he keeps watch for his brother;

And the woman who rules your house and the daughters she has given you, who know more than your head, your heart, and your belly, accept the night and subdue it and so night works for your good and that of your people;

But he who is to come is he who arises against the night and says to it, Begone:

For this death comes and does his work like a good workman earning his pay;

But all is not said because absence and presence are not opposites but one same and single thing;

For as a moment takes no time though it seems that time is a succession of moments, so a man is not gone though he seems gone: where could he go? When?

No, all is not said because he has gone and returned and goes and returns and will go and will return;

For this when you sit in the kitchen of your house ask your wife and she will tell you to open your eyes by day and close them by night, that this is best to do, because he who came and went away is to return;

No, all is not said."

The girl drew back and went to sit down beside her mother, and the blind woman said, "Within seventy days they will reach the South."

And he said, "Let's rest now."

While the emperor fanned himself in his tent, a troop of soldiers entered the first woods of the green world of the South. But the South was deserted, empty, lonely, silent. And, it must be confessed, this frightened the soldiers more than if they had met patrols, ambushes, resistance, battle. A soldier expects death; he may or may not fear it, but he expects it. If suddenly peace and silence take the place of death, his warrior's pride is useless, and he's only a poor frightened man stuck in an Imperial Army uniform.

"In my opinion, my Lord, they have fled," said General Vordoess'Dan.

The general had spent his life sitting at a desk. He was twenty when he got his first desk, a narrow, wobbly table of common wood in the barracks room he shared with other young lieutenants. At fifty he was a general and that vulgar, inadequate desk had been transformed into an immense object of scented wood inlaid with mother of pearl which took up most of the office and allowed him to see nothing of the world but the pile of folders placed before him every morning and removed every night when his adjutants had finished reading and classifying them. He had been made General of the Empire because he was of a rich and noble family and his younger sister had married the emperor's younger brother.

"They have fled," he repeated. "In terror," he added with a complacent smile.

The emperor smiled too. I believe it was the last smile of his life. He didn't even have his armor on, as in this climate it was twice as heavy and uncomfortable, and intolerably hot. He was, however, wearing a robe of yellow silk with black borders on which gleamed opal flowers, and now put on a hat of yellow plumes to protect his illustrious head from the sun. He came out of the tent and the officers and soldiers cheered him, moved by his appearance and because the general had ordered them to cheer the Sovereign every time he came out of the tent. And when the clamor died down, Sebbredel IV ordered the army to advance. And the army advanced.

Let me say, dear friends, that it was not a battle. It was a massacre, a butchery, a slaughterhouse, a feast of blood. The Northern soldiers weren't trained to fight in forests they didn't know, and though they cheered the emperor when ordered to, they were not ready to defend him or even to obey him. The men and women of the South weren't exactly an army, but they knew the forest, the water, the earth, the grass and trees, the roots and fruits, the wind, and they were ready to give their lives if the man they waited for, he who had come, fought beside them. In a few hours, believe me, a few hours, the South had defeated the North. He Who Had Come stuck the emperor's head on a spear and raised it up above the dead and the living. There's no use talking about General Vordoess'Dan's head; it got lost, and even if it hadn't I doubt if it deserved being stuck on a spear.

The men and women went back to their villages, the women singing as they went:

A badger made fun of the hunter,
A dibris danced with a spider,
A fly got suffocated in an anthill,
A worm went out fishing in a boat,
And a fool laughed and then he cried.

But all is not said, because the men of the South now danced thirty-eight dances and the last was called The Doorway, and because on the frontier between the North and South there was an encampment where more than a hundred men and women were waiting, among them He Who Had Come, Maannda, the blind woman, Rammsa, and some others who had asked or whom he had asked to stay.

And after many days the emissaries of the North sat down on the rush mats in the middle of the camp, listened in silence, and accepted. They had no alternative. The Empire had no army, it had no emperor, for Sebbredel's wife and sons and brothers, as fatuous as he, as stupid as General Vordoess'Dan, had fled the capital; it had no forces, no hopes, nothing.

This was the only time that the Golden Throne of the greatest of empires stood, not on marble, but on the earth. And He Who Had Come sat down on it, and Rammsa placed on his head a crown of green leaves, and so he was crowned emperor, and from that place he ruled the Empire under his true name.

And that's it, good people, that's all. I thank you for listening to me with such attention and patience, but what remains to be said is not really a job for a storyteller. We all know what happened in those years, anyway; and if it's possible that any of you don't, you can look at the history books and marvel at those old pages. But since not all is ever said, the temptation is great; and I can tell you, before we all go home to take a hot bath, put on slippers, and sit down by the fire, that one day he left, for he who came must go. That he walked through the green world, leading Rammsa's oldest great-grandson by the hand, that having come to the first tall trees he let the child go, telling him to run straight back home. That he walked on and was gone. That he walked into the forest and never returned. But as a consolation and a subject of meditation for just men and prudent women, I will remind you that what they say in the hot, harsh, green South is true: no, not all is said.

THE
OLD
INCENSE
ROAD

I'm an orphan," The Cat had said, and without looking at him old Z'Ydagg had answered, "So what? That's a reason why we should take you on?"

"I mean I can look after myself," the boy insisted. "Nobody's going to come making any demands on you. And I'm not a slacker. I can be useful. I've done a lot of jobs, but what I like best is traveling. And how can a poor man travel unless it's his job?"

"You'll have to talk to the boss, Mr. Bolbaumis," the old man said.

"Old man, I've already told you not to call me mister," the fat man interrupted. "What am I? some sort of la-di-da in velvet and jewels? A ballroom-dancing layabout who sleeps till noon? A parasite living off other men's work? Eh? Is that what I am? Eh? Not me! I'm an honest worker, a poor man sweating and straining to earn a pittance, hardly enough to feed his children, oh, it's a hard life!"

The question is whether The Cat joined the caravan only because Bolbaumis took him on as soon as he knew the boy wouldn't ask for wages or complain about the food. True, he was thin, too thin, and might not be strong enough for the hard work on a caravan, but it was equally true that he was thin because he didn't eat much. The fat boss took him on for another reason, too: because he saw a pleased look in the twentier's eyes. He kept asking himself what old Z'Ydagg could have seen in this halfbaked kid; but it wasn't the first time the old man had come along as twentier on one of his caravans, and Bolbaumis had learned to respect and trust him. And it should be said that the obese merchant respected very few people and trusted fewer.

"What's your name?" Bolbaumis had asked.

"Gennän," the boy said.

"I don't know why I'm taking him on," the fat man sighed, not to anybody in particular but grumbling at Z'Ydagg. "I just don't know. I'm a generous man, that's what it is. I'm sorry for him, yes sir, sorry for him. A poor abandoned boy, all alone without a father to counsel him or a mother to protect him. That's why I'm taking him on, even though he'll obviously be a dead loss. Sickly, pale, hungry, more eyes than brains, and that round mug of his—he looks more like an alley cat than a human being."

And so he came to be called The Cat.

The caravan set off to the east on a spring morning, and until they were out of the city fat Bolbaumis walked at the head of the long line. After him came five armed men. And after them the merchants, alone or with a partner, or with servants and employees. And at the end the cook with his two assistants, and the loaders and workmen. But when they left the city and walked through fields, and the fields became mountains and the mountains led down to the desert, Bolbaumis mounted his little horse and let Z'Ydagg lead.

The first thing the old man did was send the armed guards back to walk with or behind the boss; he told them he didn't need them. Then, as the path they followed kept getting rougher and dustier, he reviewed their marching order and shook his head in annoyance, reflecting that businessmen know a lot about business but nothing about the desert, while he knew a lot about the desert, and though there was no reason why at his age he should learn anything about business, it would be a good thing if these merchants he was guiding learned something about the desert. And having satisfactorily concluded this meditation, he set himself to introduce a little real order into the confusion of men, animals, and vehicles following him; only a little, since you can't do much while walking and so many things had to be seen to while making sure they kept going the right way.

But that night, out in the desert, when they made camp, old Z'Ydagg told everybody about the arrangements he wanted, and everybody, of course, agreed. When they set off next day it would be this way: he first, being the twentier (it's true some twentiers prefer to walk in the rear, and others along with the people, and there are even some who ride on a horse or in a cart, but old Z'Ydagg always took the lead, declaring that the best twentiers had invariably done so since the beginning of time), without armed guards since he'd never needed them and why would he need them now? Immediately behind him would come Mistress Assyi'Duzmaül, with her servants and employees. Why her? Not because she was a woman, not because she was beautiful, young, desirable, since she wasn't. And even if she had been, it wouldn't have mattered to the old man. So, why her? Why not Mr. Pfalbuss, a likeable elderly gentlemen whom the twentier had known for years? Why? If anybody had asked Z'Ydagg, and the strange notion of questioning a twentier's arrangements would occur only to someone crazy enough to risk expulsion from the caravan and being left alone without a guide in the desert, if anybody had asked, the old man would merely have answered, "Because."

Yet he had a reason. The woman worried him. He didn't know her, but that wasn't the problem; no guide can know every merchant on the roads of the Empire. She said she was a silk dealer. She might be, why not? She might not be, because she paid more attention to people than to the bales stamped with her mark. She said also that she was accompanying her merchandise this time because she suspected, was almost certain, that some of her employees were robbing her, and that too might be, why not? It would explain her constant vigilance. But on the other hand there are easier ways to catch a thief than accompanying a caravan on a long, hard road and doing almost without eating or sleeping in order to watch everything going on. And he didn't like her name. It was a very complicated name. The old man would have bet a finger, a left-hand finger to be sure but still one of his own fingers, that her name was false. And that is why Mistress Assyi'Duzmaül, silk dealer, was to come right after him. After her, some other traders, two or three, it didn't matter which, with their people. Fat Bolbaumis with his soldier boys, the rest of the merchants, the cook and his gear, and finally the loaders. But wait a moment, what about The Cat? Where to put that impudent and restless boy? Bah, let him be wherever he liked, with the merchants or the soldiers or the lady, that's it, so he wouldn't bother people and get them listening to him about being an orphan and the strange things he had discovered weaving rugs and assisting a magician and fishing for pearls and the rest of his fantasies.

The old twentier slept with one eye open, so he thought, and it was almost true, so that if anything happened in the caravan, or at the first hint of light if the night passed tranquilly, he got up, went over the campground, and had a bite to eat with whoever was on late-night guard. Only then, after he had a piece of biscuit and a draft of water in his belly, did he cup his hands round his mouth and call the alert. But that day, before dawn broke, the smell of fresh-made coffee woke him.

"What's the meaning of this?" he demanded.

"Coffee," said The Cat.

"I'm asking you why the devil you're making coffee at this hour."

"Because I want to drink some coffee," said The Cat.

"Insolent brat," said the twentier.

"It's strong," said The Cat, and held out a mug.

The old man was so taken aback that he started to sip it slowly, and it really was good: hot, bitter, and thick.

"Did I tell you I was an assistant in the palace cafeteria for a week?" The Cat asked, very serious.

"You've already told me too many lies," said the twentier.

"But I was, honestly."

"If the Imperial Guards saw that rascally face of yours ten blocks away from the palace, they'd take a broom to you," said the old man, no longer irate.

"I'll tell you how it was," the boy said.

"You'll tell me nothing. And go call the night guard, right now."

"I told him he could go get some sleep."

The old man choked and coughed. "You what?" he roared when he could breathe again.

"What's going on?" asked Mistress Assyi'Duzmaül.

"Coffee, dear lady!" said The Cat.

"Let's get one thing clear," said the old man, while the big woman sipped her coffee very slowly.

"Yes, let's do that!" said The Cat with enthusiasm.

Z'Ydagg sat silent a moment, thinking. A twentier doesn't lose his temper, doesn't shout, or get worked up, or strangle on hot coffee. A man to whom such things happen just because he's run into something unexpected is not fit to be a twentier. Am I getting too old? he thought. But that's stupid. On the endless roads of the deserts age is no handicap, just the opposite. A whole life of bodily and mental discipline bears fruit precisely in old age. But he'd been foolish. A bad moment. The stupid boy got on his nerves. And yet he liked the kid; he'd liked him from the moment he saw him coming as the caravan got under way: awkward yet assured, a rascal, yes, but the old man thought he saw something honest and generous in the comical face.

That's what he liked in him. If the brat hadn't been so likeable even when he was boasting and bragging, he would have made him toe the line from the start and then there'd have been none of this getting up before he did, making coffee. Even if it was good coffee.

"Here, one person gives orders," the old man said.

"Mr. Z'Ydagg, twentier of Mr. Bolbaumis's caravan," said The Cat.

"That's it. That didn't need to be made clear. It was clear. But this, too: I give all the orders. All. Got it?"

"Yes, sir."

"All means all: important and unimportant. For example, nobody can get up before I do and make coffee unless I've ordered it."

"Really? I can't?"

"No."

"You don't like the coffee I make?"

"That's not the point."

"All right, daddy, I won't do it again."

The old man was angry for a second time this morning, but he managed to stay calm. "As for the matter of the night guard," he said, "we won't discuss that, because if we did I'd end up burying you both in the sand with only your noses out and leaving you there for the sun to roast you and the ants to eat you. Which is precisely what I will do next time you take one step without my permission."

The Cat laughed. "All right, daddy, I promise I'll be good."

And don't call me daddy, the old man thought, but didn't say it. He looked at the silk dealer and saw her looking at him.

"Don't worry," she said, "I'll do whatever you say. I know what a caravan is."

Yes, she does, thought the old man who smelled lies a hundred miles away, indeed she does. And he went off a few paces and gave the wake-up call.

The Cat didn't do anything again that he hadn't been told to do. Though he could hardly be described as peaceful and tranquil, at least he didn't enrage the twentier or anybody else. He even earned the gratitude of the cook, and it's well known that caravan cooks are irritable grouches, hard to handle and generally inclined to snarl. This cook, named Nonne, hated making coffee. That is, he liked brewing real coffee, proper coffee, the kind that issues slowly and artistically from the spigot of an apparatus of copper and glass, not the hasty stuff boiled over embers in a hole dug in the dry soil swept by the dawn wind of the desert. Nonne liked cooking for caravans, creating everything from practically nothing, turning salt meat into a tender and delicious dish with a piquant aftertaste. He liked making a soft, creamy porridge of dry grain, or amazing the travelers with merely a few fibrous roots and leaves that would have been bitter if he hadn't handled them skillfully. He could even make good tea with the scanty water of the wells or their canteens. But coffee? No; coffee was worth making in the cities, the towns, houses where people live permanently, but not in the desert, on the road. So, after that first morning, Nonne thought and thought and finally spoke to the twentier, and Z'Ydagg told him all right, fine, no problem, it was even a good idea to give the boy a regular job and not keep him running here and there for every little task the men didn't want to do. And from then on The Cat was in charge of making the coffee.

And he did other things. He sang, for example. And it was he who discovered that one of Bolbaumis's armed guards played the serel.

"What's that?" he asked.

"Pipe down, kid," the soldier said.

"Is it a weapon?"

The man didn't answer.

"It's a funny shape for a weapon," said The Cat.

"I said, pipe down."

"I bet that's a serel in there."

The man turned and looked at him. "Better mind your own business," he said.

"All right, all right, no big deal," and The Cat went on forward till he reached Mistress Assyi'Duzmaül. "How come none of your children came with you, missis?" he asked her.

"And who told you I had children?"

"Nobody. But I thought so. Ladies usually have children, don't they?"

"Yes," the woman said, and was silent a moment. "So, yes, I have seven children. But they're busy, the older ones working, the younger ones studying. And anyhow I see no reason why I should bring anybody along when I travel."

After a while, she looked at him and said, "Tonight I'm going to give you one of my sleeping bags. I've got some warm ones. And you were cold last night."

But this woman never sleeps! thought old Z'Ydagg, listening to them. How did she know the boy was cold?

That night the boy slept in a fine down bag, warm and comfortable. And the next night, he sang.

He had a beautiful tenor voice, not very strong; a sweet voice that soared and dropped with ease; he sang about thieves and lovers. It was then that the armed guard opened his lumpy sack, took out the serel, tightened the strings, adjusted one or two ivory pegs, and played a few chords. Bolbaumis stared at him in astonishment. One of his guards playing the serel, what next? The soldier got the instrument tuned, played a cascade of notes, and began to accompany The Cat as he sang. Everybody else was in a circle round them listening, and one began to sway in time to the music, and another to clap, and they all ended up keeping the rhythm with their feet and head and clapping and laughing, till the old man said it was time to sleep.

Next night The Cat sang again, and the soldier accompanied him on the serel, and even sang a couple of verses along with him.

"I've never traveled with a caravan this cheerful," one merchant said.

"I've been with some," said Pfalbuss, "where you'd think everybody was born deaf and dumb, and we couldn't wait for it to get dark so we could sleep."

"Whereas the twentier has to tell us it's bedtime," said another, "as if we were children."

"More like a party than a caravan," said another.

"We're all for parties," said one of the younger merchants.

"Let's be serious," said The Cat. "Somebody tell a sad story, a really really sad story." He looked at the silk dealer.

"I don't know any stories," she said. "I'm just a businesswoman."

"Daddy," said The Cat, "won't you tell us a really really sad story?"

"There's sadness enough in store for us," said a merchant named Nayidemoub.

"There's always hope," said another.

"Louwantes was a good emperor," sighed Bolbaumis.

"Yes, he was," Nayidemoub said, "but if his nephew succeeds him, we're in trouble."

"Who says so?" another man asked. "Maybe he'll turn out well too."

"Ha!" from fat Bolbaumis.

"Look at the bright side," the merchant insisted. "Why not? You never can tell how a man may turn out."

"Ha!"

"And it could be," the merchant went on, "he won't even succeed to the throne."

"Let's hope not!" said Nayidemoub.

"Bedtime," said old Z'Ydagg.

The sun tormented them all next day. And thirst, too; the next well was a long way yet, so the old man rationed the water. Even The Cat looked discouraged. Mistress Assyi'Duzmaül kept watching him, and in the afternoon she called him. "I'm not thirsty," she said, "not at all. When we can drink, you can have my share."

"Oh, no, no," The Cat said, but the woman insisted. Maybe the boy reminds her of one of her seven, the twentier thought, and then maybe not. What does she want with the boy, a woman her age, all right, not that old, but old enough to be his mother—what does she want with him? He's young, almost a kid still, his voice hasn't even finished changing. Does she want to buy him for her bed? Would he let himself be bought? No, come on, why would he sell himself, a kid that'll have any woman he wants when he wants them. But if she offers him a lot of money? How much would it take? I don't like that woman. I don't trust her.

Night came at last and the cold wind blew from the northern mountains and the animals bowed their necks and huddled up in a corner of the corral for shelter, and the men sat around the fire, ate, drank, drank coffee; and the guard put his hand on the sack that held his serel.

"I don't like the desert," said one of the merchants.

"Who does?" said another. "Nobody."

"Daddy Z'Ydagg does," said The Cat. "He does. He likes all of it, isn't that right, daddy?"

"The world is the way it is," the old man said.

"Why?"

"Be quiet, boy," said Bolbaumis. "Don't ask stupid questions."

"It's not a stupid question," the woman said, "it's a wise one. And I'll answer it, son: The world is the way it is because men are mad."

"Could be," said Nayidemoub, "but you have to admit men have done some good things too."

"She didn't say foolish, she said mad," said The Cat. "Madness can do bad things and good things."

Kalpa Imperial

"Listen, young philosopher," Bolbaumis said, "is there any more coffee?"

"I'll make some more in a moment, boss. But, daddy, men didn't make the desert."

"No," the old man said.

"Who did make the desert, anyway?"

"It came with the rest of the world."

"And who made the world?" asked The Cat.

"That's a long story."

The soldier took his hand off the sack that held his serel.

"Before the world there was nothing," Z'Ydagg said.

"Was it really dark and scary?" asked The Cat.

"It wasn't dark because it wasn't anything, and if there isn't anything there can't be darkness, stupid boy," said the old man. "And there wasn't anybody to be scared. It wasn't silent, either, because if there isn't anything, there isn't even silence. And since there wasn't silence all the sounds and noises that hadn't been made yet could be heard. And since there wasn't darkness all the things that hadn't begun to exist could be seen. Because there was nothing, everything that was going to be in the world when there was a world could be without being."

The Cat served out the coffee.

"You're very wise, daddy," he said. "Won't you tell us how it all started being?"

He's making fun of me, the old man thought. Or is he? Or am I getting suspicious, like a cook, like some old woman peering out from behind her shutters?

"That's easy," he said aloud. "Everything that could be seen and everything that could be heard because there wasn't any darkness or silence, was all packed up together, because before the world was, there wasn't anything, not even space. And since there wasn't any time, everything joined and stuck together and melted together, and the same way those many-colored wheels on a stall at a fair go round and round till all the colors make white, so everything that was before the world was stuck together and made an eye."

"What color was the eye?" asked The Cat, who was sitting in front of the old man.

"No color, because it was all colors," the twentier said. "It was a round eye, with a very thick lens, and it had just one eyelid around it, black, round, hard, opaque. And out of this eye came a tiny speck of dust that got bigger and bigger, and then the eye saw that pinch of dust turn into a house."

The night wind whistled over the desert and the men drew in a little closer to listen to Z'Ydagg.

"It was a house of dark wood, with a lot of rooms and a balcony," said the old man, "and there was a man in every room, but on the balcony there was a woman. And the house was called *saloon*."

"*Saloon?*" said The Cat.

"Don't interrupt, snotnose," said Bolbaumis.

"Now, when the house called *saloon* was finished, with the men and the woman and all the furniture, another speck of dust came out of the eye and grew till it was another house."

"And what was it called?" Bolbaumis asked.

"Don't interrupt, fatty," said The Cat, grinning.

"The second house was called *the charge of the light brigade*," said the old man, "and it had a lot of rooms too, but it had a lot of men and women in them. But none as beautiful as the woman in the house called *saloon* was. She was so beautiful that the men of the house called *the charge of the light brigade* saw her once and never could stop thinking of her and dreamed of her night and day. But there was one of them who was so deeply in love with the beautiful woman that he wanted to abduct her. This man was called Kirdaglass and since he didn't know what the woman's real name was he called her Marillín. Kirdaglass built a ship and sailed through the air and went after the woman he called Marillín and carried her off and brought her back to his house with him. Then the men of the house called *saloon* built a thousand ships and to insult their enemies they named the ships after the women of the house called *the charge of the light brigade* and painted the names in shining letters on the round prow of each boat: Marlenditrij, Betedeivis, Martincarol, Maripícfor, Avagarner, Tedabara, Loretaiún, Briyibardó, Jedilamar, and a thousand more. With these ships named for the enemy's women, the men of the house called *saloon* sailed through the air to the house called *the charge of the light brigade* to rescue the woman called Marillín abducted from them by the man who loved her so much. Among those who sailed the thousand ships was a very brave man called Alendelón, and a wise one called Clargueibl, and another called Yeimsdín who was the one who wanted most of all to rescue the beautiful woman. In their thousand ships they sailed across the air and laid siege to the other house. But now time existed, since men and houses and women and ships existed, and so the siege lasted for twenty years. And for twenty years the men of the two houses were at war. The chief of the house called *the charge of the light brigade*, whose name was Orsonuéls, which means *the great bear*, organized the defense, and said that if one of his sons had abducted a woman, then the woman belonged to him because he'd been so brave and fearless. Then Alendelón challenged Kirdaglass to a duel, but he was in bed enjoying himself with the woman called Marillín and didn't bother going out to fight. The others did, though, they went on fighting and killing one another until there were hardly any men left on either side. Meanwhile other little specks of dust had been coming out of the eye and and turned into a lot of other houses with men and women in them. One house was called *dosmiluno* and another *rosadeabolengo* and another *alahoraseñalada* and *elmuelledelasbrumas* and *rashomon* and *puertadelilas* and *elañopasadoenmarienbad* and *lahoradelobo* and so on and so on. When almost twenty years had passed since the beginning of the siege, Kirdaglass came out at last to fight, and Yangabén, Alendelón's best friend, killed him with a poisoned arrow. Then Marillín married another son of Orsonuéls named Yonyilber, but soon, thanks to a ruse conceived by the wily Clargueible, who had had a great bear made out of wood and offered it as a gift to the besieged, the besiegers were able to enter the house, hidden inside the gigantic animal. So it was that they could set fire to the house called *the charge of the light brigade* and take back the woman and take Orsonuéls captive, and his wife Dorotilamur and his sons and daughters. The woman called Marillín married Yeimsdín and they had a lot of children and both of them lived happily ever after, till they died at a hundred and twenty. But one of the heroes who had sailed across the air in search of the abducted woman and had fought bravely through the long years of the siege, was lost with his ship. The wily Clargueibl was returning like the others to the house called *saloon* when he heard sweet voices singing that drew him irresistibly. They were the ringostars, beautiful, evil, voracious beings who used their magic voices to enchant all who heard them and attract passing sailors. Clargueibl and his crew stopped to listen and so were captured by the ringostars. One of these beings was a powerful witch called Monalisa whose smile turned men into pigs. This is what happened to Clargueibl and his men, and the ringostars shut them up in a pigsty and fattened them up until they started eating them one by one. But Clargueibl, who even as a pig kept his cunning wits, persuaded one of the pig keepers, the giant Gualdisnei, to let him live just a few days longer because he felt ill and anybody who ate him might catch his disease and then the others would punish the pig keepers for sending unhealthy food to the table. When the giant bent down to look at him more closely, Calrgueibl bit him in the neck with his pig teeth, and by drinking his blood became once again the gallant warrior he had been. Then he stuffed mud in his ears so as not to hear the song of the ringostars, stole a ship, and set off straight home. There everyone thought he was dead, and the eldest daughter of Yeimsdín and Marillín, whose parents had promised to marry her to Clargueibl when the hero returned, was on the point of marrying one of her many suitors, a silly little man named Samuelgolduin. On the day of the wedding, Clargueibl arrived disguised as a beggar, and no one knew him but his old dog Rintintín, who barked with joy at seeing him. Clargueibl came forward, weapons in hand, to the bridal couple, killed Samuelgolduin, made himself known, and married the lovely Vivianlig, with whom he went to live in another house which they named *gone with the wind* after all the adventures that lay behind them. They lived long and happily and their sons and daughters spread out across the world that now existed, formed by all the things that had come out of the eye."

"And the eye?" asked The Cat. "Where is the eye?"

"Somewhere," the old man said. "It's somewhere. But it's very hard to see."

"Did more dust specks come out of the eye?" The Cat wanted to know. "And will any more come out? And how can they?"

"I wish a doctor who can work miracles would come out of the eye now," said Nayidemoub, "one who could miraculously cure the daughter of the the dead emperor."

"She isn't sick," said one of the merchants. "She's dead too. She must be."

"Oh, don't say that, man," fat Bolbaumis pleaded, "don't say that!"

"How could she be dead, when the regent says—" The Cat began, but the fat man interrupted him: "The regent! Faugh! Ten thousand curses on the day that viper was born!"

"If one of us could see the eye, maybe the emperor's daughter would be cured," said The Cat.

"Will that snotnose shut up and let grown people talk?" said Bolbaumis.

"It's late," said old Z'Ydagg, "time to rest."

"But that damned woman wants her son on the Golden Throne," Nayidemoub grumbled, "so she keeps the emperor's daughter captive and says she's sick. She's going to kill her and say she died of her illness. And then the boy will succeed to the throne, just as she wants. I know what I'm talking about."

"And why shouldn't he govern well? Let's give him a chance," said one of the merchants.

"That she-hyena's son?" said Nayidemoub. "Forget it!"

"To bed," said the twentier. "There's been too much talking today."

"Are you going to need more blankets?" the woman who called herself a silk dealer asked The Cat.

The desert went on and on and seemed as if it would never end. But the people knew that they'd gone better than halfway, and the heat and thirst of the day, the cold of night, kept getting easier to bear. So at night they sang more cheerfully, coming in on the choruses with The Cat and clapping to the rhythm of the soldier's serel. And so the old twentier smiled, which he didn't do very often, when the boy said he was tired of singing and wanted to hear another story about when the world was new, before the Empire existed.

"Tomorrow," said Z'Ydagg, "we'll have stories tomorrow. Not now. I'm tired too."

"Don't talk nonsense, boy," a merchant said. "The Empire has always existed. It is, it was, it will be. They teach us that in school even before we learn to read."

"Who knows," said Mistress Assyi'Duzmaül.

"How can anyone even think of the Empire not existing?" a man said suspiciously, shaking his head.

"The lady's right," said the old man. "Who knows? There are legends, there are stories, and maybe not all of them were made up by blind beggar bards."

"Honest?" The Cat said. "Honest, daddy? Will you tell us one?"

"Tomorrow, I said," Z'Ydagg replied.

But the next day everybody was talking about reaching the towns on the far side of the desert, though in fact their journey's end was not yet in sight. Good Pfalbuss had a grandson expecting him in Oadast, at one of his places of business.

"Just like his mother," Pfalbuss said smiling, "my eldest daughter who died young, poor child. Just like her, my friend, the same eyes, same laugh, same business sense, same gift for seizing an opportunity."

"Your daughter was in the business?"

"Of course. She was my right hand for years."

"A woman in business? Hmm."

"Why not?" asked Mistress Assyi'Duzmaül.

"Well, of course, I didn't mean . . ."

"I believe," said the silk dealer, "that a woman is perfectly capable of any activity—business, politics, sciences, applied arts."

"Of course, of course."

"You've offended the lady, Mr. Merchant," The Cat said.

"I hope not, I certainly had no such intention."

"What would you say to a woman on the throne?" asked the silk dealer.

"Oh, well, now, that depends . . ."

"Depends on what? Have you forgotten the Great Empress? Or Esseriantha? Or Nninivia? Or the Blessed Lullisbizoa? Or Djarandé, who saved the Empire not once but twice?"

"We're camping here," said the old twentier.

"I didn't for a moment suggest that a woman couldn't or shouldn't occupy the Golden Throne," Pfalbuss said finally, "all I say is, some women yes, some women no. That's what I say."

"For example?"

"For example, that adder, the sister of our emperor who just died, that woman, no—definitely not. But Louwantes IV's daughter, yes."

Mistress Assyi'Duzmaül smiled. "I wouldn't say there's much chance of that girl reaching the throne, would you?"

"Oh, lady," said The Cat, "don't get talking politics now, huh? Look, I'm helping you with the load."

"No, no, don't do that, that's what the servants are for, those things are heavy."

She looks after him as if he was made of sugar candy, the old man thought. He said, "Come on, come on, let's have the camp ready before nightfall, get on with it. Get it all stowed, and I'll tell you a story."

What did I say that for? he asked himself while The Cat cheered and jumped up and down and everybody got to work with the loads, the pack animals, and the carts. Why am I going to tell them old stories nobody tells any more, not even the storytellers? Am I getting paid for this? No, I'm paid to lead a caravan safely, without going astray or getting delayed or losing anything, from the capital to Oadassim Province, that's what they pay me for, and pay me well because I know my job and the years have given me, maybe not wisdom, but something close. So why should I go digging up old fables about fabulous beings who were born and loved and fought and died, if they ever existed, before the Empire came to be, no, it's quite unnecessary. And therefore I won't tell them a thing, not a thing, not a word will escape my lips.

"Here it is, here it is!" shouted The Cat, dancing around him.

"Quiet, quiet down, boy," the old man said. "May I inquire where what is?"

"The camp! All ready, in order, in place!"

"Well, let's see about that, let's see, aha, hmm," said the twentier, and went about examining things, pulling at the cords that fastened the packs, testing the crosspieces that held up the corral for the pack animals, twanging straps with a finger and giving little kicks to wooden stakes to make sure they were firmly planted. He went round to the dugouts where the fires were already lighted, checked the blankets and sleeping bags, pushed the wagons to make them sway so he could hear if they creaked or squeaked, passed every person and looked at what each one was doing. At last he came back to The Cat.

"Good," he said. "Very good. I imagine you took part in this magnificently organized enterprise."

"Of course I did," the boy said. "Everybody helped, let's be fair. But I did most of it."

"I don't believe a word you say, you lazy good-for-nothing, not one word, you hear me?"

"Me? Lazy? Me? But daddy, I work all the time, day and night."

"Oh yes," the old man said, "yes, of course you do."

"But seriously, daddy. I say magic words to the animals so they won't balk or shy or kick, I keep company with Mistress Assyi'Duzmaül so she doesn't miss her seven kids, I grease axles, I tighten the girths when there isn't water and loosen them when there is, I listen to the merchants when they complain about how little money they make, I measure the feed, I give advice, I guess things."

"What things?" the old man demanded abruptly.

"Oh, things." The boy made a vague gesture as if brushing the subject aside. "And now, as part of my duties, since I have the best memory of anybody in the caravan, now I remind you that you promised to tell a story."

"The animals have to be fed," the twentier said, "and we need to eat too if we want to get on. After that, we'll see."

When the animals had been fed, the people sat around the fire and Nonne served meat and rice in broth in their bowls, and The Cat made coffee and asked softly, "Will you tell us a story, daddy?"

"An old story," said Z'Ydagg, "very old, from when the world was young and nobody suspected that it would someday contain the greatest and most powerful empire known to man. I'll tell you the story of Yeimsbón, who was the younger brother of Yeimsdín, who married that woman who was so beautiful that they said her face had launched a thousand ships into the air, you remember? Well, then, Yeimsbón got married too, when he was old enough, to a woman who was also very beautiful but bossy and ambitious, named Magareta'Acher, and they lived in the city of Erinn, where after a short time Yeimsbón was made king, on account of his valor and goodness. They had a son called Yanpolsar and a daughter called Bernadetdevlin. The two children grew up adoring their father, who was gentle and loving to them, and learned to hate their mother, who was hard and harsh and punished them often, sending the boy to work in the fields and the girl to peel potatoes in the palace kitchen. So it went on till one day Yeimsbón received a request for help from his brother Yeimsdín, who was setting off to make war on a sinister person who had been a hatmaker and now called himself Prince Chiklgruber and was trying to conquer the whole world. So Yeimsbón rode away at the head of his army, not without tender farewells to his children and his sharp-tongued wife, and leaving his cousin Yeimscañi to watch over his home, his palace, and his city. The good, brave, ingenuous king was gone for many years, and when he and the kings he was allied with had at last defeated Prince Chiklgruber, he returned to find his children grown but unhappy, his people oppressed, and his wife in the arms of the man he had trusted. The king, who had come back home full of hopes and illusions, thought to kill the adulterers; but he had brought back from the war so much sadness and weariness that he persuaded himself that something might yet be saved, and having resolved on nothing, retired to his apartment to meditate. There, creeping silently, his evil wife followed him, with Yeimscañi, the traitor. And as the king lay in his bath with his eyes closed thinking of what must be done, there they cut his throat and left him lying in the water red with his blood. But the queen had forgotten about her children, had forgotten them because she never thought about them except to make sure they were far from the palace, busy with menial work. Yanpolsar and Bernadetdevlin, who hoped their father would punish those who had abused his trust, learned of his death with pain and horror. They wept for him, of course, wept long and bitterly. But then they dried their tears and swore to avenge their father. And one night they entered the royal bedroom and pitilessly slew their mother and their uncle. Then they set free the people of Erinn from the cruel yoke that had been laid upon them when the good king left, and reigned together in peace, protected and counselled by the Erinnies, the good spirits of the city of Erinn. Yanpolsar married Emabovarí and his sister married Yonlenon, an adventurer from far away who claimed descent from the fabled ringostars who had deceived the wily Clargueibl. From the two marriages came many children who peopled the wide world, and the brother and sister slowly forgot the tragedy that had darkened their lives. Except that Yanpolsar ordered a scribe to write down the facts and keep the records, which were found many centuries later. People read this writing and told it to others, and those others told it to others, and so down through the years, and it is thus that I came to know this sad tale."

"It's not all that sad, daddy, don't exaggerate," said The Cat. "It's sad-happy. Haven't you got a sad-sad story? Or a happy-happy one?"

"It's no good, kids aren't satisfied with anything. You give them this, they want that, you give them that, they want this, and if you give them this and that, then they manage to want the other!" said the elderly Pfalbuss.

"Things aren't either sad or happy, Cat," Bolbaumis said. "They're a bit of both. The only happy-happy thing is the chink of coins, and so much the happier if they're gold."

"And why are we men and women here in the world," said Mistress Assyi'Duzmaül, "if not to try to turn sad things into happy ones?"

"Ah," said the old twentier, "a sound observation, I do believe."

"More coffee, boy, get on with it, get moving, people need more coffee," said Nonne.

The next day The Cat came to old Z'Ydagg and asked him what other stories he knew.

"Aha," said the old man, "now we can't even wait till night-time to ask for stories, eh?"

"I'm not asking you for a story, daddy, I'm asking about what others you know."

"Storytellers know many stories. All you have to do is find one in a street or a square or a tent and sit down and listen to what they tell."

"No, you don't understand," The Cat said. "I want stories about what happened long long ago, when there were no emperors or Golden Throne or regents or heiresses."

"And what does an alley cat know about emperors and their heirs?"

It was the one time the old man saw the boy hesitate. Not for long; but The Cat was silent, as if he didn't know what to say.

"Nothing, of course," he said at last. "Just what everybody knows, that's all."

And then he turned round and went back to stay close to the woman who dealt in silks.

Now I know, the old twentier thought, now I know what's going on. And I don't like it. Oh, how I wish we'd just get to Oadassim quickly, how I wish everybody would just go off their own way and Bolbaumis would pay me and I could go have a rest till some other caravan hunts me up to lead them back across the desert to the capital. Oh, how I wish the good Emperor Louwantes hadn't died, how I wish it . . .

The old man told no more stories of the incredible days when the Empire did not exist. That night The Cat sang and sang, and when he stopped he said, "Now for an old story, eh, daddy?"

Z'Ydagg answered crossly, "No stories. We need to save our strength for the arrival."

The desert was beginning to change. The color of the earth, for example, now wasn't so blinding in the daylight nor so bright at night; it was taking on a greyish hue, day and night; and the fine pale dust that covered it changed and no longer rose up at the least breath of wind. There was no need to store water because the wells came close one after the other. The day came when they saw plants, green plants struggling up among the stones. And the next day they were not awakened by the twentier's voice, nor by the light, but by the singing of birds.

"We'll camp here," said the old man on the last day, at nightfall.

The people looked at one another wondering, but they obeyed. The Cat went here and there doing this and that and mostly making noise, like a tiltill bird building its nest in the eaves. Nayidemoub came up to Bolbaumis. "Why are we making camp?" he asked.

"Didn't you hear?" said the fat man. "Z'Ydagg said to make camp."

"I know, I know, I'm not deaf, that's not what I'm asking. Why are we making camp when we could go on and be in the city before nightfall?"

"Don't rush it, Mr. Nayidemoub," said Mistress Assyi'Duzmaül. "What's the hurry?"

"The old man knows what he's doing," Bolbaumis said.

"What if we went and asked him?" Nayidemoub insisted.

Pfalbuss laughed. "Did you ever do that in a caravan? Ask the twentier why he's doing what he does?"

"No."

"Could be that daddy saw the eye," said The Cat.

"What eye?"

"The eye the world came out of. Like he told."

"Could be," said the woman.

The men laughed. Nonne was cooking, and the soldier was tuning the serel.

"I'm not going to sing today," The Cat said while they were drinking their coffee. "I'll sing tomorrow early when we come into the city. But can I ask you something, daddy? I want to know if when the world came out of the eye, the twenty directions came out of it too, that you twentiers know about."

"Yes," the old man said. "But they came out a lot later, when the eye was already hidden from the sight of mankind, and only mad folk and dying people could see it. And thus people knew nothing of the twenty directions, and thus they were divided into little kingdoms each with its own language, each with its laws and money and ambitions and madnesses, and nobody thought of the Empire, and the Empire didn't exist. And so it was that one night out of the eye came not a speck of dust but a fine thread, finer even than the hair of a newborn child, and the thread flew through the air, and flew on and on, and flew in through the window of a little hut in which a man was lying down with his eyes open. He was a humble man who worked hard to make a living, and didn't wear fine clothes, or eat delicate food; a man who didn't know how to read or write and hadn't learned chemistry or astronomy, but who thought a lot about his family, the men and women who worked and suffered as he did. And since the man lay with his eyes open trying to understand how the world was ordered, the thread that came flying through the air entered into his right eye and there split into twenty even finer threads, and the man lying in the hut saw the twenty directions, and understood."

"What are the twenty directions, daddy?" asked The Cat.

The old man couldn't help smiling at the boy's shameless boldness.

"Those aren't matters for a child to know," he said.

Next day the birds were singing when the caravan set off. The Cat walked along singing.

"We aren't in the city yet, Cat," Pfalbuss told him.

"But I feel like singing, Mr. Pfalbuss," the boy said, and went on singing.

It was a handsome city. Not very big, but handsome. Around it were green fields and woods; it rose up very bright and clear, almost white, against the morning sky.

"We have arrived," said old Z'Ydagg, looking behind him for Bolbaumis, to hand over the command of the caravan to him.

"Good, good," said the fat man.

Undoubtedly Bolbaumis meant to say more, to remark on how much he'd spent to get across the desert and how little he was going to make out of it, while he got off his mount and went forward to take the twentier's place. But he couldn't go on talking. The ruddy color the sun and wind had given him faded, leaving his face white as wax. He opened his mouth and couldn't shut it. With a shaking hand he pointed ahead of them.

"What's that?" Nayidemoub shouted.

The old twentier turned and looked at the city.

"We're being attacked!" cried the serel-player, seizing his weapons.

The five armed guards ran forward together to defend the others. For as if out of nowhere a group of horsemen came galloping towards the caravan. Old Z'Ydagg cupped his hands to his mouth and gave the warning shout. The loaders stirred up the animals to use them as a shield between the people of the caravan and the attackers. But somebody had shouted at the same time as the twentier, a powerful voice, used to giving orders. Who shouted, who was that? the old man asked himself, while he tried to impose some order on the confusion. Somebody had cut out Pfalbuss's fine, fast horse, was mounting it, galloping against the attackers. Who was it, who could it be? Whose were those woman's clothes, fluttering uselessly, while the rider galloped in the lead of Bolbaumis's guardsmen? But then, the old man told himself while he helped pile up packloads near the animals who were kicking and struggling to get loose, but then, I was wrong, dead wrong, I didn't understand. And The Cat?

"Where's the boy?" Z'Ydagg shouted.

Bolbaumis's men were fighting on the road, and with them was the man who'd disguised himself as an old woman, a silk dealer.

"I'm here, daddy," said The Cat, "but not for long. I know how to fight too!" And he ran off towards the road.

"Back, Cat, come back! Don't go!" the old man cried.

And the man who'd traveled with them dressed as a woman and now was fighting like a demon, covered with sweat and blood, echoed him: "Back, Highness! Go back!" he shouted.

"Twenty are the world's directions," murmured Z'Ydagg, the old man who knew the desert, "twenty, and the twenty lead to good and to evil, to emptiness and fullness, to movement and to stillness, to white and to black, and I'm nothing but an old man who was just about to lose his way."

One of Bolbaumis's men fell dead. Two of the attackers detached themselves from the group and spurred their horses towards the merchants. Fat Bolbaumis whipped out a weapon and prepared to defend his money. Somebody, that man, cut off a head that rolled on the road, bloody, muddy, the eyes still open, and turned to pursue the riders that were coming closer and closer to the caravan. Where was The Cat? The pack animals snorted and tugged at the ropes holding them, and a wagon tipped over, one wheel spinning in air. The old man raised his gun, found firm footing and waited, and without haste, calm, tranquil, shot the man who was coming at him through the heart. Bolbaumis took care of the other one, neatly, with a swiftness surprising in a man of his girth. Here and there, when he could,

Z'Ydagg managed to catch sight of a little figure that darted in and out of his field of vision, fired a gun, dodged, hopped back, fired again. The blood-covered demon who had been Mistress Assyi'Duzmaül drew back, sprang forward and rushed with a yell into the fray once more, killing and killing. The old man ran to join him and the guards, and standing beside Bolbaumis aimed and fired and hit, time and again.

"They're going, they're going! Reinforcements are coming! Look, look there, we're saved!" cried the merchants and the loaders.

The man they'd all thought was a woman galloped after the fugitives and would have caught and no doubt killed them if his horse hadn't stumbled, worn out or wounded. The man leaped up and came running back to the caravan: "Where is she?" he was shouting. "Where is she, you fools?"

"Here," The Cat said. "Don't worry, I'm not hurt. I know how to fight too."

Strange events, strange people were to be seen on the day Princess Nargennendia was crowned Empress. Everything was done according to protocol and tradition, but the regent, sister of the dead Emperor Louwantes IV, did not come out of her apartments in the palace to go to the throne room: she was brought under guard from the dungeons to place the crown on the girl's head and the scepter in her hands, and then was taken back to the prison in which she would spend the rest of her life, condemned for attempted regicide. And as for the strange people, they were all around the empress, elbowing ministers, dignitaries, and judges: three soldiers, one with a sack unmistakably containing a serel hung from his left shoulder, all of them uncomfortable in new uniforms; various men who were not nobles and looked a lot more like merchants or working men; another who wore on his chest the distinctive blue and gold of the Imperial Cooks; the Captain of the Empress's Imperial Guard, whose presence in the throne room was proper, but not in such privileged proximity to the newly crowned sovereign; a smiling, self-satisfied, overdressed fat man; and an old fellow in a grey tunic, wearing the soft boots of a traveler or a guide, a lean, calm old man who stood very straight at the right hand of the Empress Nargennendia I, she who passed into history with the strange appellation of The Cat, she who the tellers of tales say was nearly as wise as the Great Empress Abderjhalda but much happier; nearly as valiant as Ysadallma but much more beautiful; nearly as strong as Eynisdia the Red but much more compassionate; she who inaugurated her reign with a question to the old man who stood at the right of the Golden Throne:

"What are the twenty directions of the world, daddy?"

The storytellers say that the old man smiled slightly, like one unaccustomed to smiling in palaces, and replied, "I'll tell you what they are, my lady, but you must promise me to forget them at once."

"Yes," she said. "I promise. Cat's honor."

Then, they say, old Z'Ydagg told the twenty directions of the world, and the empress listened, and when he was done she tried to forget them. And they say that she succeeded, but not wholly: there was one, they say, that she could not forget; but nobody, neither the tellers nor their tales, can tell us what it was.

ANGÉLICA GORODISCHER, daughter of the writer Angélica de Arcal, was born in 1929 in Buenos Aires and has lived most of her life in Rosario, Argentina. From her first book of stories, she has displayed a mastery of science-fiction themes, handled with her own personal slant, and exemplary of the South American fantasy tradition. Oral narrative techniques are a strong influence in her work, most notably in *Kalpa Imperial*, which since its publication has been considered a major work of modern fantasy narrative.

Ursula Kroeber was born in 1929 in Berkeley, California. Her parents were the anthropologist Alfred Kroeber and the writer Theodora Kroeber, author of *Ishi*. She went to Radcliffe College, and did graduate work at Columbia University. She married Charles A. Le Guin, a historian, in Paris in 1953; they have lived in Portland, Oregon, since 1958, and have three children and three grandchildren.

URSULA K. LE GUIN has written poetry and fiction all her life. Her first publications were poems, and in the 1960s she began to publish short stories and novels. She writes both poetry and prose, and in various modes including realistic fiction, science fiction, fantasy, young children's books, books for young adults, screenplays, essays, verbal texts for musicians, and voice texts for performance or recording. As of 2017, she has published over a hundred short stories (collected in twelve volumes), five collections of essays, thirteen books for children, nine volumes of poetry, four of translation, and twenty-three novels. Among the honors her writing has received are a National Book Award, PEN-Malamud, Hugo, Nebula, Library of Congress Living Legend, and National Book Foundation Medal. Recent publications include *Words Are My Matter: Writings About Life and Books, 2000–2016 with A Journal of a Writer's Week, Steering the Craft, The Found and the Lost: The Collected Novellas,* and *Late in the Day: Poems 2010–2014.* Her website is ursulakleguin.com.

"Perhaps the strangest thing about these tales is how easily one forgets the mechanics of their telling. Medrano's audiences are at first reluctant to be taken in by yet another digressive, implausible monologue about sales and seductions in space. But soon enough, they are urging the teller to get on with it and reveal what happens next. The discerning reader will doubtless agree." — *Review of Contemporary Fiction*

"Unlike anything I've ever read, one part pulp adventure to one part realistic depiction of the affluent, nearly-idle bourgeoisie, but always leaning more towards the former in its inventiveness and pure (if, sometimes, a little guilt-inducing) sense of fun." — Abigail Nussbaum, *Los Angeles Review of Books*

"Gorodischer's rhythmic and transparent prose reveals the violence underlying
bourgeois respectability. *Prodigies* is both incisive and incantatory."
—Sofia Samatar, author of *A Stranger in Olondria*

Prodigies

A NOVEL

ANGÉLICA GORODISCHER

TRANSLATED BY SUE BURKE

"The right audience will have a willingness to savor, to double-
back over sentences, to bob along to wherever the author and
characters wish to take you. If you are ready for the experience of
Prodigies, it is definitely ready for you."
— Carmen Maria Machado, NPR

"This book scratched my Muriel Spark/Barbara Comyns itches,
with an extra side of the unusual." — Liberty Hardy, Book Riot